SWEET LA-LA LAND

Robert Campbell

POSEIDON PRESS

New York   London   Toronto   Sydney   Tokyo

Poseidon Press

Simon & Schuster Building
Rockefeller Center
1230 Avenue of the Americas
New York, New York 10020

POSEIDON PRESS is a registered trademark
of Simon & Schuster Inc.

POSEIDON PRESS colophon is a trademark
of Simon & Schuster Inc.

Manufactured in the United States of America

10 9 8 7 6 5 4 3 2 1

Library of Congress Cataloging-in-Publication Data

Campbell, R. Wright.
    Sweet La-La Land / Robert Campbell.
        p.   cm.
    I. Title.
PS3553.A4867S94   1990
813'.54 — dc20   89-26520
                                                        CIP

ISBN 0-671-64484-X

In memory of my father, who liked a good story

Sometimes you hear about them finding a body somewhere and you think that's the picture, but it ain't the picture, it's just the trailer.

Bosco Silverlake

Prologue

There's a clever hustler—what they call an entrepreneur nowadays but what has always been called a hustler on the streets—gets himself an old hearse, fits it out to seat twelve people, and goes around giving a tour he calls Graveland.

Besides taking his customers to Forest Lawn and Hollywood Cemetery, where he points out the stones, crypts, and mausoleums sheltering the famous dead like Rudolph Valentino and Mae West, he also drives them past the house where Marilyn Monroe took her life in 1962, the hotel where John Belushi died of an overdose in 1982, and the home of Ramon Novarro, who got beaten to death while wearing a punishment shirt of chain mail and a rubber bathing cap, in 1968.

He dispenses bits of history about others who never got famous until after they were dead and drives his clients to places like the slopes where the victims of the Hillside Strangler were found in the sixties, the site where the dismembered body of a prostitute gave rise to the Black Dahlia legend back in the forties, and the swamp called the Mud Hole on the Pacific Coast Highway, where an Oriental woman was found decapitated in the middle of the eighties.

Then there's Buddy's Place, the tavern—still operating under the same management—not more than four miles south of the Mud Hole, by another swampy patch locals call the Hog Wallow (colorful labels being as important to the freshly minted fables and myths of La-La Land as any morals that might be drawn about the perils of fast living), where back in the summer of 1975 two prostitutes and a barmaid were found, some of their parts severed and arranged according to a pattern, their breasts and bellies cut with signs said to be satanic.

Investigators from the office of the district attorney questioned Charlie Manson and members of his family, both in and out of prison, trying to find out if this was more of Manson's devilish work. He wasn't the only Devil worshiper around (if that is really what he was), and nothing came of it.

As it turned out, the police didn't have to reach very far to get their hands on a refugee from the Appalachians by the name of Daniel Younger—called Inch by all, including himself—who was a regular customer of Buddy's Place. A man come to La-La Land by way of Dog Trot, Kentucky, and Johnson City and Nashville, Tennessee, pursuing the American dream of outrageous fame and obscene wealth.

Evidence was presented that this uneducated man worshiped snakes and performed ritual sacrifice—he had indeed been a member of one of those fundamentalist Christian sects in the hills of Kentucky that danced with their hands full of rattlers in a demonstration of their faith—and had, on two or three occasions, slaughtered goats for feasts given by some of the rich of Malibu.

But he furiously denied worshiping the Devil, Satan, or Lucifer, displaying a better grasp of the subtle differences between them than the lawyers or the judge.

This naturally reinforced the jury's impression that the alien from the economically depressed hills of Kentucky, with his strangely slanted eyes and lobeless ears, must definitely be a man given over to evil.

So, in view of the fact that no witnesses were brought forward to swear to his good character or hand him an alibi, and in spite of the courtroom presence of a hugely pregnant wife and the defense contention that Younger—though he may have been drunk at Buddy's the night the barmaid, Gladys Trainor, disappeared—had not been placed on the scene the night when the whores, Carla Pointer and Janet Strum, had probably gone missing, he was found guilty on thirty-seven counts of abduction, assault, unlawful carnal knowledge of a corpse, mutilation, torture, and murder.

The judge delivered a rousing presentence harangue, stigmatizing Younger as the most depraved of men, and sentenced him to a total of three hundred and seventy-two years. It was plain that he would have been happy to sentence Younger to death at least three times over, but three years earlier the Supreme Court of the United States had declared the death penalty unconstitutional.

Although it was reinstituted in 1976, Younger was eligible for parole in 1990.

He came before the parole board of the state of California with the reputation of being one of the most biddable, easygoing felons ever to serve time, a quiet man who apparently had made few enemies and even fewer friends. A man who kept his own counsel, played twelve-string guitar in the style of Leadbelly, and attended chapel faithfully six times a week. They had no idea that he was brewing raisin snap in a cabinet built into the pulpit.

His cellmate, a New York thief by the name of Gino Macelli, was interviewed privately and asked if Younger had ever talked about the murders of which he had been accused and convicted. Had he ever admitted to the murders? Had he ever admitted to a belief in Satanism? Had he ever talked in his sleep?

"He don't even talk when he's awake," Macelli said. "It's enough to drive you bats."

He said nothing about Younger praying under his breath in a language he'd never heard before. He said nothing about the time Younger'd caught a mouse and skinned it alive with a sharpened spoon. The truth was Macelli'd known a lot of weird, hard, scary men, but none as hard, weird, or scary as Inch Younger. Macelli knew that Younger was playing a game on the system, but he wasn't going to be the one to tell them. Better Younger should be on the outside than on the inside in the same cell with him.

The authorities tried to find the wife but couldn't. He'd listed no other relations, so no one came to stand by him during his hearing.

The prostitutes had died practically friendless, the way it usually is with prostitutes who never stay in one place long enough to make lasting relationships, so their postmortem rights went unrepresented. The barmaid had a mother, a father, and two sisters when she died, but they had already disowned her. No one appeared to urge the board to refuse parole for her convicted killer.

What with things like this, that, and the other, the parole board saw in Younger proof of the liberal fantasy that prison can reform and rehabilitate, so they granted him parole.

"You understand, do you, Mr. Younger, that you must maintain steady employment, support any dependents you may have, report your earnings and debts accurately, avoid disreputable associates and places, keep reasonable hours or a curfew if one is imposed, avoid excessive use of alcohol and the use of drugs altogether, comply with the instructions of your parole officer, and submit written reports when required?"

A staff member moved in close to the chairman and whispered something in his ear.

"I'm told you have some difficulty writing."

"I read good, sir," Younger quickly said, fearful that this small matter might keep him forever imprisoned.

It was the most he'd said beyond "Yes" and "No" since the proceedings had begun, and his voice, heard even briefly, startled them. If a voice can be said to have color, Younger's had the color of rust. It was a voice that commanded attention, even though it wasn't raised much above a whisper.

"I'm sure your officer will work something out about the reports. Now, besides the matters I've mentioned, you must obtain permission to buy or own firearms, buy or drive an automobile, assume any substantial debt, marry, change jobs, or leave the jurisdiction. You understand?"

Younger cleared his throat, as though the first effort had dislodged something which was now rattling around threatening to obstruct his breathing, and said he understood.

He was told to return to his cell until the paperwork was cleared and the process for his release set in motion.

He went back and sat down on his bunk and stared at his hands.

"The sonsabitches didn't think I'd ever figure it the fuck out," he suddenly said. "I fucking figured it out."

Macelli didn't ask him what he was talking about, because he considered him as stupid as a stone, the slow workings of Younger's mind as difficult to fathom as the thoughts of a cow. He just grunted.

All of a sudden Younger stood up, raised his clenched fists above his head, threw back his head, opened his mouth, and let loose a nearly silent, hissing scream of triumph. The sound of an animal about to hunt and kill.

1

Six o'clock in the morning. A sweet day like the day outside the plate-glass window of Gentry's, a coffee shop down the block from the corner of Hollywood and Vine along the hookers' stroll, doesn't come that often to La-La Land, which had, once upon a time, been a small-town beauty with golden hair and clean breath and a figure just full enough to be interesting without being fat. She'd had her scandals and even a movie murder or two, but there was something oddly innocent about her sinning.

The years had passed and she hadn't aged very well. She'd been too much used and abused, and now the snowbirds, pack rats, barn owls, and assorted freaks fed upon her bones, doing things to her that would drive a person crazy if they weren't already certifiable.

The man everybody called Whistler, a professional private eye, as they once called it when Hammett was getting drunk and Bogart was wearing his trench coat, was more than a little shopworn, too.

Some people in the know said that Whistler knew La-La better than anybody else—except for a kiddie cop named Isaac Canaan; Bosco, the one-armed counterman at Gentry's; and a pimp with a glass eye by the name of Mike Rialto—and had been done by her more than most.

All the same they were a loving couple, La-La and he, she working out of her purse and he working out of his hat.

On a good day like today they even looked young again, their hopes and dreams jingling like coins of gold and silver in their heads.

Bosco came over to top up Whistler's coffee cup, the pot in one hand, a copy of Thoreau's *Walden* caught in the pit of the arm that wasn't there. When he saw the look on Whistler's face he sat down across from him in the booth and matched Whistler's sad smile with his own.

"You tell me your dreams and I'll tell you mine?" Bosco said.

"How did you know?" Whistler asked, looking at Bosco without much surprise because it was a well-known fact that Bosco talked to ghosts and knew things ordinary people didn't know.

"Know what?"

"That I had a dream."

"It's always six to one that somebody's had a dream. Everybody dreams."

"But how many remember their dreams?"

"That's another matter."

"I had a dream about a girl I once knew by the name of Faye. It was the middle of the seventies."

"Don't talk to me about the seventies," Bosco said. "I lost my arm in an argument with a shotgun in the seventies and wasn't feeling all there."

Whistler went right on as though he hadn't heard a word of Bosco's grim joke. "In the dream I was nosing up to thirty, sitting here waiting for my sweetheart to come walking around the corner over by the Chinese. While I'm watching, she stops and puts her shoes in the prints left by Myrna Loy."

"How do you know they was Myrna Loy's?"

"It was a dream and you know things in dreams you wouldn't know when you're awake."

Bosco nodded, agreeing to that without dispute.

"I run across the street and hug her from behind," Whistler went on. "When she turns around, I can see she doesn't recognize me. I try to kiss her but she turns her head away and says she doesn't kiss men she doesn't know. I feel the tears start up and she touches my cheek and says, 'Hey, why are you crying?' And then I wake up and I've got the blues, which won't leave me. They've been hanging on all morning. But it's not bad, you know what I mean? It's a sweet sadness and I'd just as soon it didn't go away just yet."

"The Chinese is twelve blocks down the boulevard," Bosco said, "and Gentry's wasn't even here back in the seventies."

"Something was here. We're walking on ghosts. Besides, dreams don't care about that."

"You don't want to get in the habit of living inside dreams or moving pictures," Bosco said. "It thins the blood and turns the brain into spaghetti. You shouldn't take dreams, flicks, or promises from ambitious women too seriously."

"Don't you ever have sweet dreams?"

"Oh, sure. I dream I'm sitting in this booth with one hand on my crotch and the other on a redhead's thirty-eight-D's."

"How do you feel when you wake up?"

"I feel like I only got one hand and a coffeepot in that."

Isaac Canaan walked in and spotted Bosco sitting at the table with Whistler and the coffeepot. He snagged an empty mug from the counter before sitting down and pouring himself a cup.

"That's lukewarm," Bosco said.

"So, go get me hot," Canaan said, continuing to pour the mug full. He put down the pot, picked up the mug, and took a swallow.

"Battery acid," he said.

"I told you," Bosco said, getting up. He bent toward Whistler for the last word. "I'm telling you, you got to watch this dreaming. If all of a sudden a man gets pushed into the real world out of a sweet dream, the shock could stop his heart."

"I'm not going to let you do it to me," Whistler said, turning to look out the window again. "I'm not going to let you push me out of my dream. Here I am, and Gentry's isn't even here because it wasn't here back then, and you weren't here either."

"Was I here?" Canaan asked, not even knowing what they were talking about, just wanting a piece of the conversation because he'd just stepped in off the streets, where he'd been talking to runaways and vagabonds and children drowning in the sewers, every one of them looking at him with leery eyes, doubting his good intentions.

"Why, for chrissake, I don't even know you," Whistler said. "I never even met you. So how can you be sitting here talking sense to me?"

Bosco reached out and put his hand around Whistler's wrist, but Whistler didn't move an inch.

"I don't feel a thing," Whistler said. "There's nobody there. I'm just sitting here waiting for my honey." He straightened up as if he'd been stabbed, his face losing color, and for a minute there Bosco thought that Whistler had, indeed, been rudely evicted from his fantasy and was having an attack.

"What the hell?" Bosco exclaimed.

"Likewise," Canaan said.

"I think I dreamed so hard I just made it all come true."

Whistler was out of the booth and out the door before Bosco could say another word.

Bosco sat down again. He and Canaan watched as Whistler charged across the boulevard without looking left or right, fending off the cars with nothing but his waving hands, making his way through the pimps, hookers, undercover cops, and dealers to the spot where a small woman with short pale yellow hair and many rings on her fingers stood staring down at her sandals and the brass celebrity star in the Walk of Fame between her feet. Whistler put his arms around her from behind. She turned around, startled, and ducked away as he put his face close to hers. Then he lifted her off her feet and held her in the air a long time, looking up into her face as she looked down into his, suddenly laughing, her hands touching his cheeks, both of them showing all their teeth as though they were in a rage of happiness.

"You think our friend's in trouble?" Bosco asked.

"We're all in trouble," Canaan said. "Where's my hot coffee?"

2

Paul Hobby was a Hollywood legend in his own time. Fresh out of business college back in the late sixties, he'd taken three thousand dollars of his own money, three thousand of his brother's, and ten of his father's and talked himself into a two-hundred-and-fifty-thousand-dollar loan from the bank to make a motion picture.

Bubble, Bubble, Boil and Blood, into which everything was thrown, including but not limited to jiggly-juggly girls in peril, motorcycle bandits with towels stuffed in their crotches, women cut in parts with chain saws and ripsaws, tarantula attacks, monsters from outer space, and the punk rock band Three Cocks and a Pussy, grossed a hundred times its cost and gathered a cult following that was still going to late-night showings twenty years later.

He followed it up with other low-budget exploitation flicks, grabbing on to trends the minute they surfaced and rarely failing to rake in the shekels.

He beat the big studios to the punch. Shooting flicks with multiple cameras in five days. Re-dressing one set so he could shoot a piggyback production for the same rental fee. Stealing ideas with the boldness of an airport pickpocket. Creating look-alike imitations of winning titles with the imagination of a Moonie scrambling to con a rabbi for a buck.

When the epic *Cleopatra,* starring Elizabeth Taylor and Richard Burton, was ready for release, he beat them to the screens with *Clio,* starring Harriet Pilbreck and Roger Fermier. When Dustin Hoffman did *The Graduate,* Hobby released *Graduation* a month sooner. When they made *Guess Who's Coming to Dinner,* he made *Look Who's Staying for Lunch.*

But it was in mining material about Satan and satanic cults that he found his specialty. Quickie knockoffs of *The Omen* and *The Exorcist* and some half-assed original notions about the Devil made him rich.

He was known by some as the King of Sleaze, by others as the Prince of Thieves, and by still others as a penny-pinching, devious, crooked, low-life bastard who'd sell his mother for a quarter and his girlfriend for a buck.

He had an office suite in a building he owned on the lower end of Hollywood Boulevard, an apartment out in Culver City, a rent-controlled flat back in New York City, an estate on one of the outer islands of Hawaii, a house in the Colony at Malibu, and a twenty-room mansion in Brentwood. He owned plenty of other real estate, not for personal use but for investment.

He was not married but was intending to get married a week or so after he finished shooting his latest epic, *Witches in Heat.*

His wife-to-be, Sharon Allagash, was an attorney working for a fashionable firm in Century City.

His girlfriend, Mae Swift, often waited for him in the two-room sleep-over apartment at the back of his offices in Hollywood, ready to offer care, comfort, and a tongue bath at the end of a difficult working day.

Some people would consider it perverse that he was about to marry one woman and was still seeking comfort from another—an impossible conflict of interest, agreeable only to a very unreasonable man.

He was an unreasonable man.

He prided himself on being unreasonable because he had nothing but contempt for nearly everybody. Treating people badly and making them kiss his ass while they hated his guts proved to him, over and over again, that the average person would do the same things for a thousand bucks they condemned him for doing in order to make millions.

"We got the fireman on the set?" he demanded of nobody in particular.

The grips were putting finishing touches on the second-story gallery of the great room of the castle, the electricians were wiring up the incandescent enhancements for the real flames that would be burning in the iron chandelier and the sconces along the wall, the makeup people were getting Eddie Minkus and Joanne Smalley into their ape suits, the cameraman was ordering his gaffers around, moving lights and adjusting spots and gobos, and the principal actors were in their dressing rooms snorting coke, quaffing vodka, or firing off farts just for the hell of it.

"We got a fucking fireman on the fucking set?" Hobby shouted, lifting his voice in the special way he had that signaled one and all that the big honcho was getting pissed off and was about to cut off heads and stamp on testicles.

"We got a fuckin' fireman," Boomer Bolivia shouted, taking a couple of steps and giving it to Hobby right in his left ear. "Why don' you sit down, let us set the shot? Then you come over, do your t'ing, say you don' like this or tha', fire tha' one, fire this one. Off the fuckin' set, Paul. Leddus do it?"

"I ought to kick you in the nuts," Hobby said.

"You try it an' I cut off your dingus and shove it up your sweet patootie," Bolivia said. He was the only one in town who'd give Hobby's crap back twice without paying for it one way or another.

Most people thought that Bolivia, of all the people around Hobby on a regular basis, got away with his challenges because they were such old friends. Because there was real affection between them. Because they'd been known to raise hell around town in their youth. Because they'd shared the same women.

A couple of insiders said that it was because, around picture three or four, Hobby had made a filthy remark about Bolivia's mother. It was supposed to be taken as a joke, but Bolivia didn't understand such jokes and his Latin machismo couldn't allow the insult. He took Hobby to a private place and punched him in the stomach until he vomited all over his shoes and then told him if he complained or tried to seek revenge in any way he'd come back and fix his belly so he wouldn't be able to hold anything down for a month.

A couple of really inside insiders said it was because Bolivia had come up from Colombia, Brazil, or maybe even Bolivia—which was why he called himself Bolivia, not his real name—for a celebration of the Age of Aquarius held on the beach above Malibu. The Age of Aquarius is due to begin sometime around the year 2000 and is supposed to be an era of international harmony and service to others. But it has also energized a lot of cults dedicated to the glorification of evil, which are trying to take it over. In either case, many believers have been jumping the gun and exploiting the

Age of Aquarius forty, fifty years early. Bolivia, these inside insiders said, was a voodoo priest, a *hungan*, who knew all there was
to know about calling up demons and paying them off and so forth,
and therefore he had Hobby scared to death of him.

There were other inside insiders who said that was all a lot of
crap.

"Ready?" someone shouted.

"Ready."

"Okay, Jimmy?"

"We're ready to go live."

"All set, Harry?"

"Go, go, go."

"Willy?"

"Ho!"

"Ready on the set!"

"Principals?"

"Take out the stand-ins."

"Stunt ready to go?"

"Ready."

"Jake? You the safety man?"

"Standing by."

"The fireman takes the call from Mr. Hobby. He got that?"

"You got that, Benny?"

"Sure, I got it. Whattaya think, I'm brain-stunned?"

"Don't get smartass," Waco, the assistant director, said.

"We don't want another *Twilight Zone* here. We don't want anybody killed," Jake said.

"I couldn't do the time," Hobby said. "Who's on the stopwatch?"

"I've got it," Jake said.

"Give it to me," Hobby said. "You've got to be right there with
the extinguisher."

Jake handed the watch to a grip, who walked it over to Hobby.

"So are we ready or are we ready?" Hobby said.

"We're ready," Waco said.

"All right. Let's make a picture. Everybody pay attention to me,
people. I'll say 'Action' and I'll say 'Cut.' Let's do this one time and
one time only."

"Minkus and Smalley on their marks," Waco said.

The stuntman and -woman shuffled over to a spot underneath

the iron chandelier, which had been lowered and its gas candles lit. They were buckled into harnesses of chain and hooked up. Two grips stood by ready to winch them up the second they were torched.

Nervousness and urgency crackled like electricity in the air.

It looked like a simple stunt. Fire suits covered in fur and doused with gasoline, faces protected with masks. Stunt people set alight and lifted on the chandelier up toward the beams crossing the width of the great room constructed on the soundstage. Held suspended there for thirty seconds. Suits rated for ninety. Plenty of leeway, plenty of time to lower them so Jake, the stunt coordinator, and Benny, the city fireman, could put the flames out with hand-held extinguishers.

But everybody knew that it was the simple stunts that killed.

"Settle down, everybody," Waco said in a soothing, normal tone of voice. "Actors?"

The actors in the scene were at their places, mysterious yet gaudy in their medieval costumes.

"Camera?"

"Rolling."

"Speed."

"Torches!"

The ape suits were set aflame. The grips ducked out of camera range.

Waco looked at Hobby and thumbed the crown of his stopwatch.

"Action," Hobby said, and thumbed his.

The winchmen worked the handles and raised the chandelier and the blazing stunt people up to twenty feet.

The actors acted, the crew watched fascinated, the stunt people burned, the cameras turned, and Waco hit the button on the stopwatch at thirty seconds. He turned to look at Hobby, who'd forgotten all about the watch and was staring up at the flaming human beings with an expression of odd delight. He seemed mesmerized, in thrall to some powerful emotion.

"Thirty-five seconds!" Waco shouted.

"Hold it, hold it! Another five!" Hobby yelled.

Waco looked at Bolivia, neither one of them knowing what to do.

Jake yelled, "Down, down! Bring 'em down!" But Hobby yelled "No! Five seconds!" even louder.

Everyone began to babble or yell out instructions. There was a rising wave of sound, like the sound of a crowd witnessing a disaster.

"Five seconds! Five seconds!" Hobby was yelling.

"Fifty-five seconds in!" Waco shouted.

"Down! Bring the fucking rig down!" Jake ordered.

But nobody listened, nobody moved. They were waiting for the director. Hobby had said it was going to be his call. They were waiting for it.

Bolivia started moving toward Hobby, making a fist, setting his huge arm for the punch. He was going to coldcock Hobby right where he was standing. Afterward, everybody who was there would say that's what he clearly meant to do.

"Sixty seconds!"

"Cut!" Hobby screamed. "Get that fucking fire out, you assholes!"

3

Bosco watched Whistler growing younger right before his eyes. It was something in the way he laughed and flung his hands around as he told the woman one story after another, catching her up on a hundred things. He was acting enthusiastic, out of control, not all there. Nuts!

It made Bosco a little nervous because he'd long since come to believe in that old quotation that God first made mad those he would destroy, although he insisted he didn't believe in God but only the *idea* of God, some *intention* in the beginning that there should be a God.

"So Spencer Tracy's standing there waiting to get the next day's call from the assistant director," Whistler said, "and all this time Harry Bagley's looking up at him—with the usual big cigar stuck in his mouth—giving Tracy the eye. So Tracy figures he maybe met the guy on another picture but forgot who he was. He says 'Hi, there. How's things?' And Bagley says, 'Never mind that bullshit. Where do I know you from?'"

"Oh, God, old Harry," she said, laughing at a story she'd clearly heard before. "How's he doing?"

"He's gone," Whistler said, twisting his mouth, one side up and one side down, making light of death because what else could a sane man do?

When Shirley Hightower, the only waitress in a year who'd lasted more than two weeks, went over with a refill, they didn't even notice but just went on looking, talking, and holding hands.

Whistler kept on saying "Faye" and she kept on calling him Sam, whatever the hell that meant.

They were manufacturing an atmosphere in the shop. Bosco finally figured out what it was. He was sitting in on a rerun of Bogart and Bergman meeting in Rick's saloon in *Casablanca*.

If they'd only warned him, he thought, he would've rented a piano and hired a piano player.

"I can't believe it, Faye," Whistler said.

"I can't believe it, Sam," she replied. "How long's it been? Fifteen years?"

"Just about fifteen years, give or take."

"Give or take what, Sam?"

"Two or three lifetimes."

"Hey, you making like a clown again? You making like old Sam the Sandman, the Sad Man?"

Whistler winced as though she'd struck a nerve. He pasted a smile on his face so his memories wouldn't show through.

Without his clown makeup on nobody had recognized Sam the Sandman, the Sad Man, fifteen years before, sitting in the courtroom watching the pregnant woman who'd once been his woman go through hell as they laid out all her husband's sins.

She'd turned around once or twice, nervously looking at the curious piling into the courtroom but turning back right away as though afraid of their power to hurt her. Each time she'd looked, Whistler had hidden his face, because he didn't want her to see him sitting there and think that he was gloating over the man who'd stolen her away from him.

Still, when the chance came along to see the man who beat you shown up and brought down, it took a saint not to want to be witness to his downfall. And it was only human nature, or at least a man's nature, to hope that the woman who'd refused him *would* see him sitting there, not gloating but just sitting there—not that she'd make the comparison and regret the choice she'd made but just that she'd see him sitting there.

If she spotted him and saw how faithfully he'd kept her in his heart and threw herself into his arms to beg forgiveness the first chance she got, well, that was only fair, that was only justice.

When Younger had been brought in, wearing the orange jumpsuit issued to prisoners, Faye stared at him and then suddenly turned around and looked Whistler full in the face, staring into his eyes across the room that was filled with people come to watch her humiliated and wounded.

His face felt like wood. He couldn't smile. Didn't know if that would be the thing to do anyway. He wanted her to know he was there for her even if he couldn't put his arms around her and comfort her the way he wanted to.

Before he could get the right expression on his face, she'd turned around front again and the principal actors had started filing in and everybody'd clattered to their feet as the clerk called the court to order and the judge swept in and the case started that would send her husband away.

"What's the matter, Sam?" Faye asked.

"Memories."

She took her hands away, picked up her cup, and took a swallow of coffee.

"Me too, Sam," she said. "How come you didn't come over and talk to me in the courtroom?"

"I wanted to."

"I saw you looking at me that once. You just stared at me like you couldn't stand the sight..."

"Oh, no."

"...so I didn't look again. It hurt me so."

"My God, I would've picked you up and run away with you if I thought I could. If I'd thought you wanted me to."

"I wanted you to."

"How come you disappeared after the trial?"

"What was I supposed to do, Sam? I was—"

"Nobody calls me Sam anymore."

"What, then?"

"Whistler."

"Whistler? Okay. That's good. I'll try to remember. Don't you want to hear?"

"Sure, I want to hear."

"I had a baby. Inch Younger's baby. Maybe it should've been your baby if I'd done everything right, but it wasn't yours, it was his, and I went away to have it."

"You didn't have to go away."

"You don't think so? The wife of a man they said butchered three women in a shack in the middle of a mud hole? I was a news item, what do you think?"

"It blows over. Somebody else gets murdered."

"That's nice. A person's got to wait for another horror movie before people will stop paying attention. That right? No, that's not right, Whistler. See, I remembered, I didn't forget. Nobody forgets. They keep on remembering every couple of years. I wanted to get out from under it, I couldn't get out from under it. My kid couldn't get out from under it. No matter where we went, people found out, sooner or later. I don't know how that can be but that's how it is. You meet a person who knew you at a party, at a football game, here and there. It always happens. Sooner or later. No matter where you run."

"I can't believe you're sitting here," Whistler said. "How long you been back in town?"

"Two and a half years. Close to three."

"Where you living?"

"Up on Franklin."

"No. You're kidding me. You've been living up on Franklin all this time?"

"Only the last four months. When I first came back I lived in Santa Monica for about a year. Then I moved up to West Hollywood."

"Even so, I can't get over it. I mean this town isn't so big a person who knew another person wouldn't bump into that person, living as close as this."

"You live here?"

"Well, I've got a house above Cahuenga, but I'm here more than I'm there," he said.

"Still checking the trades? Still in the industry?"

"I've been out of the industry a long time."

"How long?"

"Fifteen years."

"Oh?"

"I gave it up. It gave me up. A woman killed herself while she was on the phone talking to me."

"I heard about it. It wasn't your fault. You were just the host on a call-in show, filling in between the reels."

"I didn't know what to do. I had her in my hands and I lost her."

"You ever find out who she was?"

"Just another dreamer."

"Aren't we all?" she said, giving him back the other half of the line from some old ballad, her lips twisting up a little bit as though the taste of the words in her mouth were too bittersweet to bear.

"So what is it, Faye? Why did you come back?"

"I came back because I came back."

"I can't believe you're sitting here," he said.

She laughed softly and said, "How many times are you going to say that?"

"Well, I mean I can hardly believe it," he said, laughing, too. "What are the chances, two people meeting like this after fifteen years and how many miles on the road?"

"This is nothing but a small town. You said it."

"Up on Franklin," he said, shaking his head in disbelief. "Where you working?"

"I'm working where I live."

"What do you mean?"

"I'm the assistant director of a halfway house for homeless girls. Runaways. Throwaways. It's called Magdalene House."

"I know that place. I've got a friend, a cop, Isaac Canaan, steers kids to you when he can."

Her eyes got wide. "I know Isaac."

"I can't believe it."

She looked at her watch. "I've got to go. Oh, Jesus, I got to go. I've got to relieve the duty desk." She slid out of the booth.

"Wait a second. You've got to give me an address. You've got to give me a telephone number. I don't want you disappearing on me again," Whistler said, standing up and reaching out to grab her sleeve.

She handed him a card she took from her pocket. "This is one of the cards I hand out to the kids. I ask them to call me when they've had enough and want to have some shelter for a while."

"I'm a candidate," Whistler said, taking the card.

She moved in close to hug and kiss him again, started to leave, then turned around and looked at him for a New York minute. "We might not be able to pick it up where it left off," she finally said. "We might not be able to find Sam and his girl again."

"That's a chance."

4

William Twenty, the star of Hobby's latest, said, "Can we have one for the actor?"

"What the fuck's that supposed to mean?" Hobby said.

"I think I can get the scene better."

"You already got the scene good."

"I think I can make it better."

"It's good enough for me."

"I'd like to try it one more time."

Hobby looked at the assistant director. "You got the hours?"

"You're fifteen minutes till double time," Waco said.

"So fuck one for the actor," Hobby said, looking Twenty square in the eyes.

"Don't want to spend a dime, do you?"

"I spent a dime when I hired you." He walked the two steps, the mountain going to Mahomet, and threw his arm around the actor's shoulders. "I'm beat to the rocks."

"You mean your socks."

"I mean my rocks, my nuts, my balls, fachrissakes. I'm so tired I won't get it up for a week. I'll have to send you in to stand in for me on my honeymoon."

Twenty grinned. They both knew he didn't like women.

"So don't make me crazy, 'one for the actor,'" Hobby said. He grabbed his crotch. "This for the actor."

"If you were only twelve," Twenty said, putting his mouth close to Hobby's ear, whispering his secret.

"Next time we'll do a picture about the Devil in a boys' school. You'll play the headmaster. Go home. You got a call for tomorrow?"

"I'm resting."

"So rest. But don't forget my party at the beach."

Twenty walked away, mollified by the attention.

"Fucking 'one for the actor,'" Hobby murmured under his breath as Bolivia came up to him.

He was looking worried, looking pale under his permanent suntan.

"What's the matter? You look like you seen a ghost," Hobby said.

"I'm still shakin' from tha' fire. You could've burned them two stunts to deat'."

"You getting chicken in your old age?"

"Maybe I am."

"So you don't have to be so goddamned serious about it," Hobby said, knowing there had to be more.

"Tha' Younger's gettin' out," Bolivia said.

"What?"

"They parole' him."

"Who the hell told you that bullshit?"

"No bullshit. It'll be on the news by tonight."

"But how come you..."

"I been keepin' tabs on him."

"All these years?"

"Only the las' five or six."

"So what about it, he's getting out?"

"Suppose he comes lookin' for us, askin' us questions?"

"Questions he didn't ask at the time of the trial?"

"He's had time to t'ink about it. He's had time to remember t'ings."

"He was stoned out of his skull. If he didn't remember then, he ain't going to remember now."

"Wha' if he does?"

"Then fuck him. I toss him a bone. I give him plane fare back to the hills."

"Suppose tha' ain' enough?"

"Then we do what we got to do."

"Not me."

"You really are getting old, ain't you?"

"Older. It's differen' now. I gotta wife. I got t'ree kids. I ain' wild an' crazy like I used to be."

"But you're still full of shit, ain't you?"

"If tha's wha' you wanna say, go ahead an' say it."

Bolivia walked away.

"Hey, Boomer!" Hobby called.

Bolivia stopped and turned around.

"The next time you raise a fist to me, be ready to throw it."

This time Hobby walked away and Bolivia stopped him with something more to say.

"Hey, Paul. You still wan' me comin' to your party tomorrow night?"

"Certainly. What do you think? I didn't say we wasn't still friends."

5

Lawry's Prime Rib is one of the few things that doesn't change all that much in Hollywood. It's been sitting in the same spot along restaurant row for a few decades. Big silver serving carts are still wheeled around. Under their lids repose chunks of cow, sliced up by a white-hatted chef, served up as you like it. The seasonings on the table are available for purchase in take-home jars and bottles. If you forget to take some home, you can stop in at your friendly supermarket along the way and buy it there. Everybody's learned to reach out for the extra buck.

It's not an intimate restaurant. It's not the sort of place a man hoping to seduce a woman would choose. It had been a favorite place when they'd been sleeping together—after the first couple of times—eighteen, nineteen years before. When they could afford it.

It was too brightly lit, too noisy, and too insistently jolly for seduction. Whistler felt he'd made a poor pick and wondered if Faye was thinking he was sending her some sort of message unread by the sender. Was he saying that he wasn't any surer of the revival than she was? Maybe fifteen years wasn't long enough for a new production of *The Boyfriend* or *Guys and Dolls*. Maybe nostalgia worked only after thirty, forty years, when all wounds were healed and all memories had turned sweet. He didn't think he was reluctant to pick up where they'd left off, but he was smart enough to know he couldn't swear to it.

They didn't say much while their meals were served, watching the carver with the same bright-eyed, self-conscious interest as every other tourist and couple out on the town.

"I told you what I do for a living," Faye said. "What do you do for a living?"

"I'm a detective."

"A cop?"

"Private."

"I never would've thought."

"Me neither."

"You like it?" she asked.

"I don't know if I like it. It's just that I feel as though there's nothing else I'd rather do. Not now. Not here. How about you? You like your work?"

"It's a payback."

"What?"

"I'm paying off all the wrong I've done. Okay. I like it. It's not what I dreamed when I came to town with my little dancing shoes, but I like it."

"Your kid live with you?"

She turned her head away as though he'd slapped her.

"I say something?"

"What I did to my boy is part of what I'm trying to make up for."

He didn't ask her what it was she'd done. He knew she was going to tell him. He cut a square of roast beef and forked it into his mouth along with a piece of Yorkshire pudding, looking out into the dining room as he chewed, giving her time to make up her mind how much she wanted to tell.

"I'm afraid when you hear what you're going to hear, you'll get right up and walk out." Her mouth twisted up and her eyes looked stone-washed all of a sudden, the blue faded out by a film of tears.

He reached out and took her hands. "You don't have to tell me anything."

"I want to. I don't want to."

"I think you better try me, then. If I walk out on you, it'll mean I wasn't worth much to you anyway."

Faye stared at him for a moment, then made a sound as if she was actually thinking about the breath she took and looked away.

"After he was put on death row, I just turned my back on Younger. There was no charity in my heart, let alone any love."

"You'd just had the baby," he said, as though that could be excuse enough for practically anything.

"I had no love or charity in my heart for the baby either. It was a boy, and I kept thinking how he might grow up to be like his father, living on women, cheating and seducing them, even doing worse. Even doing what Inch ended up doing."

Whistler could hear it coming, the breast-beating and the confession. He'd heard enough of it years ago on the call-in show to last a lifetime. And heard plenty of it since—the drunks and dopers and child molesters spilling out their pitiful, ordinary mischiefs, and some not so ordinary, staring into his face, necks thrust forward to receive the knife, chests exposed for the bullet, ready to take whatever punishment he might want to dish out. Delivering penance.

When he didn't respond fast enough, she took back her hands, clutching them together as though in prayer, determined to tell him everything.

The tears were running down her face like the tracks of snails, making shining rivers on her cheeks, pooling up in the corners of her mouth. She cried without a sound, showing Whistler her grief and shame because she couldn't hide from him—not from her *confessor*—but not making a curtain scene out of it, not in front of someone she'd known and loved so long ago.

"I busted up in little pieces. I ran home to Johnson City with my baby in my arms, but when I got there my mother was dead and my father wouldn't have me. He was living with a woman. We'd have been in the way."

There wasn't any escape for Whistler. He had to sit there and listen. He made his face a neutral mask.

"My own father wouldn't have me and the baby, so I got into this rage and went up into the hills of Kentucky where Inch Younger'd come from," she went on. "I left my child with his old man, who lived in a falling-down shack and made pot whiskey. What was I thinking about?...What was I thinking about?" She looked at Whistler as though he could really give her the answer. "Inch told me how his father had beat up on him when he was little, after his mother had run off on them, and still I left my baby with that old man."

"How old was the boy?"

"Four and a half. I'd held on to him that long. I'd done that," she said, as though asking Whistler to put that down on the plus side of her book.

"How'd you get along?"

"I worked as a waitress sometimes. I worked in stores." She was watching him like a hawk. "I took up whoring."

He didn't flinch, didn't bat an eye.

"I was a mess. Drinking and doping. I dove right down to the bottom of the well."

The tears had dried on her face. Her hands were loose on the tabletop.

"Then there was a night when..." She stopped in the middle, let it go by, deciding whatever she was about to tell him she shouldn't tell him.

"Something happened that woke me up. It wasn't something as big or bad as other things I'd done, but it turned the lights on."

"That's the way it happens."

"Four years ago I sobered up, cleaned up. I went back to get my son."

"He'd have been ten? Eleven?"

She didn't seem to be able to answer. She put a hand up to her throat as though it was full of words she couldn't spit out and couldn't swallow.

"The kid was all right, wasn't he?"

"He was gone," she finally managed to say.

"Run away."

"Sold. That old man sold him."

"What?"

She winced as though afraid he'd strike her for letting such a terrible thing happen. "My father-in-law was dead, but there was an old woman, Granny Hours, who told me old man Younger'd sold John six months before."

"John? That what you named your kid?"

"I wasn't going to name him for his father." Her mouth twisted as though she'd bitten into something bitter. "So I named him after my father, and my father turned us away."

"Younger sold him how and to who?"

"Just sold him for cash to some travelers passing through."

Put that in a book, put that in a moving picture, nobody'd believe you, Whistler thought. He remembered what Canaan had told him one time: "I can get you a child between the ages of six and four-teen, boy or girl, delivered to your doorstep, no questions asked, do with it what you want, twenty-five hundred dollars."

"Where do they come from?" Whistler'd asked.

"Central and South America. Mexico. Asia. Some right out of the barrens in the Southwest or the Appalachians back east. Stolen away or bought for cash."

Whistler cut another piece of meat. She'd thrown herself on his mercy. You ask a person to judge you, you can hardly jump into bed with him an hour after. She'd made him a confidant, a confessor, a shoulder, an uncle. She'd made him a father, the kind she never had.

Women believed that was how to treat a lover, telling him old history and old sins, testing the depth of his understanding, the tenderness of his heart, the strength of his feelings for her. He knew otherwise.

6

Every day for just over fifteen and a half years he'd awakened to the sound of the goddam bell ringing up the morning, ringing away the night and the sleep that was his only comfort.

Every night he lay on his bunk, staring up at the bottom of the bunk above him, where some con, the latest a guinea named Macelli, slept, and worked over the series of events that had landed him in the shit up to his neck.

They said he'd murdered and butchered three women. They tried him and convicted him and dumped him in a cage. When he thought about that night at Buddy's he couldn't remember going back to the shack behind the tavern with Gladys Trainor, or cutting her throat with the linoleum knife they presented in evidence. His linoleum knife. He remembered fighting off the cops when they kicked in his door and dragged him out of his own house, out of his own bedroom with his pregnant wife crouched, cowering, in the closet. He told them later he thought they were thieves or rapists invading his home, but all they said about that was, What would thieves be doing breaking into a house with nothing in it? What would rapists be doing going after a woman ready to pop?

What he remembered best was the taste of bitter beer on his lips when he was startled out of drunken sleep by the sound of shouting men, with Faye not in the bed, reaching for the pistol he kept in his slipper on the floor. Having an unregistered gun in his possession counted against him. The prosecution made out that it was just another proof of what a violent man he was. He hadn't even had the chance to fire the goddam thing. They were all over him like shit on a bean patch, screaming in his ear, twisting his arms up behind his back, with him not knowing what the hell was happening.

Oh, there'd been plenty of surprises in store for him. Maybe not so surprising after all, when you stopped to think about it.

Those women getting up on the stand and testifying how he'd seduced and cheated them. You'd think they were living back before the turn of the century, when women hid their ankles under long skirts, staying out of saloons and having the vapors every thirtieth of the month. For God's sake, even Charlotte'd got up there and made him out to be some kind of devil. Charlotte, who'd showed herself naked to half the men who passed through New Orleans. Who knew how many she'd laid down for?

And maybe it wasn't so surprising that the only thing Willard Everleigh, testifying as to his character when they were boys back in the hills of Kentucky, could come up with was that Willard had seen Inch butcher hogs at the age of ten or eleven, like his daddy'd taught him. Which was supposed to make him out to be a man capable of killing and butchering women.

Then there was that business about the snakes. Did he dance with his hands filled with rattlers and water moccasins? Did he dance until he fell down in a fit? Well, he'd said, the only dancin' he'd done in eight, ten years was the rock and roll. It got a laugh, but he'd been dead serious. Did he speak in tongues while in a frenzy? Had he once claimed to be an itinerant preacher and gone around the Southeast telling innocent young women that he'd been sent by God to show them the key to heaven? Had he showed so many of them the key that his bastards were scattered from Atlanta to New Orleans?

He didn't admit to it, but he didn't deny it either. The women in the courtroom and on the jury had looked at him in that sneaky way they had when they got to wondering about a man who didn't give a damn about them except he wanted a piece of ass. Curiosity and speculation got more women under the covers than sweet talk any day in the week. Except Sunday maybe.

He was and he wasn't surprised at first that Faye hadn't come to see him. There was her having the baby practically hours after he was sentenced and carted off to San Quentin. And the recovery after. And a lot of trouble for her after that. But she should've come visited sooner or later. Let him see her face. Because if he'd ever loved anybody, he'd loved her. Otherwise why would he have gone to the trouble of marrying her? She'd had no money to speak of, and chances of her making it as a movie star had been slim to none. The very least she could've done was bring the kid at least once so he could've seen how his seed turned out.

The very least she could've done was call him on the telephone or write him a letter so he wouldn't have to feel so cut off from the world and all.

No woman should be so cruel to the man she'd slept and fucked with and whose child she'd had. Once a woman had a man's child they were more than man and wife. They were a family. They were blood. And blood was supposed to be thicker than water and the strongest tie that bound there ever was.

Well, so he'd hate her forever for turning her face away from him and never letting him lay eyes on his boy.

What'd surprised him most of all, thinking back on it, was Paul Hobby coming to see him.

He'd hardly known the man, having no connection with him except for doing a couple of small jobs around his beach house, killing the goats for a couple of roasts, bending the elbow with him and Bolivia down at Buddy's once in a while. Getting roaring drunk a couple of times.

He remembered how they'd asked him to dance for them like he danced with snakes back up in the hills. There was a woman in the crowd who wore a silver robe with odd black markings on the back. She'd been naked underneath, and he remembered sometimes, in sparkling flashes that could've been real and could've been otherwise, how they'd stripped him buck naked and forced him to fuck her while she lay on her back across a boulder on the beach.

Even so, when Hobby showed up during visitors' hours to say how sorry he was for the trouble Inch was in and how he'd do what he could to keep an eye on Faye and the baby, it was more friendship, coming from a stranger, than he'd gotten from people who claimed to be his friends.

Hobby said that, knowing Younger was an independent-minded man, a proud man, disdainful of charity, he'd brought along a paper for him to sign, giving Hobby the right to exploit the case in any way he could, book or film. He'd support Faye and the baby out of the proceeds and put what was left in an account for the time, if and when, Younger got out of prison.

Hobby told him not to mind the things they were writing about him in the papers. How he was known to be a violent man of unpredictable temper, skilled with knives and familiar with guns, fighting off the arresting officers, pulling a gun on them with his pregnant wife right there in the line of fire.

A mountain man of disturbingly odd attraction for the ladies. The newspapers made a lot out of that.

Some reporter wrote that Inch Younger had the evil face of Pan and called him the Pagan Killer. He described Younger's hair as soft as fox fur, sticking up all around his head, worn long in back.

Jaw like an ax blade. Eyes almost lidless, Oriental eyes, dark eyes with a peculiar luster, shining out of a face like tanned leather. Small ears without lobes, set close to his head. A hard, straight upper lip, ticked underneath his nose and at the corners with small indentations like the points in a strand of barbed wire, lower lip soft-looking and curved like a woman's. A man who looks like a man changing into an animal or an animal changing into a man. Caught there in between. Not particularly handsome but, according to female witnesses, a man of undeniable fascination.

Hobby commissioned the reporter to write a book. It failed to find a home with a New York publisher and finally ended up a paperback original put out by a quickie publisher in San Fernando Valley. The title was *The Hog Wallow Murders*. It sank without trace. Maybe there were too many other similar stories crowding the news about that time. Maybe nobody saw a television special in it. Hobby lost interest in doing a film.

He went to visit Younger again and told him that he'd tried to locate Faye so he could give her some money to live on, but couldn't because she'd disappeared, infant and all.

Well, Younger'd thought at the time, you could believe that or not as you pleased. It didn't matter much. He didn't care about seeing that Faye had any money, and the chances of him getting out were slim to none anyway.

That was the last he'd seen or heard of Hobby.

Younger was slow but he wasn't entirely stupid. Nobody did anything for nothing. Hobby'd wanted something from him, but it didn't pan out, so that was the end of that. He probably never tried to locate Faye at all. It was the kind of shit Hollywood assholes said because it didn't cost them anything.

He thought about the goddam linoleum knife. That was the piece of evidence that probably decided the jury that he'd killed those three women, even though he told them that he *thought* he'd lost it a couple of weeks before the two whores were supposed to have been murdered and cut up. Where, when, and how he'd lost that knife came to him in dreams, but he never could remember the details when he was roused from sleep by the goddam bell.

He lay there thinking about all that. It was like swimming around in a stew. He knew that the New York guinea, Macelli, was watching him.

"Why you lookin' at me, Macelli?" he asked.

"I ain't looking at you."

"You think I don't know you're lookin' at me?"

"I was just thinking how you're going to be out on the street."

Younger didn't crack a smile, but when he said, "Yeah," you could hear that he was smiling with satisfaction all over his face.

"What you going to do when you get out?"

"I'm going to follow the rules. I'm going to work in the car wash. I'm going to go to school nights and get to be a automobile mechanic. I'm going to make something of myself."

"What're you *really* going to do?"

Younger finally turned his head, so Macelli could see his mouth as he said in a jailhouse whisper, "First, I'm going to drink a bottle of booze and get drunk. Then I'm going to get me a woman and screw her blind. Then I'm going to find my wife and ask her why she never come to see me, never brought my kid to see me, turned her fucking back on me. And I'm going to go looking for the sonsabitches that tricked me into here and make them pay me back for fifteen years."

7

They were lying on the bed but not in the bed, in Whistler's bedroom, in his rickety house that perched on stilts over the Cahuenga Pass. Not under the sheets. Not naked. Just lying on top of the bed, fully clothed except for their shoes, their heads on the pillows, looking up at the ceiling and murmuring in the ruddy gloom of sunset.

"Why didn't you come back sooner?" he said.

She didn't answer.

"Why didn't you come back after Younger was put away?"

"I told you."

"Tell me again."

"The town went sour on me, or I went sour on the town."

"It wasn't because of me? I mean looking at you in the courtroom and not knowing what to say?"

"No. The trial wrecked me. Knowing what I'd been living with wrecked me. That's why I couldn't love the baby."

"Are you crying again?" he asked, even though she made no sound. Even though he could scarcely see her face in the shadows of the room. "If you don't want to talk about it..."

"I can't not talk about it," she said. "Maybe if I'd talked about it when it happened I wouldn't have fallen into the bottle."

He made a sound as though he'd been punched in the stomach.

"I had nobody to talk to," she said, "so I became a drunk. I had a little boy that needed me, and I became a drunk."

"I hear you."

"I kept wanting to tell the story because I was hoping somebody could make some sense out of it for me. I mean I came out here full of big ideas, grand dreams, and I tossed it all away for a hillbilly, just what I'd left, a hillbilly with funny eyes."

He lay there next to her, hardly touching, wanting more than he'd wanted in a long time to undress a woman, to undress Faye and pull her close to him just to see if their bodies would fit the way they used to long ago. He wanted to touch her, put his hand on her thigh or breast or belly, but he knew she'd be offended, even angry. She'd accuse him of being insensitive—though he sensed she wanted touching as much as he—and being interested in nothing else after all this time. After this miraculous rediscovery. Then she could vent some of her rage on him because—as Bosco often said—when you had nobody to hate, anybody to hate was somebody to hate, even if it was only for a second, just long enough to burn a little of the accumulated pain and grief away.

"You don't have to say unless you want to say," he said. "You want to take the fifth with me?"

She turned her head on the pillow, trying to see his face in the gloom. Take the fifth was AA jargon. It meant for one alcoholic to listen to another alcoholic tell all the worst. Not to comment. Not to advise. Not to forgive. Just to listen. An ear was better than a wall.

"You in the club?" she asked.

"Ten years sober. Ten years without a drink."

"Good God, Sam, we've both had our troubles, haven't we?"

He rolled over on his side and kissed her. She didn't open her mouth or give him her tongue. It was as though they remembered what it was like to be lovers and were sad because they might not be lovers anymore.

"I'll share that time with you," she said. "The time I almost told you about in the restaurant. It was the night I bottomed out. It was really Christmas morning."

It's nearly always Christmas, Whistler thought. That was the worst time of the year for practicing drunks and recovered alcoholics.

"Four years ago. I was in this fleabag hotel all by myself. Not welcome in my father's house. Separated from my kid—I didn't even know where he was. I weighed about eighty pounds. I looked like a bone with a hank of hair on one end. I was lying on the bed so hungry I wanted to cry, dying for a drink but too weak to get up and go do what I'd have to do to get one. I managed to reach out and open the room door. There was nobody around. I could tell the whole hotel was practically empty. I started to panic. I thought I was really in a tomb, that I was already dead. I'd died and this was going to be my hell. A dirty, empty hotel, with nobody to bring me a drink and no strength to go looking for one.

"I was just about ready to start screaming, when I heard a door open and close down the corridor. I reached out and pushed the door open a little more. I saw this man walking toward me, putting on his overcoat. He was wearing a hat."

Whistler didn't ask what all these little details had to do with it. He understood that the details had everything to do with it, the horror of that waking dream.

"I coughed and he glanced in at me. He smiled but kept on going. Then he must have stopped and stepped back, because there he was sticking his head inside the door a little.

"'Something the matter?' he asked. 'Are you not feeling good?'

"I told him I just woke up after flying all the way in from Miami or someplace, ready to surprise my sister for the holidays, only to find out she'd gone to their cabin up in the woods. So, when I felt up to it, I was going to get packed and dressed and take the bus upstate to spend Christmas Day with my family.

"I said it was nice he stopped to ask if I was all right. He said what else could a decent person do, Christmas or no Christmas. But especially at Christmas people should care about one another. He was away from his family and he understood how bad it felt to be alone. Nobody to have a laugh with, a meal with, maybe a little drink.

"Who was kidding who? I didn't believe he had a family and he didn't believe I had a family. I knew what he was and he knew what I was. Just a couple of tramps.

"I said I'd offer him a Christmas drink if I had any to offer, and he said he could probably buy a bottle downstairs. So he went away and came back with a pint. We had a drink. I started feeling better. I could feel the color coming up to my cheeks. I told him to turn his head while I got up and went into the bathroom to run some water on my face and comb my hair. When I came out he had his overcoat and jacket off and was sitting on the bed. We had another drink and then we had sex. He left his socks on. It was pretty bad.

After it was over, he didn't have to play the game anymore. But he was a very decent guy. He left what was in the bottle and laid two ten-dollar bills on the dresser."

She became very quiet remembering the shame. Whistler knew the story wasn't over. The terrible punch line was yet to come.

"And do you know what?" she asked, working him the way a comedienne works a cabaret crowd. "I thought so little of myself, of the merchandise I'd tricked him into buying, that I made him take ten dollars back."

"You crying?"

"Not about that Christmas Eve. About all the Christmas Eves I didn't have with my kid. It haunts me I let my boy get lost," she said.

"You ever try to trace him?" Whistler asked.

"Yes, I went looking."

"Where'd you look?"

"Old Younger'd saved a matchbox he got from the people he sold John to."

"How was that?"

"Matches don't come with tobacco up in the hills. You can't pick them up all over the place like you can in cities. Everybody usually lights up from the fire or the kerosene lantern. The old man was wanting a light for his pipe, I suppose, and this man handed the box of matches over."

"And he kept it for six months?"

"He gave it to Sue-Sue, this twelve-year-old girl—for favors done, I wouldn't be surprised—and she saved it. It was a pretty matchbox covered with foil. She kept needles and pins in it. It's the sort of thing children do, especially children from the hills who don't have much by way of pretty things."

"What kind of place was giving out the matchboxes?"

"The Motel Royal in Johnson City. I went there, and that's where my luck ran out. They said they didn't keep registration cards more than three months. I stayed around for a while, hoping for I don't know what, then I moved on."

"I'll look for your boy," he said, and kissed her again. This time she opened her mouth.

"How can you do that?" she asked. "It's been so long."

"There's things to do and places to look. I'm not making any promises but I'll find him if I can."

He kissed her again.

"I know I'm in your bed, but I don't do it on the first date," Faye said, trying to make it funny.

He ran his hand up her leg beneath her skirt.

"I wasn't expecting anything."

She fumbled with the belt of his trousers.

"Sure you were," she said, "and so was I."

They didn't even bother getting undressed the first time.

8

Bosco was on duty.

"Where's your morning man?" Whistler asked.

"He keeps railroad hours. I only see him when the run from Chicago pulls in. About three times a week. That's a little restaurant humor. I don't care. What else have I got to do? You want coffee?"

"Ham and eggs and coffee."

"You're going somewhere."

"What makes you say that?"

"You never eat breakfast unless you're going somewhere."

"I can't get over you," Whistler said. "Bosco, the wonder man. Knows all. Sees all."

"Tells all," Bosco said.

"How's that?"

"Don't do it," Bosco said.

"Don't do what?"

"Don't go chasing sparks from old fires."

"I wish you'd stop talking like your average friendly street-corner philosopher and spit it out."

"What you was ain't what you are now. Take it from me, you bump into this guy Sam on the street and you wouldn't even recognize him. You probably wouldn't even like him. The same goes for Faye."

"Hey, Bosco, give me a little credit. I look at Faye I don't see eighteen, and she damn sure don't see twenty-five or whatever."

"Okay, so where you going?"

"Kentucky."

"What's back in Kentucky?"

"That's where Faye lost her boy."

"How long ago was this?"

"The last she saw him was eleven years ago. The last anybody else she knows saw him was four years ago."

"Let me make sure I just heard what I thought I heard. You're going back to look for a kid gone missing four years ago."

"That's right."

"What do you give your chances? Twenty million to one? A hundred million to one?"

Whistler turned his head and looked out the glass door.

"You ducking the conversation here?" Bosco said.

"I'm watching for Faye. She's going to drive me to the airport."

"Say even two hundred thousand to one. Say that. Those good enough odds for you to go back and forth across the country?"

"Stop with the odds. What are you all of a sudden, a bookie? You read about how brothers and sisters, separated when they were kids, find each other after forty years. You read about mothers finding sons and daughters and vice versa."

"It ain't commonplace. Tell me you don't think it's commonplace."

"So it's not commonplace."

"Okay, I'll give it to you. It happens. But you can go crazy looking for a lost kid."

"You don't want to make me a breakfast, I'll get a breakfast at the airport," Whistler said.

Bosco went off to fry up a pair of eggs and a slice of ham. He came back with them on a plate with some hash browns, and the coffee.

"You could be doing her an unkindness, Whistler," he said as he put them down.

"How's that?"

"Building up her hopes."

"There's Faye," Whistler said, slipping out of the booth.

"You want me to take care of your car and your house?" Bosco asked.

"Faye'll do it," Whistler replied, and was out the door and on the sidewalk, walking toward his beat-up Chevy waiting at the curb in somebody else's care.

Bosco sat down and started to eat Whistler's breakfast.

"Woman enters the picture," he mumbled under his breath, "and your whole diet goes to hell."

9

They wouldn't call him Kentucky like he wanted them to. His name was John but he liked Kentucky better. Sometimes he called himself Dan. There was power in names. He told everybody to call him Kentucky, but everybody called him Bitsy. That was a hell of a name for a leader, a caretaker.

You had to work like a sonofabitch to establish your authority when you were only fifteen years old, five feet two, a hundred and ten pounds soaking wet. Not that he wanted to be the boss. He didn't really want to be the boss. He'd like it a lot better if Hogan, who was seventeen, eighteen, maybe even nineteen—who could tell?—five feet ten, a hundred and fifty, would be the boss.

When Hogan came on the scene a month, two months ago, in from Idaho, Nebraska, someplace like that in the Midwest, all he had to say when anybody asked his name was "Call me Hogan," and everybody called him Hogan. Bitsy didn't think that was his name. Nobody used their real names on the street. They used made-up names like they used made-up histories.

What the hell was a Hogan anyway? What the hell was anybody doing calling himself Hogan like some fucking character out of a John Wayne movie? He wanted to be John Wayne, why couldn't he be the boss and leave Bitsy in peace?

Why was it left up to him? And if it had to be left up to him, why couldn't they call him Kentucky like he asked them to?

Being the leader, taking care of a goddam crowd of eight, ten kids, all ages, all colors, all persuasions, meant he was the last one in bed, making sure there was clean water in case anybody got thirsty in the night, making sure what food they had left over was covered up and put away in the tin-lined box so the rats wouldn't be attracted.

First one up in the morning, making sure nobody had taken sick during the night, or got up half zonked, half asleep, and shit in the corner where it'd attract flies and other vermin.

Dipper forgot and did that every once in a while because Dipper wasn't all there and really should have been in an institution instead of out on the streets. Except there were no institutions for people like Dipper. Some asshole governor had fixed that a long time ago. Sent everybody out of the institutions, all the morons, all the half-wits, and told them to take care of themselves or let the neighborhoods take care of them. So the neighborhoods didn't take care of them. The city put some of them up in hotels, where they got beat up, pissed on, poked up the ass.

So Bitsy had one of them, Dipper, on his hands, too, along with big lazy assholes like Hogan and baby whores like Sissy and Mimi and Moo.

Bitsy thought Mimi was beautiful. She dressed in torn underwear she called shifts with openwork lace all over the front and a satin bed jacket over that and a short skirt that was ripped up both sides and high-top shoes and fingerless gloves. She was heavy on the makeup and her hair was screw-curled. Moo dressed the same and Bitsy thought she was beautiful, too.

They wanted to look like tramp rock singers, and Mimi even sang one of the latest numbers for him when Bitsy found her up on the roof a couple of times, leaning her elbows on the rotten wooden rail and staring out over the city, singing under her breath. She wasn't a very good singer—even Bitsy could tell that—but she pooched out her red mouth in such a way that Bitsy couldn't keep his mind on his ears.

One thing he really liked about her, she didn't give it away to anybody, not even to Hogan, who acted like he was doing a girl a favor if he pulled down her pants.

He heard her tell Hogan right off the bat, "Twenty dollars is my price for friends."

"Don't make me laugh," Hogan said. "Twenty's the best you ever get out on the street."

"So, they're all my friends," she said.

"I get fifty for my ass," Hogan boasted, and walked away, strutting his buns like they were filled with raisins.

"Thinks his shit don't stink, that one," Mimi told Bitsy. "What he don't know is I'd do it for five dollars for a friend. For a real good friend I'd even do it for nothing."

Bitsy decided right then and there he'd save up a fiver and ask her, in a kidding way, if she'd meant what she'd said, so in case she said she wouldn't do it for the fiver—what'd he think she was, a cheap whore?—his feelings wouldn't be hurt so bad.

But he never saved up the fiver because he had this terrible hunger that wouldn't let him rest, and every dollar he managed to get his hands on went for eats.

Still, he intended to save the fiver someday, even if he died of starvation the next minute after they'd done it.

He was alone in the abandoned, boarded-up building. All he could hear inside the shell was the drip-drip of water somewhere and the scattered patter of rats and mice. A stub of a candle guttered in the corner where he sat on his pile of rags and blankets. After dark everybody went out on the hustle, rubbing their eyes, rubbing their bellies, ready to prowl, ready to do what had to be done for the price of a meal, new Reeboks, a lid of smoke, a chunk of crack.

Sissy and Mimi and Moo out there on the stroll selling their tender asses. Hogan and Roach and Duckie strutting their buns.

My God, the things you had to do to make it through the night and the next day. Feeding appetites. Pleasing perverts.

"I'm no fucking faggot," Hogan always said. "I don't take it in the ass. I poke them in the ass. I don't suck nobody off. I just lay back and let them do me. I can't stand faggots. Fuck 'em all."

Bitsy remembered the first time he'd been had, in a freight car traveling west. The big fucking coon had bent him over. What was there to say? He'd been raped. That didn't make him a queen.

"Light a candle in the window, Mother. I'm coming home," he said, grinning wryly, grinning at his filthy hands.

He got up and put out the stub of candle. Put it in his pocket. Got out his pencil flash and made his way out of the wreck of a building, out into the streets. Out with the lights and the crowds and the good times.

10

It gets cold at night in La-La Land.

Faye was wearing an extra pair of socks inside her boots. She had on a quilted anorak and kept her hands in her pockets.

Jojo, her partner for the night, blew on his hands every now and then but that, she knew, was more because of dead nerve ends from mainlining in the past than because of the weather. He was big and black and had a mass of keloid tissue on the right side of his jaw and neck from a time when he'd been set afire—had been burning and scarcely knew it—which frightened everyone who saw it until they got to know him. He was free of drugs. Born again in Christ. Out there trying to help where he could.

They knew what few others knew. Living on the edge was a high, with or without drugs. Danger was living. Death was something to be dared.

They figured a runaway kid was addicted after thirty days on the streets of any city. Addicted to cocaine or crack. Addicted to speed or heroin. Addicted to the high of surviving from day to day. Out there on the corners with their friends, selling their bodies, shooting up between their toes, sucking dicks, eating cheeseburgers and tacos and slices of pizza. Slurping Cokes. Guzzling ice cream sundaes. Living the life. Why the hell else did anybody think whores call it the life? Because they like it. Not all the time. Not every hour of every day. But mostly they like it.

That's what Faye and Jojo knew.

They were getting known along the hookers' stroll around Hollywood and Vine.

Faye wondered why it was, if Sam'd been sitting there in the window of Gentry's regularly, he'd never seen her doing the missionary scene night after night. You had to wonder, was there such a thing as fate? Was there such a thing as God?

"You doing all right, Sissy?" she asked a child with parti-colored hair, underwear top beneath a fake-fur shrug, torn-off jeans so tight the seam nearly disappeared in the fold of her crotch.

"My tits are freezing off," Sissy said.

"Why don't you wear a bra?"

The kid named Duckie, wearing the colors of a gang from a city far away and a baseball cap with "Detroit Tigers" stitched on the front in orange thread, laughed and said, "She ain't got enough to worry about." He bit the last piece of ice from a Popsicle and threw the stick in the gutter.

"She's talking about keeping warm, not showing the booty, you silly sonofabitch," Sissy said, laughing and striking out at him. Puppies at play.

"How about some warmer underwear at least?" Faye said, very seriously, as though she were a doctor prescribing for a patient. "You get a chest cold out here in southern California, it can hang on for a month."

"What is it? You her mother?" Duckie asked, belligerent all of a sudden because Sissy had called him a sonofabitch.

"What's the matter with you, Duckie?" Faye asked. "Get up on the wrong side?"

"Wild hair up his ass," Sissy said, digging it in.

"I ought to smack you in the mouth," Duckie shouted in a burst of anger.

"Hey, hey," Jojo murmured.

Duckie raised his arm. "Smack you right in the fucking mouth!"

"Well, pardon me. What'd you have to eat, makes you so mean?" Sissy said. But she didn't move an inch.

Mimi and Moo moved away from the side of the building where they were showing the goods in a neon glow, attracted by the ruckus. Something to see. Something to do.

"What's the matter, Sissy?"

"Nothing. Duckie's got a wild hair—"

"I'm warning you. I'm going to smack you," Duckie said, and reached out to grab Sissy by the fake-fur shrug.

"Hands the fuck off," she said, jerking away. "You got Popsicle all over your hands. You got sticky shit all over your hands."

One of the girls moved in and grabbed him by the arm, pulling him away. When he threatened her with a raised fist, she whirled away, laughing.

"I'm gonna give you a slap in the mouth, you don't watch out, Mimi," he said.

"I've got some flannel tops over at Magdalene House," Faye said.

"Flannel tops?" Duckie shouted. He started to laugh like a maniac, slapping his knees and walking down the street and back, one foot on the sidewalk and one in the gutter. "I'd like to see that. I'd like to see Sissy in long johns."

"They're not long johns," Faye said, paying no attention to Duckie's antics. "They're little tops with short sleeves and sweetheart lace edging."

"She wants to get you in there, lock the door, turn you into a nun," Duckie said.

"Duckie," Faye said, finally getting annoyed, "why don't you find a place to sit? Leave us alone."

"Why don't you find a place to shit?" Duckie shouted as though he'd made a clever comeback.

"You can't do anything with Duckie unless you give him something sweet," Mimi said.

Jojo went into his pocket and came out with a candy bar. He broke it in half and gave one part to Duckie and kept the other.

"Big deal," Duckie said, stuffing the candy in his mouth.

"Now, go away for a minute," Jojo said. His voice was deep and dark, like a chocolate river.

Duckie walked off, munching the candy bar, lifting himself on his toes with every stride like a kid who'd won the game.

"You could come over and get a couple of those tops," Faye said.

"Me too?" Moo asked.

"You too, Moo," Faye said.

The girls started to laugh.

"Maybe you could sit around," Faye said.

"You too, Moo," Mimi said.

"Have something to eat."

"Who? You, Moo?"

"Maybe even stay the night."

"You blue, Moo?"

"The doctor's coming around first thing in the morning," Faye said, knowing she was losing out to silliness.

"Why you blue, Moo?" Mimi shouted.

"Well, if you change your mind," Faye said.

Faye and Jojo walked away, with choruses of children shouting and laughing behind them.

"Twenty minutes from now one of those girls or boys is going to be in the back of some car earning their keep," Faye said.

"Try. All we can do is try," Jojo replied in his bitter-chocolate voice.

11

The Malibu house was being used for Hobby's bachelor party, Sharon Allagash, the wife-to-be, having already moved into the Brentwood mansion.

Bolivia; Ira Konski, Hobby's agent; and his attorney, Melvin Yibna, the friends who'd volunteered to throw the do, complained that they hadn't been able to invite every dear friend Hobby had. They'd have had to hire the convention center. So he'd just have to make do with a hundred and twenty of his nearest and dearest.

A better selection of clever barracudas, ass-sucking lampreys, and sweet sharks could not be found anywhere, except maybe at a convention of evangelical ministers.

Now, in actuality, a hundred and ten of those gathered beside the beautiful Pacific were no more than business associates or mere acquaintances. The friendship status of half a dozen more was doubtful. The truth was, if only true friends had been called and mustered, they could've held the party in a telephone booth.

The trick was to find out which of the four remaining would declare themselves, without reservation, Hobby's bosom buddies.

Ira Konski was in charge of refreshments, chili catered in from Chasen's, cold cuts and salads from Canter's on Fairfax, and liquor from the Liquor Barn, discounted twenty cents on the dollar.

Melvin Yibna, being a lawyer and having contacts, was supplying the entertainment—X-rated cassettes, playing nonstop on the forty-inch projection screen, and a live act starring a young woman who nursed the sick by day and exposed her crotch by night.

Bolivia, a man who could get things done—and everybody knew

it—had recruited twenty hookers, who would present themselves at the likely moment in a most dramatic way.

The invitations had advised that dress was optional, so there were a hundred and nineteen men and one woman—Hobby was later to brag that there hadn't been any no-shows—outfitted in everything from leathers and denims to business suits and tuxedos.

Monsignor Terence Aloysius Moynihan, the show business priest, was wearing a two-hundred-dollar pair of slacks, Italian walking shoes without socks, a silk shirt, and a cardigan sweater instead of his formal black outfit with the little cape trimmed and sashed in purple.

The labor lawyer, Frank Menafee, wasn't looking very well. The news was passed around that he was dying of cancer. As a professional courtesy and for old times' sake, Yibna told the dancer to give the old attorney some special attention.

Pig-Nose Dooley, said to be a contract killer, was wearing a madras dinner jacket that burned the eyes of everyone who looked at it.

The one woman present was wearing a gown that pretended it was lime-green skin, grabbing every curve and dimple with a death grip, skirt slit up her thighs to the spots where her hips swelled, bodice cut so loose her tits were exposed about eighty percent of the time—a very frustrating thing for nearly every man in the room.

Eve Choyren, bogus Russian countess and practicing Satanist, had no use for most men except as pals, happy to be one of the boys but unwilling to hop into the sack with any but a special few, preferring the delights available with women.

She was present because she'd known Hobby about as long as anyone else there, because she possessed the clout that had obtained Hobby his star in the Walk of Fame along Hollywood Boulevard, and because she could be depended upon to do a lesbian act with one of the hookers or the dancer when the time arrived.

Hobby had stood up there in blue denim work pants and shirt, a handkerchief in the crotch of his pants, shirt opened to his navel displaying plenty of chest hair and gold chains, greeting arrivals for about an hour. But now he was sitting with Monsignor Moynihan, Bolivia, Pig-Nose, Eve, Yibna, and Konski—maybe four of these were the four real friends—and a screenwriter by the name of Jack Tensas who, it was rumored, had lately grown a conscience. They were all in the conversation well, half circled with a kid suede couch in front of a driftwood fire. Some were eating from plates, some were not. Some were drinking and some were not.

"You want to turn me down, go ahead and turn me down," Hobby was saying. "You got a right. You don't want to do a little horror picture with me..."

"If it was classic, Paul..."

"...that's okay with me..."

"...it'd maybe hit me a little differently, but..."

"...I'll get somebody else. Somebody younger. Somebody cheaper."

"...what you want to do is the same old crap, cutting up screaming girls."

"I was only doing you the favor, Jack, because the word is out that you're hurting."

"I've had expenses."

"I think you're right, Jack," Eve said.

"Right about what?" Hobby asked. "Right about he's had expenses? Right about I'm making the same old crap?"

"Are you going to do another of those disgusting pictures where you turn the theater into a butcher shop?" she asked. "Then that's what I think Jack's right about. Why don't you cut up some men once in a while?"

"I do. For Christ's sake, Eve, you know I play fair. I'm not out to pound on women. I chop up men, too. You've got to understand, what I'm doing in these pictures is in the best tradition of the Grand Guignol."

"What's that?" Pig-Nose murmured to Yibna, who was sitting at his elbow.

"French cabaret theater of horror, violence, and sadism, popular in the nineteenth century," Yibna murmured back.

"Like the flicks Hobby makes?"

"Yeah, like those."

"Up your grand gigi, Paul," Eve said. "Give us a break. You're not doing anything in any tradition except the tradition of making as much money as you can doing anything you can and having some kicks while you're doing it."

"What do you want me to do? You want me to make the Bobbsey

Twins? You want me to make documentaries for charity? You want me to go broke?"

"That would be nice," Monsignor Moynihan said. "I don't mean go broke, Paul. I mean it would be nice if you put your considerable talents and resources to work in a higher cause from time to time."

"Like Mother Church?"

"We have a Sunday dramatic anthology that could use your help."

"I'm not even a Catholic."

Monsignor Moynihan smiled the smile that fluttered a lot of female hearts around town and some that were male but wanted to be female. "I have time for your instruction in the faith any time you want to make a conversion."

"Conversion from what? I'm not anything."

"We're all something, Paul, even though we might not know it."

"Okay, say I do a little something for the church. No violence. No blood. No torture. Right?"

"I'd say we could do without."

"I mean your show is for a family audience, right?"

"That's correct."

"Little kids watch it?"

"Yes."

"So we don't want to show anything that'll give the kiddies bad dreams, do we? Like a bleeding heart with thorny vines curled around it, dripping blood? Or like some half-naked gazoony tied to a post with arrows stuck in him?"

"You're making—"

"As a matter of fact, we don't want to show some poor sucker nailed to a cross by his hands and feet, with a spear wound in his side, do we? Nothing like that?"

"Hey, Paul, you can' compare," Bolivia said, casting nervous glances at Monsignor Moynihan and leaning forward so that the cross around his neck dangled free.

Fucking whattayacallit, *hungan*, from the fucking jungle, used to dance around with his fucking shlong hanging out, all of a sudden he's a Catholic, he's religious, Hobby flashed. But he had no time for making the point to Bolivia that it was a long way from cutting up whores to wearing a cross around your neck right side up. He

had other fish to fry. He was on a roll, sticking it up the monsignor's nose.

"I can compare," he went on. "I make pictures—other people
make pictures—they start biting our asses about. Legion of De-
cency, this and that, gets up in arms. What are we doing scaring
little kids? So what I'm asking the monsignor here is how come
little kids aren't supposed to get scared about a man hanging on a
cross, and a face dripping blood from a crown of thorns, and a
bleeding heart hanging on the wall?"

"The symbols of a faith. The revelation of Christ's passion is a
message of love, joy, and redemption," Monsignor Moynihan said.

"How's that? Because your Jesus Christ was supposed to have
walked up out of the tomb?"

"His is a message of resurrection and life everlasting."

"So, in three of my last six flicks, Sally Bothner gets turned into
cutlets. She's up and at 'em for the next picture, good as new. If that
isn't resurrection, what the hell is?"

"You're getting yourself all upset over nothing," Konski said.

"While we're on the subject, Ira, let's take a look at the God of the
Jews. What a beauty he is, you want to talk about blood and sadism. Turns that Lot's wife into a box of Morton's—'When it rains
it pours'—just because the sucker turned around and took a peek
to see if she was standing there. Asked that other gazoony to sacrifice his son. Got Noah drunk so he'd screw around with his daughters. That bandit, Jephthah, made a deal with God to kill the first
person who comes out to meet him from his house after he kicks
the shit out of the Ammonites."

"How do you know all this?" Konski asked, genuinely amazed
and dumbfounded.

"What do you think? You know me all these years and you still
think I'm an illiterate, for Christ's sake? So who's the first person
comes out of his house? His only child, his daughter. So what does
he do? He offs her. He kills his child because he made a lousy deal.
Wonderful stuff to be teaching kids."

"They're stories meant to teach a lesson," Yibna said. "Parables
and moral fables."

"How do you know that isn't what I'm making?"

"Well, now, Paul..." Konski started to say, a smirk curling his
mouth.

"Now, Paul, what? Just fucking what? You people. Every one of you holier than fucking thou. But get into a little financial trouble and see how quick you'll sell your ass, write me a scene where cats eat out a baby's belly, or at least turn your face the other way when a client like me does it."

"Fuckin' right," Pig-Nose said.

"This is your bachelor party, fachrissake," Bolivia said. "We shouldn' even be talkin' abou' heavy t'ings like this. We should be talkin' abou' all the swee' ladies you goin' to miss as soon as Sharon ties a hal'er aroun' your neck."

Everybody laughed and went "Ho!" trying to ease the strain and turn the subject.

Then the dancer, who'd arrived with her protector—though what the hell the skinny asshole could do against a hundred and twenty if they decided to gang-bang his ward was anybody's guess —unseen by those gathered in the well, came tippy-toeing out on the wooden floor. Somebody had rolled up and pushed aside the ten-thousand-dollar rug so she could tap.

"My name is Fawn," she announced, all tricked out in tight black shorts, white sleeveless dickey, bow tie, top hat, and dancing shoes with bows on the toes.

Monsignor Moynihan stood up gracefully and stuck out his hand to Hobby. "I guess it's time to take my departure," he said. "My blessing upon your coming marriage and my every wish for your perfect happiness."

It wasn't long before Fawn's hat was tossed aside, the crotch of her pants unsnapped, and the dickey parted to show everything she had. She wasn't tapping anymore but was whirling around barefoot, until she spotted Menafee sitting all alone in a big over-stuffed club chair and went over to crawl up his legs and put her treasure in his face.

While everybody was getting joy out of that and Fawn was work-ing Menafee's zipper, Bolivia gave a yell, drawing attention to the pool on the terrace on the other side of the sliding glass doors, between the living room and the sand, where he'd arranged banks of lights which suddenly blazed to sensational effect. Out of the middle of the pool erupted fire, roaring up out of hidden gas jets. Then from everywhere naked women materialized like the succubi of dreams, body chains glistening around their waists and slave bracelets at their ankles. Treasures fluffed and sprinkled with glit-ter, nipples lipsticked, hair protected from the water with sequined caps as they all dived into the pool. Twenty grade-A hookers came out wet, their naked bodies glistening and silvery like giant fish.

Eve Choyren took off her dress, picked out a likely redhead, and went at it on a poolside chaise under a lavender spot.

Bolivia got behind Hobby and bent over to whisper in his ear. "You shouldn' bring up religion at these events," he said.

12

The hardest thing was getting a hot shower when you were out there living in the streets. The girls and boys who were selling their asses could manage a shower after every trick, unless the only place they had to turn the trick was an alley, an empty doorway, or the back of a car.

Bitsy didn't get picked off the stroll all that much. He was skinny and he didn't smile charmingly. There were a few faggots who liked boys who looked younger than they were instead of the studs like Hogan, and Bitsy, looking nine or ten, filled the bill. But there were real nine- and ten-year-old hustlers out there selling, and it wasn't easy making a score.

Gas stations and restaurants were on to street people buying a cup of coffee and then disappearing into the john for half an hour, maybe more, taking a whore's bath in the basin, using up the hot water, offending people with their bare asses when customers came in to do their business.

Bitsy had a morning schedule that started whenever he decided to get up—could be 11:00 A.M., could be 2:00 A.M., could be high noon.

It was midnight.

He walked by the Shell station and popped into the men's room, using a key he'd conned out of some gonif a month before.

They had liquid soap in a tilting jug over the sink. Bitsy used it to wash his feet and crotch with the washrag he carried rolled up in a towel. Then he washed out his socks and rolled them up in the dry end of the towel, with the washrag in the other end, so after he walked around all day, looking like a kid on his way to the beach, he had a clean pair of socks for the next day. He put on yesterday's pair of dry socks and put his Reeboks back on.

Maybe once a week, in good weather, he'd hitch a ride down to Santa Monica Beach and wash his jeans in the surf with a cake of saltwater soap. He'd spread them out on the sand to sun-dry and sit there in a pair of shorts—you could think they were swim trunks —watching guys toss Frisbees for their dogs, and girls oil themselves all over.

He had the best-looking faded jeans. Everybody said so.

He left the rest room and went across the street to the International House of Pancakes, where he had his wake-up cup of coffee. The waitress gave him the eye and at first he thought she was going to ask him to take a walk, but instead she asked him if he wanted a day-old Danish on the house. So it wasn't a bad start.

He paid for the coffee from the small change in his pocket and left the waitress a dime. Then he went into their rest room to take a dump because they kept it cleaner than the attendants at the gas station kept the one over there.

While he was sitting on the toilet, he checked his money stash, which he carried around with him in a matchbox with a layer of matches on the top. In case any musclers tried to rob him, all they'd find was some small change and the lights for his cigarettes. He'd usually get to keep the matches, where maybe a deuce, maybe a fiver, was hidden. He didn't have that couple of bucks, he could get so hungry he'd get dizzy and fog out right while he was walking around. It made him sick. It made him have crazy ideas. Visions even that were almost real. He sat there rubbing his thumb over the embossed foil covering the top of the matchbox. The embossing was pressed almost flat he'd been carrying it and rubbing it so long, the bright metallic colors almost worn away.

Now he felt good all the way around, so he walked over to the four corners at Hollywood and Vine, practicing the pimp roll that made the black hustlers look so cool.

Hogan was already there, walking up and down, five paces one way and five the other, hands on his hips, shirt unbuttoned, blond hair brushed high on the sides. Moo and Mimi were standing by the curb, Moo leaning on Mimi as if she wasn't totally awake yet.

"Uppa, Bitsy," Hogan said.

"What?" Bitsy said.

"Dibba-dobba, Bitsy."

"I can't understand you."

Mimi and Moo started giggling.

"Ungowa-buttawa, Bitsy-Itsy," Hogan said.

"What's the matter with you? You sick? You crazy?"

Mimi and Moo fell all over themselves. When Bitsy glared at them they made their mouths into O's and covered them with their fingerless gloves.

"Shubba, shubba, shubba," Hogan said.

"You're a asshole," Bitsy said.

Hogan stopped grinning. He stopped strutting. The girls were stamping their feet and whirling around each other with glee. Hogan walked over and invaded Bitsy's space.

"Back the fuck off," Bitsy said.

"What do you mean, back the fuck off?"

"Just what I said."

"You call me a asshole? Did I hear you call me a asshole?"

Mimi and Moo stopped laughing. They stood there watching Hogan bully Bitsy, put him down, take his balls away. First they'd been amused and now they were eager, wanting to see somebody humiliated. Bitsy would do.

"I said you were *acting* like a asshole."

"No, you said I *was* a asshole. Mimi? Did this wart here call me a asshole, didn't he call me a asshole?"

"He called you a fart," she said.

"I didn't. Fachrissake I never did," Bitsy said. He could feel tears rising in his throat. They were testing him. Testing his leadership. Anybody who knew anything about human nature would know that.

They were gathering a crowd.

When there's nothing to do, anything to do is something to do. When there's nothing to see, anything to see is something to see.

Bitsy hoped there was a cop standing around there. Somebody in a purple string shirt or a leather vest, scoping the street for early-morning action, ready to leap in and save him if Hogan started hitting on him.

"So it's getting worse, ain't it?" Hogan said. "I don't know if I can stand here and take your insults."

"Cut it out, will you? Just cut it out," Bitsy said, smiling his thin, nervous smile. "I'm in no mood for kidding around first thing in the morning."

"Oh, shit," Hogan said, turning away, suddenly losing interest in the game of torture. He whirled around, then whirled around again and threw his arm around Bitsy's neck, making it look affectionate. But with Bitsy's neck in the crook of his elbow he gave it the squeeze, letting Bitsy know he could do him some real damage if he wanted to.

"Where's Dipper?" Bitsy asked.

"How the hell do I know where's Dipper?" Hogan replied, letting go.

Mimi and Moo were back at the light pole, jiggling around as if they couldn't stand still.

"You see Dipper?" Bitsy asked them.

"What are you, his mother?" Mimi asked.

She laughed as though she'd just said something very funny. Nobody else laughed except Moo, and even she didn't laugh very much.

"I'll bet he's still back at the house," she said, taking mercy on Bitsy.

"Anybody want to go down to the beach?" Bitsy asked.

"It's the middle of the night," Mimi said, as though she wasn't sure about Bitsy's sanity.

"I got to make breakfast," Hogan said.

"Why didn't you say so? I'll spring for breakfast."

"Well, alllll right," Hogan said, "let's go do breakfast and then let's go do doo-doo and then let's go do the ba-ba-ba beach."

Mimi and Moo laughed so hard they almost fell down in the gutter.

It didn't take much, Bitsy thought, to make some people lose their minds.

Hogan walked with him across the street, his arm around his shoulders again. Just a couple of buddies going over to the coffee shop for a little eggs and bacon, a little Danish, a little coffee. No girls allowed.

What he didn't like about being so small was that, even though you were the leader, when somebody bigger than you put his arm around your shoulders it made it look like he was pushing you around where he wanted to go.

He searched his pocket with his outside hand, seeing if he had enough for two meals. Sonofabitch. He'd have to go into his stash. He'd have to take out the tenner buried under the layer of matches, and everybody'd have a look at his stash. He fumbled the matchbox open inside his pocket and cut the tenner out without having to let anybody see it.

"What the hell you doing?" Hogan asked. "You playing with yourself? You playing pocket pool?"

He laughed again. Bitsy laughed, too, because otherwise it'd look as though Hogan was making fun of him again.

13

The 7:30 A.M. flight to Atlanta arrived only forty-five minutes late, giving Whistler nineteen minutes to make the plane leaving for Tri-City.

An hour later he was on the ground again, feeling every mile of the trip on his skin and in his bones. Since they'd picked up three hours crossing time zones west to east, it was around four-thirty in the afternoon with maybe another half hour, ten miles by surface transportation, into Johnson City still to go.

Tri-City served Johnson City and Kingsport in Tennessee and Bristol in Virginia. None of them being exactly a metropolis, there was bus transport but not a lot of taxis lined up waiting for the rush.

Whistler looked over the three cabs sitting there as he walked from the terminal to the curb, and decided on the one that needed a wash the least.

The driver, leaning against the fender with a toothpick in his mouth, looked like the kind of Volunteer who watched the Grand Ole Opry every week and dreamed of being its comic star. He was old enough to know some stories and young enough not to be tired of repeating them.

The other drivers were about to hawk him, when Whistler opened up the passenger door to his chosen taxi and tossed his bag onto the seat.

"Johnson City," he said.

The driver marched around to the left side and slid in behind the wheel while Whistler settled himself in the back and checked the name on the license behind the plastic-windowed holder.

"You know the Motel Royal, Doke?"

"You really know how to live high, don't you? And it's Hoke, not Doke. My sonny was playing with that license and smudged it with his little fingers."

"Do I detect a note of contempt for the accommodations I just named?"

"It'd make a nice kennel for your dog, if you hated your dog."

"Well, I don't know it by experience or even reputation."

"How do you know it?"

Hoke's eyes kept flickering to the rearview mirror, checking Whistler out, reading his clothes, his haircut, how he smiled and when.

"I know it from the matchboxes it used to hand out."

"Oh, them."

"Are they a local joke?"

"Used to be, when Millie and Wendell bought five thousand of them from some huckster on his way to Knoxville. It's one thing to try to make a silk purse out of a sow's ear, it's something else to paint a pig white and try to sell it as an albino mare."

"They still gilding the lily?"

"Hell, no. When the five thousand ran out they put the old box of kitchen matches on the counter and called it a customer courtesy. That was—Jesus—must be a year ago."

"They lasted a long time."

Hoke tossed him another appraising look, wondering how come this stranger would know that five thousand matchboxes had lasted three, three and a half years. "They didn't hand them out to just anybody."

"Millie and Wendell still own the Royal?"

"Well, they both own it but only Millie runs it. They split up last year and neither one would sell out to the other. So Wendell said okay, he'd let Millie keep the manager's apartment and she could run the goddam place and cheat him if she wanted to. He took a house on the edge of town and pays the motel a lot of surprise visits just to keep her honest."

They rode in silence for several minutes and then Hoke asked, "You still want the Royal? I don't want to take any money out of Millie's pocket but I could recommend something better."

"I'm sure you could, Hoke, but I think it's the Royal for me."

"Sounds like you got business there."

"Well, it's what brought me here."

"What business you in?"

"I'm looking for somebody who disappeared from around here about four years ago."

"We got lots of those."

"Disappearances?"

"Disappearances. Runaways. Here we are."

When they pulled into the driveway and stopped alongside the office, Whistler saw that the Royal was every bit as tattered as Hoke had led him to believe.

"Wait for me," Whistler said.

"You're on the meter."

"I wouldn't have it any other way."

"Take as long as you want. Hey, you mind if I go in with you and say hello to Millie?"

"That's all right with me. Any questions I've got to ask, the more people hear them the better."

Hoke followed Whistler through the glass door, with a tarnished gold decal crown slightly off center, into the office. The four- or five-foot counter was made of triple ply. The edges hadn't been finished and there were little dribbles of glue that had come out of the ply here and there. A counter display advertising Hamm's beer was half filled with travel brochures praising Appalachian sights, and some timetables for the Greyhound and the Tri-City Airport. There was a summons bell and the open box of kitchen matches, just as Hoke had said there'd be.

A small color television on a shelf up in the corner under the ceiling was on but the sound was off. Anybody sitting and waiting in the one chrome and vinyl chair shoved against the wall would have had a bad angle on the screen. It was positioned for the bene-fit of the person behind the counter.

On the plywood-paneled walls were maybe fifty, maybe a hundred little black picture frames with registration cards in them. Whistler identified the signatures of a couple of southern governors he remembered, some football and baseball players, and even some movie and television stars. But he doubted very strongly that Jack Nicholson or Robert De Niro ever spent the night at the Motel Royal. More than likely they were the registration cards of people with the same names, who might even stop back just to see their signatures framed up on the wall, borrowing a little namesake glory the way people sometimes do.

A door in the back wall was open, leading to the manager's apartment. Part of the living room showed—some red drapes and half a fake mantelpiece displaying one of those statues of a naked Nubian slave girl walking a leopard. A radio was playing country and western somewhere inside.

Whistler hit the bell. It sounded cracked. He hit it again.

He could hear somebody grunting and complaining from inside the apartment, and then the sound of shuffling feet. Pretty soon a woman in the kind of wraparound housedress his aunt used to wear years ago came scuffing across the gritty linoleum like a sand dancer.

She was fifty, maybe fifty-five, with enough coquette left in her to make her adjust the front of the housedress and touch her hair when she saw a man as likely as Whistler standing at the counter. She flicked a blue eye at Hoke and it was clear to see there was no love lost between them, though they grinned at each other and made purring noises the way cats do.

Whistler suspected that Millie was mad at Hoke because he didn't recommend the Royal to travelers and Hoke was mad at her because she probably wouldn't pay him a commission for the service, and here he was bringing in a customer just to show her that he wasn't as tightfisted and small as she was.

"Room?" Millie trilled.

"Please. The best one you've got."

"The one with the view of the fishpond," Hoke said, sly and sarcastic.

Millie spun the Leatherette registration-card holder around facing Whistler and handed him the ballpoint fixed to the counter with a chain.

He signed in and turned it around facing her.

"Gary Cooper?" she said. "Ain't that somethin'. You was my favorite before you died."

"I'm not that Gary Cooper," Whistler said, giving her a lopsided grin he thought looked a little Cooperish.

Millie blushed and said, "Well, I know that. Don't you think I know that? But ain't it somethin' havin' the name of a movie star?"

"I'd like it better if having it would save me money like it saved him money."

"What do you mean?"

"Cooper's business manager signed all the big checks so Coop wouldn't have the bother, but Coop signed the little ones—anything less than a hundred—himself."

"Why'd he do that?" Hoke asked, as interested in the story as Millie.

"Well, alot of folks who got a check from Coop signed by his own hand just naturally saved it as a keepsake and never cashed it. I was told he saved ten, maybe fifteen thousand dollars a year that way."

Millie cocked a blue eye at Whistler and gave him a flirty smile. "You ain't plannin' on payin' for your room with a check, are you?"

"Cash," Whistler said.

"Well, I just wondered. Because I want to tell you right now I'd cash the check, Gary Cooper's name or no Gary Cooper's name."

Whistler took out his roll. It was thin but he kept a fifty on top.

"Sixteen fifty a night," Millie said. "How many nights will you be stayin'?"

"As long as it takes me to do what I came here to do."

"Nothin' naughty I hope?"

"Well, if anything naughty comes to mind, you'll be the first to know."

Millie blushed again, enjoying every minute of it.

Hoke was looking at him shrewdly, wondering what the hell a good-looking big-city man was doing buttering up old Millie.

"You want to pay by the night, then?" Millie asked.

Whistler laid down a twenty. She made change and handed him his key.

"Last cabinette on the right. Ice machine and soda machine is just around the corner."

"By the way," Whistler said, "these celebrities really stay here, or they just named-alikes?"

Millie waved a hand, making small of it. "Was just one of my husband's hobbies. I always thought it foolish. But he liked to sort through the registration cards every now and then, looking for funny things like that."

She waved at Whistler as he and Hoke left the office.

When Hoke was getting Whistler's bag out of the cab, he said,

"Fact is, the registration cards was about the only thing old Wendell got out of the separation. He's got a room full of 'em."

"Why's he saving them?" Whistler asked, reaching for the bag.

Hoke swung it aside and held on to it. They started walking back to the cabinette.

"He says you never know when someone'll get famous and he'll have a card with the same name on it," Hoke said.

"A friend told me that they only kept the cards three months."

"That's all your friend knows. Millie probably told your friend that. Anything she can do to spoil even a little bit of Wendell's fun, she'll do."

They reached the accommodation Millie called a cabinette, which she surely supposed gave the Royal another extra bit of class at no expense. Hoke stood there, waiting for Whistler to open the door.

The room, Whistler saw, was not all that bad. Cheaply constructed, with tacky drapes and pictures of a Victorian lady and a bellowing stag in frames screwed to the wall, but a cut better than some rooms he'd slept in.

While Whistler checked the bathroom, Hoke set the suitcase on the luggage rack and stood there, with his eyes half shut and his head tilted a little to the side, peering at the chromo of the stag.

"You think Millie and Wendell really suppose anybody'd steal that damn thing?" he asked when Whistler stepped back into the room.

"People have stolen worse, I suppose. What's on the meter?"

"Eighteen dollars and forty cents. Ten-dollar surcharge in from the airport."

"L.A. prices," Whistler said.

"Supply and demand."

"How much would you charge me by the day?"

"A hundred dollars and gas," Hoke said without a moment's hesitation.

"A hundred and you supply the gas."

"Where you want to go?"

"Up into the Kentucky hills. Place called Dog Trot. You know it?"

"I wouldn't say I knew it. We know about Dog Trot around here because it gets a laugh and because there was this killer—did the dirty out in your town, by the way—come from Dog Trot."

"Places get famous for the damnedest things, just like people."

"Like having a movie star's name?" Hoke said, with a look in his eyes that told Whistler he didn't believe all that crap about Whistler's name being Gary Cooper.

"Like that," Whistler said right back.

"This killer lived here in Johnson City for a time. I knew him. Inch Younger he called hisself."

"How well did you know him?"

"Not that well. I just knew him to have a beer with now and again. You here about Inch Younger?"

"I'm here about his kid."

"I didn't know any kid."

"He was up there in Dog Trot with his grandpa until about four years ago."

"Then where'd he go?"

"That's what I'm trying to find out."

"How old a boy?"

"He'd be fifteen now. So he was eleven then."

"You a detective?"

"How'd you figure that out?"

"Oh, I got an eye. Parents hire you to find this runaway?"

"Mother did."

"Kid eleven years old runs away he must've had strong reasons. I don't think you got much of a chance of finding him."

"He didn't exactly run away. He was taken."

"By who?"

"That I don't know."

"Four-year-old kidnapping . . . what chance have you got?"

"I've got to try."

"Well, sure, a fella's got to make a buck."

"So can you drive me up to Dog Trot?"

"Not in my cab. It's forty miles, then forty miles up into the hills."

"I had a look at a map."

"It's a wonder Dog Trot's on it."

"Hard country?"

"Very hard, and hard people. Not to be poked and prodded, you know what I mean?"

"*Deliverance* country?"

"What do you mean, deliverance country?"

"You see that motion picture with Burt Reynolds?"

"Oh, sure, I saw that." He laughed. "I don't know is Dog Trot that kind of deliverance country. They got their share of close-bred half-wits, and I suppose there's more than one rascal would corn-hole anybody, woman, man, boy, or goat. I guess there's even some would shoot you for your shoes but, hell, you'll be safe enough with me."

"What you said about the cab."

"Oh, I just meant it wouldn't make it over those back roads. We'll have to go in my four-wheeler. Eats the gas, does that four-wheeler, so why don't we say a hundred plus gasoline?"

"You'll have to take a check," Whistler said.

"Well, as long as you don't sign it Gary Cooper."

14

The way they show it in the movies sometimes, prisoners are
let out of jail in the early morning. Sometimes the actor has a bun-
dle wrapped in brown paper and string. Sometimes he's got a
cardboard suitcase. He's got a whitewall haircut and a fedora
that doesn't fit.

Prisoners get out in the afternoon. Sometimes late. There's a lot
of administration, a lot of paperwork, and everybody's jumping
around getting breakfast, taking a dump, doing what they got to do
early in the day, and everybody's running two hours late by the
time ten o'clock rolls around.

Younger spent the morning passing out his goods. Things he'd
collected. Some books. A child's doll he'd carved out of wood with
the tongue of his belt buckle, some little animals made out of bread
dough and then painted.

The guard gave him a new blade for his razor, even though it was
the middle of the week and you usually got the new blade on Sunday. Gave it back when you were finished, then got it again the next
morning. Most of the time you got your own blade back because the
office was afraid of spreading impetigo and other such diseases of
the skin. Used the one blade all week and then got a new one the
next Sunday. But the guard brought him a fresh blade on this
Thursday and said, "Going to miss you, Younger. You've done good
time."

Younger didn't say anything. He didn't say fuck-all all morning.
He didn't even go to breakfast. Nobody asked him why. Everybody
knew why. There were bastards inside could hate your guts and
you didn't even know it. They'd start up with a man waiting for

release. Get him into a bad fight. If the power's in a bad mood, you end up in discipline, your parole revoked. It doesn't happen often, but you hear about it. Maybe it's all lies, but why take the chance?

He refused a haircut and the guard said, "That's okay."

There was no interview with the warden. The warden was up in Sacramento arguing for this or that. Assistant warden couldn't be found. The captain of the guards shook his hand and said, "You going to be all right?"

"I hope so."

"They got you a job?"

"I start at a car wash first thing Friday morning."

"You got a place to stay with people?"

"My people are all back in the mountains."

"What, the Sierras?"

"The Appalachians."

"You going to go home?"

"One time. If I can."

"So, you've got no family here?"

"Nobody."

"You got a room, though?"

"They got me a room in this hotel."

"That's good."

"I hope so."

"You going to be all right?"

"I hope so, Captain."

"Good boy."

He got on a bus and rode with two prisoners going down to Los Angeles County for appearances, looking out through the grillwork over the windows at a world so pretty he could hardly stand it.

They let him out the door in front of Parker Center with a new suit, a pair of Adidas running shoes, a pair of jeans, a work shirt, extra underwear and socks in a canvas carryall, and eighty dollars in cash.

He went over to the bus stop and waited for the first of three buses that would get him to the hotel on Western Avenue.

15

Hoke looked like a different man behind the wheel of his four-wheeler. Stronger, bulkier, more substantial in every way, as though he took strength from the shotgun and the rifle racked behind him.

"Are we expecting trouble?" Whistler asked, indicating the weapons with a gesture of his head.

"Everybody travels with a gun or two this part of the country we're going into," Hoke said. "Always a chance we could get a shot at a deer."

"Is this the season?"

"Season? Nobody bothers about season up here. Who's going to check it out? Game warden don't come nosing around these hills much."

"Deliverance country."

Hoke laughed and slapped the wheel, liking the idea that the slicker thought there was real danger behind every tree and down every hollow.

He turned off the two-lane blacktop along a packed-dirt track that climbed up toward a distant ridge.

"How far?" Whistler asked.

"We got to rolley-coaster over three of them like that ridge up ahead."

Even the hard-packed surface of the road disappeared after a little while, and there was nothing but a trail scratched on the flanks of the hills, sandy in spots, dangerous with accumulated flints in others.

Once, they flushed a ring-necked pheasant right in front of them and Hoke said, "Damn."

By the time they got to the one-pump gas station and store, near a small collection of shacks scattered along another trail that seemed to peter out in the thick stand of loblolly pine up ahead, Whistler's kidneys were giving him hell from all the rattling around.

There were two old men and a younger one sitting on the porch, which leaned off to one side as though ready to give up the fight. They were chewing tobacco and spitting out a spurt of juice every now and then, making patterns in the dust.

There was no fey-eyed child picking away on a banjo, as there'd been in the moving picture. That gave Whistler a sudden, odd pang of disappointment.

The younger man was wearing an apron, marking him as the proprietor.

"Hello, my name's Hoke. Up from Johnson City," Hoke said, getting out of the four-wheeler. "This here is a friend of mine from Los Angeles, wanting to have a look around."

"Hunting?" the storekeeper asked.

"Nope."

"Handicrafts?"

"Nope."

"What then?"

"Old news."

That seemed all right with everybody, because they all nodded.

Whistler put one foot on the porch step. "Could I use your rest room?" he asked.

"My what?"

"You got a public toilet?"

"You got to take a crap, there's an outhouse the other side of the stream. You got to take a piss, you can do it right over by that tree, save you the trip."

The storekeeper and the old men stared at him as though he was being tested.

He walked over to the tree and unzipped. That seemed to decide everybody that he was okay. While he stood there enjoying the release of the flow, which disappeared into a clump of leaves and mushrooms at the base of the tree, he heard a screen door slam. He looked over his shoulder and saw a girl in blue jeans and flannel shirt, watching him and smiling.

He caught his breath and cut off the flow for a second, then let go and finished the job, wondering why a man felt so much more concerned about his dignity in front of a beautiful girl than a homely one.

He zipped up and went back to the porch, looking up at the girl and smiling into her face.

Up close she wasn't as beautiful as she'd first seemed. There was a scar on her upper lip that lifted it a little, exposing a little bit of tooth like a dog making a threat display.

She had a body though that could give a man persistent dreams.

"This is Sue-Sue," the storekeeper said, as if he knew the effect the girl had on men and was amused by it.

"You still have the matchbox, Sue-Sue?" Whistler asked.

"How do you know about my matchbox?" she said, putting special emphasis on the last syllable of the word, drawing a few snickers from the men. Even Hoke was having a laugh the way Sue-Sue was playing with the stranger from the big city.

"Your matchbox's famous," Whistler said, giving it right back to her. "Your matchbox is known all the way back in Hollywood, California."

"You from Hollywood?" Sue-Sue asked, her eyes changing, her manner changing, anxious now to make a good impression on this man who came from such a magic place.

She fingered her lip, and Whistler could practically read her mind as she dreamed an old dream about getting it made right so that she'd be as pretty as she thought she might be, given half a chance.

"I read how they can fix things about a person back there in Hollywood."

"They can fix things about a person right over to Knoxville or Nashville or Chattanooga for that matter," Whistler said. "But I suppose you're right. The best ones would be where the money is, in New York or back on the coast. I can leave my name with you. If and when you ever find yourself back there, I might be able to help you find whoever was best at fixing things about a person."

The storekeeper didn't like the sound of that. "I don't think Sue-Sue's going to do much traveling any time soon."

"I didn't say soon. I said if and when. I don't put any time limits on a promise or a favor."

Sue-Sue knew enough not to worry the man, who might've been a relative or might've been her husband.

"Well, don't hold your breath waitin' for a call from me," she said, but smiled in such a way that Whistler knew she was thanking him and saying that—if and when—he shouldn't be surprised if he heard from her.

The storekeeper was no fool—he got part of the message—but he decided, especially with Hoke standing there to witness, not to push it any.

"So you still have the matchbox?" Whistler asked.

She held up a finger and went into the store, the screen door slamming shut behind her.

"You go to any of them parties back in Hollywood?" one of the old men asked.

"What parties is that?" Whistler replied.

"Where movin' picture actresses run around bare-assed fuckin' and suckin' everybody."

"I used to hear rumors about such parties," Whistler said, "but that was some time ago. I don't hear much about them anymore."

"Well, I asked did you ever go to one?"

"I was never invited."

The old man turned away in disappointment and spit a stream of tobacco juice into the dirt.

Whistler felt as though he'd walked onto a movie set where a bunch of character actors were doing a bad job of it.

The screen door slammed behind Sue-Sue again as she came out with a little foil-covered matchbox in her palm. She handed it to Whistler. The foil had tarnished over the years and the embossed crown and "Motel Royal" were pressed almost flat, as though Sue-Sue had run her thumb over them time and time again.

Whistler had the notion that the glittery little matchbox had once been a kind of wish stone for a small girl.

"You can't have it," she said.

"I wasn't thinking of asking. I was just wondering where you got it."

"Don't you know? I mean whoever told you about it all the way back in Hollywood must've told you who give it me."

"Younger?"

"That's right, old man Younger."

"Matt Younger give it her," the storekeeper said.

"You remember where he got it?"

"From some of his kin was passing through," Sue-Sue said.

"How do you know they were kin?"

"Well, the old man gave them Inch's boy, John, didn't he?"

"You knew that?"

"Everybody knew that," the storekeeper said. He looked around. "You see any crowds around here? What one body knows everybody knows."

One of the old men leered sideways toward the storekeeper and Sue-Sue and said, "We got no secrets here. We're nothin' but an open book."

"What one body knows everybody knows," the other old man said, repeating the storekeeper's words.

"I can see how somebody gives a kid away to somebody else, you'd naturally think they were family," Whistler said, "but have you got any reason to know that for sure?"

They looked at one another as though he was asking a question just too difficult for them to fathom.

The storekeeper shrugged.

Sue-Sue smiled her small, dog's snarl and said, "Their name was Bosley."

"How do you know that?"

"I heard old man Younger call the man Mr. Bosley."

"There any Bosleys living around about?"

"Not that I ever heard of," the old man who'd been curious about Hollywood entertainment said.

"Wasn't from around here. Was from Pickett County," Sue-Sue said.

When they all looked at her as though doubting her little bit of information, she said, "I saw it on a sticker on the back window of their car. 'Pickett County Fair' it said."

"They could've just been visiting the fair."

"They could've," she agreed.

"Anything else you remember? The make of the car? The license plate? Anything like that?"

"You must be jokin'," the storekeeper said. "It's been four years.

She was twelve. It's a wonder she remembered the things she already told you. If she remembers."

Sue-Sue looked at him with disdain but made no protest. Then she looked at Whistler again and he could hear plain as if she'd said it aloud how a little girl of twelve could remember every least thing that happened to her in this godforsaken crossroads. She'd remember names of passing strangers and stickers on car windows and she'd treasure a little matchbox wrapped in colored foil, for lack of much else.

"The car was a brown sedan," she said. "The woman was fat and lame."

"Now how in the hell would you know a thing like that?" the storekeeper asked.

"While the man and you and old man Younger was inside drinkin' beers, the lady asked did we have a toilet and I showed her where she could take a pee. She almost slipped on the stones because she had these metal braces on her legs."

Sue-Sue looked triumphant.

"Did anybody tell Faye Younger any of this?"

The faces of the men closed down, and Sue-Sue backed off a step as if she didn't want to hear what they'd have to say.

"Faye Younger was a whore, though she wasn't giving any of it away around here. Did her whoring down in Johnson City. Left her goddam brat on Matt Younger's doorstep, then took off after her own pleasure. Husband suffering in jail, but she didn't give a damn. Comes back five years later and expects to see her kid all scrubbed and shiny-faced? Sheee-it! No use for her kind anyhow. City tramp. Never should have married Inch Younger. He was a hill man."

Faye must have offended every single soul in Dog Trot, the way the old men were looking and Sue-Sue was ducking and the storekeeper was carrying on.

Sue-Sue reached out and took the matchbox from Whistler's fingers.

"John Boy's got one of these, too. You find him and ask him can you have it."

16

It was Bosco's day off. It was Isaac Canaan's day off, too. They could have gone to the zoo, down to one of the beaches, out to Griffith Park for a horseback ride, up to the Angeles Forest for a taste of pine. They could have hung around the Polo Lounge at the Beverly Hills Hotel.

But they would have felt uncomfortable in any of those places, aliens marooned in strange worlds.

So they were sitting in a booth at Gentry's, Canaan wearing summer-weight slacks and rubber-soled plimsolls, a short-sleeved shirt with a dead alligator on the pocket, and a bandanna tied around his neck. He was still wearing his old felt fedora.

Bosco had on a pair of slacks and a white shirt with one sleeve pinned up.

They both had cups of coffee in front of them. They were both reading newspapers. Bosco also had a copy of *Magister Ludi* close at hand.

"What the hell about this?" Bosco said.

"About what?"

"About this killer gets out on parole today."

"Where do you see that?"

Bosco named the page and, when Canaan turned to it, tapped the columns, two of them above the center fold with a cut of Younger.

Canaan read it through, his lips moving slightly. "Sonofabitch bastard," he said.

"You know the gazoony? You have anything to do with him?"

"I was on the fringe. I was working vice out of Venice Division when it happened. I got to do some digging."

"Small world," Bosco said. "What was it like?"

"What was what like?"

"What you found when you was digging."

Canaan's jaw twitched, which was for him a severe expression of disgust.

"It says here there was evidence that Younger was a member of some satanic cult," Bosco said.

"Well, the bodies were marked."

"Marked with what?"

"Three sixes."

"Sure." Bosco closed his eyes and recited: "'Let him that hath understanding count the number of the beast, for it is the number of man; and his number is six hundred threescore and six.'"

"How do you do that?" Canaan asked, as close to showing admiration as he could get.

"Do what?"

"Quote things like that?"

"I read a lot."

"I read, too, but I don't remember the way you do."

"Some things stick," Bosco said, modestly. "So what else?"

Canaan stared at Bosco for a minute as though he was thinking about whether he wanted to go on with this conversation. Maybe he was only trying to remember, like Bosco closing his eyes. He took a marker pen from his shirt pocket and snatched a napkin from the dispenser.

"It was like this," he said and drew a diagram as he talked. "The coroner reported seven or eight slashing wounds—I don't remember exactly—on the breasts and belly of Carla Pointer. Plus the six sixty-six and something like this, a star, carved on her next to the numbers."

"A pentacle," Bosco said.

"That's right. That's what somebody called it. The other woman —Janet Strum—had something almost like this carved into her chest."

He drew a design that looked like a pentacle, except there were lines joining the legs of each point so it looked like five letter A's woven together.

"Like that," he said.

"Pentalpha," Bosco said. "Used for fortune-telling and calling up spirits."

"So," Canaan said, going back to his drawing, "one of them had both arms cut off at the shoulder and laid over her spread legs like this." The drawing of the severed and rearranged limbs made a diamond. "The head was off. The next one—Janet Strum—was partially clothed in bra and panties. She had about twenty-five defensive wounds on her hands and arms. Two slashing wounds on her throat. One finger had been severed. It was found on a shelf four feet away. Both legs were partially severed at the knee. The left leg severed at the hip but still joined to the body. An attempt was made to remove her head, too, but it wasn't finished."

"Something interrupted him."

"That's the way it looked."

"It says here there was three bodies," Bosco said.

"Third one was the barmaid. She was wearing all her clothes. What there was of them. Somebody'd cut her throat, but there was no attempt to cut her up or mark the body in any way. She had some slashes on her hands and arms though." He turned the napkin around facing Bosco. "This is how all three were laid out. The barmaid, Gladys Trainor, being the last one buried."

He'd drawn three paper dolls that seemed to be holding hands, whirling around in a dance caused by a passing wind, their paper arms and heads and legs torn from their bodies, their separate parts overlapping in places.

"You keep on saying slashing wounds, Isaac. How's that?" Bosco asked.

"Because the weapon used to inflict them was of a type that couldn't be used for stabbing. There was a linoleum knife with dried blood in the seam of the guard and handle. You know the kind? About five inches long, curved along the spine so it makes a hook. That's what got Younger convicted in the end. It was his knife. It had the initials IY burned into the handle with a hot nail. He said he'd lost it doing an odd job for some homeowner, but he couldn't remember where. That's what he said, but they didn't believe him."

"Fifteen years. How do you remember all that after fifteen years?"

"Some things stick," Canaan said.

17

Granny Hours could have been a hundred. She was certainly more than eighty. Mountain years, which some say are different from any other kind of years, were in her face and body. She looked as if she could walk the hills and leave a city man like him far behind, Whistler thought. Kill and dress a hog in the morning. Do a family load of wash by hand in the forenoon. Chop a cord of firewood after lunch. Lime the walls of her cabin and put up forty quarts of preserves before dusk fell, and read a chapter of the Bible before going to her bed.

She smoked a pipe, not a corncob but a decent briar with a hard rubber bit she'd chewed nearly in two with the four teeth left in her mouth.

Beneath the dappled shadows cast by the trees above her shack, when she turned her head just so—the rag wrapped around it and her hair turning color—she reminded Whistler of photographs he'd seen of the writer Isak Dinesen. Noble faces popped up in the strangest places.

When Whistler and Hoke had approached her door, she was sitting on a stool just beside it, smoking her pipe and taking the sun. She watched them approach halfway up the path before reaching out a clawlike hand with a finger pointed at Whistler and saying, "Just you."

Hoke took no offense but turned back and went to sit and wait on a tree stump beside the road.

"How come you wouldn't let my driver come along up here?" Whistler asked.

"The man from Johnson City? No reason, except it's you come

here for my help, and though you may be willin' to share what you know with everybody in the whole wide world, I am not."

"Is it all right if I ask you some questions?"

"If you've got more than three, you might as well sit down. Reach in. There's a chair just inside the door."

Whistler got the straight-backed wooden chair and set it down beside Granny Hours's stool.

"You were a friend of Matt Younger and his son, Inch?"

"Dan'l. He was Dan'l before he changed his name. A man shouldn't do that. It marks him out for special pain."

"Yes, I suppose that's true."

"We were neighbors—could even be distant kin—for as long as means anythin'."

"Not friends?"

"Neighbors is one thing, friends another. I never liked Matt Younger. He was a mean-spirited man given too much to hurtin' creatures what couldn't fight back. Used to beat Sara and the children, every one. Used to beat Dan'l most of all, until the boy growed into his hands and feet and threw a rabbit stew into the old man's face one suppertime."

She laughed at that, remembering, taking small joy out of the past.

"Did you much like Daniel Younger's wife?"

"What I saw of her wasn't much good. Even a hound dog'll lick and warm her whelps, except she's crazy or a bad'un. But I reckon she had her fears and reasons."

"How about her boy? You have much to do with John?"

"A dark-destined child, full of hurt and sorrow, that one, twisted at the moment of his birth like a leg broken and left unset. I could see it in his face."

"See what?"

"His fate. I could see he'd end up murdered or doin' murder. His father gave him the blood, his mother threw him away, and his grandpa, old Matt Younger, burned the mark deep."

"How did he do that?"

"He was proud of his boy, Inch. Proud that he'd made it to the big city. Proud that he'd been in the newspapers."

"For murdering three women?"

"Why a body's famous don't make any difference to some people.

It's just the being somebody other than just another one in the crowd."

Whistler knew that was true. He'd often said himself that if Charlie Manson was let out of prison, there'd be people by the hundreds waiting with his photograph, asking him to autograph it.

"Inch Younger had his face in the Sunday supplement," Granny Hours said. "A writer even writ a book about him. A book with pictures. Somebody back in California sent Matt a copy. He wrote back with some money and asked for ten more. He gave one to the boy as a treasure. Very proud he was."

"The boy?"

"I mean Matt Younger, but the boy was proud, too. Carried that book with him everywhere. Pored over it like it was the Bible."

"If Matt Younger was proud of his son, was he proud of his grandson, too?"

"Couldn't have been too proud. Couldn't have wanted the boy, selling him off the way he did."

"Why did he do that?"

"The boy was trouble and Matt Younger knew he'd run away sooner instead of later. So why not get the price of some tobacco and whiskey out of it when he had the chance?"

"You know who bought the boy?"

"They was strangers to me."

"Sue-Sue says they could have been relations to the Youngers."

"That might be so. I couldn't say."

They'd come to the bargaining and Whistler knew it. He reached into his pocket and took out his money clip. He peeled off a twenty-dollar bill.

"People tell me you know just about everything," he said.

Her eyes flickered down at his hands. He peeled off another twenty.

"You think money buys everythin' and anythin', don't you?" she said.

He peeled off a third twenty. "I think it could buy a little comfort with no harm to anybody."

She turned her head and looked like Isak Dinesen again, distant, wise, and proud.

He knew she was being stubborn because it gave her more pleasure to pretend to be about to help the stranger, but just as apt to send him away empty, than to simply make the bargain.

He folded up the sixty dollars and put the rest away. Then he folded the bills twice more and put the little bar of money into her unresisting hand.

"Sue-Sue said she heard the man called Mr. Bosley," he said.

"First name was Bosley," Granny Hours said. "Last name was Trencher. Bosley Trencher and his wife, Kate."

"You know them?"

"Just as much as I've told you."

"How come you know that much?"

"Younger told me one time when he wanted something from me."

"You traded for information you had no use for?"

She grinned and opened her hand, showing the sixty dollars. "Information's like nuts and corn. You can store it away till it's needed."

Here he was, Whistler thought, sitting beside a one-room cabin in the hills of Appalachia, talking to a woman who'd probably been no farther than Johnson City—and hadn't liked that much—in her whole life, who was talking, thinking, and dealing like a big-city politician or a street hustler.

"Favor for favor?" he said.

"That's what makes the world go round," she said.

"You happen to know where Bosley Trencher and his wife live?"

"That I couldn't tell you," Granny Hours said.

18

Sharon Allagash would never perform naked, would never deliberately and with titillation aforethought remove her garments one by one in a tantalizing way for a bunch of men or even for a man not her own.

She knew all about Fawn, with the little patent leather tap shoes and breakaway crotch, the twenty hookers, fluffed and oiled, the lesbian show put on by one of the nameless whores and Eve Choyren, the most notorious thrill merchant in town. It was all right with her that Hobby wanted to wallow in the stinks and sweats of frenzy one more time before settling down.

But Mae Swift—she knew all about Mae Swift—was not negotiable. She had her marked down in her Daily Organizer, an item on her agenda. Things to do. Things to get rid of. Mae Swift had to go. Sharon wouldn't have some professional floozie washing her husband down with her tongue, doing the hootchy-kootchy on a tabletop in black stockings and a garter belt, feeding an appetite for odd and acrobatic pastimes.

He'd have to learn more wholesome ways. She wasn't about to be third party to a case of AIDS.

He liked to call her the Ice Maiden in the dark of the night as she lay absolutely motionless underneath his hairy body, allowing her flawless, cool, sweet flesh to be violated by the beast.

It wasn't that she was too shy, too prudish, to undress in front of him. She just denied any intent to tease or arouse him. It was a game she played with him and herself. A casual pretense. She was well aware that her offhand way of taking off her clothes excited him much more than any striptease could have done.

With her back to him, as he sat on the bed, she removed her sensible shoes one after the other, bending each leg and reaching down to slip them off, exaggerating the thrust of her buttocks just a trifle.

The zip on her skirt sounded like paper tearing. She stepped out of the skirt and clipped it evenly on the hanger. She removed her half-slip and stood there in blouse, tie, vest, suit jacket, stockings, and briefs.

Sometimes, in a teasing mood, he'd say something like "Show me your briefs," and when she pretended not to understand, he'd say, "A little legal humor there. Get it?"

She had wondered sometimes how such a stupid man could make so much money, until she thought it out and came to the conclusion that a stupid man was just that much more likely to be successful in a world of stupid people. It wasn't true that a one-eyed man would be king in a nation of the blind. He'd be found out and murdered for the terrible threat he posed. How could it be any other way?

She took off the briefs, a wisp of silk not much larger than two maple leaves, rolled them into a small ball, and placed them on the dressing table.

He made so much more money than she that it had frustrated and angered her when they'd first met. He'd asked her how much she earned, and when she told him a hundred and fifty thousand a year he'd smiled and said how good that was, as though he didn't think it was very good at all. She knew that no matter how high she rose in her profession, he would always generate more income than she. She might even find herself working for him as a hired legal gunslinger.

She unbuttoned the single button on her man-tailored jacket, removed it, and draped it on the hanger over the skirt. Sometimes he'd take it from her and hang it up in the closet, playing at being her maid. But now he just lay there on the bed, staring at her as though he could hardly see.

Worn out from last night's orgy, she thought, amused at such childish excesses.

She went into the walk-in and hung the suit up herself.

Most of her clothes were still at her condominium. There were six suits in the Brentwood house, one for each day of the working week and another in case she had to make a Saturday meeting. All lined up on the rod, worn in sequence until—barring accidents, which she rarely allowed to happen—they were sent to the cleaners every six weeks and another six suits were brought into use.

She stepped back into the bedroom to go on with the show.

The vest was quick, the stockings took a while.

Her tie, bought off the display at Brooks Brothers, fifty-two dollars, slid from her neck like a snake. Hobby hadn't moved an inch, though his eyes dropped to the pale growth of fine hair at her crotch. She pretended not to notice, looking at her fingers as she unbuttoned the blouse and slipped it off her shoulders, standing there before his eyes, finally naked, wearing no bra because she didn't have that much to contain. Her body was as smooth and pale as alabaster. The perfect sacrificial lamb, Eve Choyren had once called her.

The one way to get a lot of money, Sharon had finally decided, was to marry it. It would cut her time getting the things she coveted by at least twenty years.

She went to the bed.

He finally seemed to become aware of her. "Have a hard day?"

Her eyes went to his crotch, where he hung flaccid. "No, but I see you had a hard night."

"Good-bye to all that." He tried to smile.

She pushed the newspaper off the bed. It landed with the story of Younger's release facing up.

"You want to tell Mommy what's the matter, babe?"

19

Whistler understood a lot more about why the registration cards had been saved when he met Wendell, once the co-manager of a nothing motel halfway to nowhere, husband of a woman who could be described in much the same way.

He and Hoke found Wendell sitting in a seat-sprung and tattered easy chair rescued from some dump, in front of a falling-down house beside the country road, waving to the cars that went by from time to time. The chair's stuffing poked out here and there, just like the tufts of hair under Wendell's hat and the whiskers coming out of his shirt collar and his belly sticking out between the bottom of the shirt and the top of his Levi's.

The yard was awash with every sort of machine, device, folly, extrusion, molded artifact, rag, and scrap that could be salvaged from a civilization given to throwing things away before their time. The stuff seemed to be tumbling out of every door and window, though Wendell had constructed tunnels through the mountain of things so that he could at least get into the house and under cover when it rained.

"How you, Hoke? Long time no see," Wendell said.

"It's been a time or two," Hoke agreed. "Want you to meet a friend, Wendell. This here is Whistler. Come from over to California."

"How you?" Wendell said, looking past Whistler and waving at a passing truck, which hooted back.

"Can we sit?" Whistler asked.

"You can sit as long as you got something interesting to tell me. Or you can sit and do like I do."

"How's that?" Whistler asked, sitting down on a three-legged kitchen chair which had one leg on a brick to balance it on the uneven ground. Hoke took another.

"You can just wave and smile like I do as the folks drive by."

There wasn't more than one car or truck every ten minutes along the stretch of road.

"Heavier traffic in the summers, when the city people come down to cool their asses," Wendell said once.

They were all silent otherwise until Wendell finally spoke again. "So, now that we know each other better, what did you come to me looking for?"

"I see plenty I'd like to buy and own," Whistler said, "but I doubt I could carry it back with me."

"Transportation can be a problem and I don't ship," Wendell said.

"But maybe you've got a little something I could tuck into my pocket," Whistler said, reaching into his pocket and taking out a five-dollar bill.

"That'll buy you something bigger'n little. What's on your mind?"

"You remember a man and wife, stayed at the Royal, named Trencher?"

"You must be having me on."

"First name of the man was Bosley.'"

"Bosley Trencher. That's got a ring to it, ain't it? Well, I don't remember, but if you know the month they stayed here, it'll be easy to find."

"I wouldn't know the month."

"How about the year?"

"Four, maybe four and a half years ago."

"No trouble."

"How's that?"

"I got all them registration cards sorted according to year, month, and last initial."

"Will you take a look?"

"I'll have to get up and go back into the house."

"Could you do that?"

"It's a long way to go and it ain't easy me getting up out of this chair once I get into it."

"You got to get up every once in a while to take a pee, don't you, Wendell?" Hoke said.

"Sure. But I don't got to pee right this minute."

"You happen to have any of those matchboxes covered in colored foil?" Whistler asked.

"Saw one of them boxes, did you?" Wendell said, looking pleased.

"Yes, I did."

"All the way back there in California?"

"That's right."

"Only bought five thousand of them, you know?"

"I only want one." Whistler took out another five-dollar bill.

"I always said them matchboxes would make us a profit," Wendell said, snatching the money from Whistler's fingers. "I might just have one left."

"So why don't you see if you can work up a pee, and we'll mind the store while you find what my friend's looking for?" Hoke said.

Wendell thought about that and then asked for a hand up. He made his way through the debris along a path planted with rusty bedsprings and broken trellises, stopping halfway to turn around and yell, "Don't forget to smile when you wave."

They smiled and waved for maybe half an hour until Wendell came lumbering back with a white card in his hand. He handed it over before sitting down.

"People come from Moodyville," he said.

Only that was written on the card.

"How about my matchbox?" Whistler asked.

Wendell took the little box out of his sweater pocket and handed it over between thumb and forefinger as though it were a jewel of great price.

It lay on Whistler's palm, brightly colored, the foil only slightly tarnished, like a sign of better things to come.

20

If you don't watch out, saving souls can get to be nothing but a job. Ask any priest or minister.

Day after day Faye took her turn managing the routine of Magdalene House, seeing that the household laundry got done, the groceries scrounged, the meals cooked, the rugs vacuumed, and the garbage taken out to the fifty-gallon drum. Rousting sleepy girls out of bed just as if they were her slugabed teenage daughters and she their mother.

Except they weren't her daughters, they were somebody else's daughters. And they'd been kicked out, pushed out, scared out, molested out, or had just plain taken a walk out of bad scenes, because they were too restless for their own good. They looked like young women but they didn't have the heads of young women. They had heads filled with more pain and hard times than most people suffer in a lifetime. Bodies to match. Tired out. Worn out. Stretched out. Fucked out.

For Faye the chores and duties of the day were the job.

The nighttime on the streets was the calling.

That hadn't turned into a job yet. Not for her and not for Jojo. The hours were long, the successes few, but still they felt light walking along the gutters and through the alleys, into wrecked buildings where rats did dances on the ceilings above their heads and doped-up children cried out in their troubled sleep. Following the yellow beams of the six-cell flashlights into places of sorrow, like Dorothy and the Scarecrow skipping along the yellow brick road.

"I think we got a chance with the one calls herself Sissy," Faye remarked.

"What makes you say that?" Jojo asked.

"Instinct."

"The last time I had an instinct, I walked into a basement by myself to see if a kid that needed saving was holed up there. What I got for my instinct was I stumbled into a crack deal and they took me for a cop. Got cut on the arm."

"I still got a feeling about Sissy."

Mimi and Moo were standing around in the middle of the block, past the bookstore, laughing and giggling and shaking the booty. Hogan was strutting around them, schoolboy's ass in tight jeans, blond hair prettier than a girl's. Bitsy leaned against a plate-glass window, his white skin gone blue in the neon, looking like a corpse propped up there, glaring envy at Hogan and the girls.

Faye and Jojo came walking up in their two pairs of socks and boots and sweaters and anoraks, flashlights tucked under one arm, thermoses full of hot chocolate under the other.

"Hi," Faye said. "Cold, cold night."

"A bitch," Hogan said.

"Traffic's thin."

"Well, you know what the man said who built the million-dollar custom Rolls."

"What's that?"

"I only need one customer."

Everybody laughed. You'd think they were friends who'd bumped into each other while strolling through the park, except it was one o'clock in the morning.

Faye turned her attention to Mimi and Moo. "You've got to be cold in those skirts. I mean you can't tell me you're not cold."

"Only when the wind goes whistling up their cooze," Hogan said.

"Don't mind him, Faye, he's just being funny."

"*Thinks* he's funny," Bitsy said from where he was leaning against the window. On the eary. Hearing every word that was spoken. The monitor of the street. Dipper laughed as though Bitsy had said something very funny.

Faye glanced at him.

Bitsy went into the bookshop doorway and Dipper crowded in with him.

"Who's that?"

"That's Bitsy."

"He new?"

"Oh, no. He's been around five, six months."

Bitsy took out a paperback book, squatted down, and pretended to read. Dipper imitated him, even though he had no book.

"Who's that with him?"

"We call him Dipper."

"He's not all there," Hogan volunteered.

"He shouldn't be out on the streets, then."

"Where should he be?" Bitsy said from the doorway, practically shouting it.

"Why don't you go the fuck home?" Hogan shouted back.

"He should be in a facility. An institution," Faye said.

"Like hell!" Bitsy shouted.

"You crazy, yelling like that?" Hogan demanded. "First thing you know, the fuzz'll be around, shovel our asses into jail for disturbing the peace."

"We tried to get some help for Dipper once. They kept him three days and let him out. Said he wasn't functionally impaired," Mimi said, stumbling over the last two words.

Faye glanced at Jojo. He walked over to see if he could talk Dipper and the other kid into maybe going to one of the shelters. There were a few churches and union halls that took the homeless in for the night. Before he could get there Bitsy and Dipper got up and ran east down the boulevard, laughing wildly.

"Is the other boy retarded, too?" Faye asked.

"Bitsy?"

"Yes, Bitsy."

"He's an asshole but he's not loony," Hogan said.

"Bitsy's all right," Mimi said. "He just thinks he's our mother."

"He on something this minute?"

"Oh, sure. I think he got his hands on some crack."

"Is he an IV user?"

"I don't think he does heroin. Does Bitsy do heroin, Hogan?"

"I don't know. He could do speed maybe."

"I don't think so," Moo said. "He's afraid of needles. He told me once."

Faye watched the two figures grow smaller and smaller, running down the middle of the street now, dodging the traffic, light as it was.

"Where's he going?"

"Home."

"Where's home?"

"We've got a building down at the end of Sunset."

"What's the address?"

"Never mind," Mimi said, and smiled.

"Sissy around?" Faye asked.

"I haven't seen her today," Mimi said.

"I heard she got picked up by some rich dude in a stretch limousine. She's away on a long party," Hogan said.

"I heard she left town," Moo said in a small voice.

Faye glanced at Jojo and he shrugged, because they both knew it could easily mean that Sissy was in bad trouble with some crazy sex pervert or sick in some pile of garbage or dead on some rooftop.

Almost every night the teams on the morgue wagons picked corpses off the roofs and out of the alleys, throats cut, heads battered, hearts blown away with dumdum bullets.

"Why don't you give it up for the night, Mimi?" Faye said. "Come back to Magdalene House with us. I can find you a bed. Give you something hot to eat and drink."

"Oh, no," Mimi said. "I got to make a little pocket money."

"How about you, Moo? You want to sleep warm tonight? It doesn't have to be forever, you know. It'll only be for one night if you don't like it."

"I don't think so, thank you very much."

It all seemed so ordinary. An older person asking a couple of younger persons if they'd like to come home and have some food and stay over.

"I hope you don't get insulted, Faye—and it's nice, you stopping by to invite us over—but you and Jojo standing here is going to ruin any chance we got to make a connection. You look like a couple of cops, and the customers just go cruising by," Mimi said.

Hogan raised his fist and yelled, "Honk if you want to get fucked!"

Jojo shook his head.

"If you change your mind," Faye said.

They went back to the van, drove down a couple of blocks,

parked, and went looking around for kids to save.

It went on like that until three-thirty in the morning, poking around Dumpsters and cardboard boxes, passing out condoms and small bottles of bleach and drinks of hot chocolate. They worked their way down the boulevards until they got to the derelict building to which Bitsy and Dipper had fled.

They shone their flashlights through the half-boarded door. Jojo found the trick of it, pushing aside a panel that had been tied off so the barricade could be swung aside as though it were on a hinge.

"Call it a night?" he said.

"This one's the last," Faye said.

They picked their way through petrified dog shit and old plastic clamshells from McDonald's and busted syringes, the garbage that was taking over the city. They found the stairs and climbed to the top, throwing long blades of light into this room and that. Battered and rusting filing cabinets. A broken chair. Busted walls and plaster from collapsed ceilings. Glittering stretches of broken glass. Signs of fire. More fast-food wrappings and aluminum cans everywhere.'

In one room they saw nothing but piles of rags and blankets in a corner, the rest of the floor looking almost as if it had been swept.

"Somebody sleeping here," Faye murmured.

They soft-footed it over to the burrow. Faye squatted down and pulled the corner of an old blanket away from Dipper's face.

She looked up at Jojo and whispered, "It's the retarded kid."

"Dipper," he said, and his voice, though low, seemed to boom in the empty space.

Another body in the pile of rags and coverings stirred. The voice of a sleepy child said, "Cut it out. Go to sleep."

Faye moved to the place where Bitsy slept. She partially shielded the flashlight with her fingers and shone it on Bitsy's face.

It looked like the face of a fox, she thought. Pointed chin, soft mouth, big eye sockets. Eyelids closed in sleep, as pale as alabaster, almost translucent. His fine brown hair clung to his forehead. It looked damp.

Something stirred in her. Memories of a four-year-old looking something like this, helpless in sleep, vulnerable to anything that might want to hurt him.

She reached out and touched his cheek with the back of her hand, then placed her palm on his forehead.

Bitsy jumped as though she'd stung him. He sat straight up and cried out, knocking her hand away, backing away from the light, throwing up his hands, ready to fight.

"It's only us," she said, all in a hurry. "The people from Magdalene."

"What the hell you doing nosing around here, shoving that light in a person's face, waking them up?"

"You've got a fever. You feel okay?"

"I feel all right."

"I just thought you might like to come with us. We could drive you to emergency. Get you something for the fever."

"I don't want anything. I just want you should leave me alone."

"Please let us help you."

"I don't want any help, lady. Do me a favor, you want to do me a favor, go away and let me get some sleep."

"How about some hot chocolate at least?"

"Fuck off, will you?"

"Okay," Faye said, getting to her feet, ready to let go but not wanting to let go. Unable to shake off the feelings of old pleasure and new pain. Unable to forget how she'd gone to little John in the dark hours, seeing his damp hair clinging to his forehead. Touching him—testing for fever—in the small hours.

21

Whistler sat in the front of the four-wheeler with Hoke.

"You could've rented a car in Johnson City cheaper than having me drive you all the way to Moodyville," Hoke said. "You city people must have money to burn."

"You're my luck, Hoke," Whistler said. "You're my charm. I come into the hills a stranger and they see you with me and every door opens up."

"They was getting a kick out of you."

"What the hell. I'm not rich but you're my man and worth every penny it's going to cost me."

Whistler stuck his head halfway out of the window, as foolishly happy as a dog with the wind in his face for no reason he could say except it looked as if he could do something for Faye. For his lady love. For his best girl. Old flame. Number-one squeeze, as the kids on the stroll would say.

It was going to work out. He was going to find the boy and take him back to Faye, and they'd get to know one another and after a while Faye and he would get married. On Saturday afternoons he'd take John over to Griffith Park and get into a game of softball. On Sundays Faye'd cook a chicken or a roast. He'd get a regular job, start a new career. They'd buy a house out around Woodland Hills or Thousand Oaks maybe. He'd commute to work every day and home to his family every night.

He wouldn't sit in the window of Gentry's night after night, feeling sorry for the whole goddam world.

After a while he pulled his face back in.

Moodyville was not much bigger than five Dog Trots in a bunch, maybe six or seven hundred people. Hoke stopped in the center of the town.

The post office was in the grocery store. The woman behind the counter looked suspicious when Whistler came in wearing a suit and tie. He bought himself and Hoke cold soda pops, taking them out of an old chest filled with ice.

"I just come from over to Dog Trot visiting relations," Whistler said, affecting just the trace of an acceptable drawl, like a hill man gone from home and giving in to city ways.

"Don't know it."

"Over by Johnson City."

"That's a fair piece. You still ain't said what brings you here."

"I'm a friend of a friend who was the friend of a family up there in Dog Trot."

Her mouth quirked as though what he said or the way he said it amused her.

"I was coming by here and was asked to look up this child of this friend of mine," he went on.

"Yes?"

"The child was left with his grandfather, but the old man was getting too old to stand a boy around the house—or so I was told. The old man's dead, so he can't say different. Old grandfather sent the boy along with the Trenchers for upbringing. You happen to know them?"

"Bosley and Kate Trencher? I know them."

"They still living around here?"

"Kate is."

"Bosley pass away?"

She looked sly, amused by the special knowledge the stranger didn't have. She was bubbling with it. Then she let it come.

"Bosley ran off with Kate's sister, Charlotte, and the boy. No good, that one. Never was. Charlotte, I mean. Danced without her clothes on down in Memphis and New Orleans, so they say. So that's why Bosley used to live with Kate. Ran off with Charlotte and the boy."

"Whose boy was it?"

"Charlotte's child, I suppose. A bastard. Bosley's child...some say. Left Kate all alone out there in the dust. Poor crippled woman. Hard for her to get around. Precious hard for her to keep the house out there along the dirt road with the dust kicking up every time the wind blows. Stuck in the mud every time it rains."

"They farmers?" Whistler asked.

"Used to be. A long time ago. Dried up, give out, and blew away. Bosley was working over to Harriman in the hardware."

"How far is that?"

"Forty miles. It was hard on Kate even then. Bosley away all day. Off at sunup, home after dark. It wasn't so bad when her sister and the boy were here. But that didn't last long. I could've told her what was going to happen. Her sister kept her figure, you see."

"How long ago was this?"

"Two years and a little maybe since they went away—boy was here maybe two years before that. Charlotte maybe only six months. Whole thing seems funny to me. Anyway, they're gone now. I could've told Kate what was going to happen with that sister what danced without her clothes on and kept her figure."

"You think Kate Trencher knows where they ran off to?"

"I doubt it."

"Maybe I could ask in person?"

She gave him the directions to the Trencher place with some reluctance, suddenly secretive and protective.

"You stop in on your way back, you hear?" she said as she waved him out the door, clearly wanting to know what he might find out and would be willing to tell her.

Out on the dusty street, Hoke complained of the heat and the glare.

"If you trust me with your vehicle, I could drive out alone," Whistler said. "Shouldn't take me more than a couple of hours. You could stay inside the store in the shade and suck on soda pop until I get back."

Hoke one-eyed him and handed over the ignition key.

The Trencher place was about ten miles outside of town, nothing but a house gray with age and neglect standing on a bare patch of ground. There was wire fence strung on metal stakes along the front but none on the sides. It had either fallen down or never been built. There was a gate in the fence, though all you had to do was walk maybe twenty feet in either direction to go around the fence without bothering with the gate.

Whistler could understand its purpose. The fence marked the

place they owned, and in wet weather the gate identified the way along the stone path that led to the door.

There was a porch with rotting steps. Two wicker rocking chairs were self-destructing in the overheated air. A screen door, torn in one corner, was a black mouth proving that the front door was open, promising a little coolness inside.

When Whistler put his foot on the first step, a gray tomcat came racing out of the hole in the screen and crouched with its ears laid back, as though ready to attack. Inside the house a dog set up a terrible racket.

The body and head of a bullmastiff appeared behind the screen. Having given warning, the dog was silent now, staring at Whistler with solemn intent.

"Who is it? Who's there?" a thin complaining voice called from deep inside the house.

"I was passing through and I thought I'd stop by for a visit," Whistler shouted.

He waited, afraid that his voice had been swallowed up by the heat and emptiness. He couldn't imagine a silence so full as the silence that surrounded the staring house in the middle of nowhere.

"Who are you?" the voice cried at last, a little closer now. "Do I know you?"

"I know the Youngers over to Dog Trot."

The silence lasted longer this time. Then, softly, he heard a whisper and a shuffle and the sound of wheezing breath taken in and pushed out with great labor.

A shape loomed behind the screen, behind the dog, and stopped.

Whistler was aware of someone staring at him, testing him for danger.

A hand like a starfish appeared on the screen. It pushed open the door. A mountain of a woman stood there, one aluminum crutch dangling from her forearm, the other planted on the floor. A purse as big as a satchel was slung over her shoulder.

"How do you know the Youngers? Which one you know?"

"Inch Younger," Whistler lied.

"You from prison?"

"Lady," Whistler said, as though warning her off any such questions.

"Who'd you go to see up to Dog Trot?"

Whistler knew she was waiting for him to mention the boy. Then she'd have learned something useful to her.

"To see the old man."

"He's dead."

"I found that out."

"How come you didn't know he was dead?"

"Inch never mentioned."

"Well, that could be right. No love lost. Maybe Inch don't even know."

"He asked me to stop by Dog Trot and see how the boy was. When I didn't find him there, I came looking here."

"Who told you to come looking here?"

"The people own the Motel Royal. The husband collects registration cards."

Kate Trencher sighed as though she just couldn't bear her own weight anymore.

"I'm coming out on the porch and sit," she said.

Whistler started to climb the rest of the steps.

"No, you stay where you are until I tell you different. The dog'll go for you, you come near me."

"Whatever you say. We can forget about the whole thing, I'm causing you any bother."

"Oh, no, oh, no," she said, and Whistler could tell, for all her surly suspicion, she was hungry for company and conversation.

She adjusted the second crutch and came out through the screen door sideways, scuttling over the sill and step by step across the porch, which creaked under her weight, like some monstrous crab, until she reached one of the wicker chairs. It screeched like a wounded animal as she gave her weight into it, her legs in their steel braces straight out in front of her. She struggled on one side and the other and undid the locking levers. She shook off the crutches and settled the huge shoulder bag on her lap.

The cat still crouched on the porch, but the dog stayed inside.

"I don't have reason to come out here and sit very often," she said. "The chair's used to me, but one of these days it'll break apart when I sit in it and drop me on my ass. Then I'll just have to sit and pray somebody comes along and finds me. I don't get much mail and nobody much passes by, so that could be a while. They could just find me laying here dead."

"Too bad they didn't leave the boy."

"What for?"

"Give you a hand. Do for you."

"More likely do me than do for me. Surly little bastard. Born to be hung. Well, what could you expect, a mother like that, dumping him on old Matt."

"I guess she had her troubles."

"Oh, yes, we all got our troubles."

"Would it be okay if I sat down on the step here?"

"That's all right."

Whistler settled himself on the top step. The sun was slanting down the sky, throwing shadows, and a coolness drifted up from the low ground.

"How come your sister, Charlotte, wanted to get the boy from old man Younger?"

"She knew that Younger was up for parole. She thought she'd surprise him and get the boy for him. His own mother never even took the boy up to see Younger in prison, you know. That's no way to do, keeping a boy from seeing his father, no matter what the father'd done."

"Your sister expect Younger'd get in touch with her?"

"Well, if he didn't get in touch with her, she'd get in touch with him."

"Maybe that's why she got the boy, so she'd have a good reason to get in touch with Inch."

"She used to live with him one time. Followed him out to California. Then he took up with that other woman."

"The one he married?"

"Yes, that one. Didn't work out, did it?"

She looked self-satisfied. Even though her sister had done wrong by her with her own husband, blood was thicker than water.

"If she was going to try to pick it up with Younger again, how come Bosley went away with Charlotte?"

"You sure do know a lot, don't you?"

"You don't have to say. I understand."

"Well, now, you don't understand as much as you think you understand. My husband just did her the favor and drove her and the boy back to California because they wanted to save the fare."

"That was two and a half years ago and he's still not back?"

For a moment she looked as if she was going to cry, her face coloring up and her jaw going soft, but she shook herself, the way a dog will do, and said, "None of your business."

"I'm going back there. You want me to look Charlotte up? See if she knows what happened to Bosley?"

It was a temptation too strong for her.

"If you'll give me your sister's address. If you know it?"

"Oh, I know it all right."

She went into the satchel and came out with a piece of paper and a stub of pencil. She wrote out the address, with the tip of her tongue peeking out between her lips, concentrating like a child.

"Ask her to write me, will you?" she said, handing it over. "Tell Charlotte, or Bosley if he's there, I don't hold no ill feelings. Just tell one or the other to write and let me know what's going on so's the mailman'll have reason to come out and stop by."

"What else can you tell me about the boy?"

"He was always brooding about his father. Carried this book somebody'd writ about Inch. It had pictures in it. He was forever looking at the pictures, asking did he look like his pa."

"Did he look like Inch?"

"Nothing like. Well, yes, maybe around the eyes. Inch had funny eyes, you know?"

"I know. Like a wild creature."

"That's right," she said, settling back, finally ready for a real chat.

She took a package of cigarettes and a disposable lighter out of the huge purse, shook one out, and lit it without offering the pack to Whistler. The first drag went down to her toes.

"Well, Inch'd marked the boy, didn't he? Having a killer for a father ain't something a body can take off like an old sweater. It'll show somehow," she said.

She rummaged in the purse and brought out a bag of hard candies, then popped one into her mouth and stared at Whistler as though deciding if she should let him have one. She decided against it.

"You don't happen to have a picture of the kid?" he asked.

"Sure I do. We took him places, you know?" she said, searching through her bag again, as though taking a boy places meant taking pictures, documentary evidence that he'd had fun when he was a child. Proof of how good they'd been.

She found what she was looking for and handed a picture to Whistler. It had been taken at the county fair and was encased in plastic.

It was a good photo, the faces small but very clear and sharp. Kate Trencher was in a wheelchair, her arm around a frail child with a face older and a body younger than his years. He was bent sideways as if he resented her embrace but knew he had to put up with it. A man was stooped down with his face close to Kate's. It looked as though the effort he made to smile was almost more than he could handle. The other woman, Charlotte, had a good figure, just as the postmistress had said. She looked composed but pained, like a person forced to attend the funeral of someone not even kin.

Whistler brought the photo up closer to his eyes.

He thought he knew the boy in the picture, had seen him before along the stroll, among the army of runaways and throwaways. He knew the face, plucked out of hundreds. No special trick. He saw them day after day. Canaan would know the boy in a million. And would know his name and police record as well. Whistler reached out for the name but it wouldn't come. Still he was sure this kid in the picture and the kid often seen along the stroll were the same.

He thought Charlotte looked familiar, too, but knew it starts that way, thinking you recognize one face in a photograph and then believing you recognize others.

"Can I take this picture with me?"

"What for?"

"Give it to his father."

"Well, all right," she said grudgingly, hating to give up any little thing that belonged to her. "I got others."

Whistler stood up and put it in his pocket.

"Don't go," she said. "It'd be all right now for you to sit in the chair beside me. The dog won't mind."

"I've got a long trip ahead of me."

"Oh, just another five minutes," she said. "I can tell you something else you might want to know."

She was playing the coquette. It was grotesque and pitiable, yet there was a longing for human contact in her face so strong it was like a scream.

Whistler sat for five minutes as the sun slipped down the sky.

After a while she said, "The boy had a Devil's mark on him."

"A Devil's mark?"

"Shaped like a toad's foot."

"Where'd he have it?"

"They're always in secret places. With men and boys usually under their eyelids or inside their groins. The boy had his under his armpit."

22

Younger wasn't the sort of man to be scared of work. He'd been working since he was six, one way or another. But looking around at who else was working at the car wash made him feel small. They were blacks and Chicanos and women and dopers with hair down their backs.

"I got hopes for you," the manager had said in the morning, when Younger reported in for work.

"How's that?"

"Take a look. I got sixteen people working the line, not counting the checker and the cashier. Sixteen people on the washing line. By the end of the day I could've already lost one or two. By the end of the week maybe four. Who knows? But there's one thing I can tell you for sure. Half of who you see won't be here at the end of the month. They come and they go. The turnover breaks my back, you understand what I'm saying? I spend half my time showing new people how to drive the cars onto the conveyor the right way. How to wash the rags. How to put the wax in the reservoir when it runs low. You understand what I mean? I got a lot riding on you. The owner don't want to take on a con. He says, 'How about you get some sonofabitch suddenly gets a wild hair up his ass, drives off in a brand-new Mercedes, a Beamer, maybe a Maserati? How does the insurance work on a thing like that?' I says, 'This ain't a car thief we're trying out. This ain't a gonif steals purses, robs banks. This is a murderer.'"

Younger stared at a spot right between the manager's eyes, but it didn't do a bit of good—he just went rattling on.

"'You read up on your crime and punishment and you'll find out that murderers are very dependable. Wardens use them for servants

in the house with their women and children there,' I says. 'Murderers is trustworthy,' I says. So I got my reputation riding on you.
You understand what I'm saying? Well, one thing, you don't talk a
lot. Come on, I'll show you how to wash out the rags."

All day Younger wiped off the cars as they came off the washing
line. All day jumping in and out of cars, climbing in the back with a
bottle of window spray and a rag, wiping off the inside of the windows. All day drying off the side panels and the hoods and the tire
rims.

It felt good bending and stretching. Climbing in and out. Holding
the rag up when the car was finished, signaling the customer, re-
extending the aerial in hopes of the extra tip. Adjusting the side-
view mirror when the driver got behind the wheel. Not saying anything except "Thank you, sir," or "madam." Not doing anything
when they stared at him as though they knew. Just shrugging when
one of them asked, "Do I know you?"—the newspaper with his
picture sometimes sitting right on the seat next to them.

The black man he was partnered with was as untalkative as he
was. It was hard to tell his age. There was some white showing in
his hair, though, and his eyes looked sad instead of half angry. He'd
said hello and how are you? and that was that—until the end of
the day, when he walked over, looking at his hands as though they
should be paler with all the time they'd spent in water, and said,
"You want to get a beer down the block?"

"What's your name again?" Younger said.

"Everybody calls me Preacher."

"You a man of the cloth?"

"I ain't ordained but I try to do God's work."

"You figure I'm in need of charity?"

"Any man alone in the world is in need of a friend."

"You reckon to be my friend?"

"If you want."

"What makes you think I'm alone and need a friend?"

"I see the papers."

"You want to save my soul?"

"All I want to do is ask you over for a beer."

"Only one trouble with that."

"What's that?" Preacher's face closed down. He could hear it
coming. He'd heard it often enough before.

"I don't drink with niggers."

23

The picture was a couple of days from being wrapped up. The trick was to finish all the principal scenes not yet shot so that he and Sharon could take their two-week honeymoon in the Virgin Islands.

With his house at Malibu and his estate in Hawaii, with her condo in Aspen and her house in Palm Springs, they had to go to someplace new—five hundred dollars a day—for their honeymoon.

He was pushing the crew overtime to get the footage. Coming home ten, eleven at night with his eyes burned out of his head from the lights.

She was managing a corporate merger, putting in hours just as long, coming home eleven o'clock, midnight. Sometimes not coming home at all. Sleeping on the couch in her office, too weary to make the journey home along the freeways.

So it was one o'clock, and Hobby was in the Brentwood house, sitting all alone in the library, in front of a fake log fire fueled by gas. Sitting there in his shorts and a tatty robe made of toweling. Going over his notes for the next three days' shooting. Figuring out the shots, the long ones, the establishings, the inserts that he could turn over to his assistant director in case he didn't have the time to get them all.

There was a glass of brandy on the table next to him.

"You shouldn't drink alone," Eve Choyren said at his back.

He jumped a foot and landed on the floor in a crouch, the pages he was working on scattering all around, the glass of brandy tipping over and spilling across the wood and leather tabletop.

"Fachrissakes. For Jesus H. Christ's sake, why the fuck do you do that? I could drop right the fuck down fucking dead with a heart attack the way you do that. How the hell do you do that? How the hell do you get through locked doors and past alarms?" He stood up and closed his robe around him.

She was dressed in a long black coat which overlapped high black suede boots. She was wearing a black fur hat tilted at an angle on her black hair and a black scarf around her neck.

"If you don't know by now what powers I possess, Paul, why do you continue to ask the questions?"

"Is that what you're going to do? You going to jump me from behind, scare the shit out of me, give me a fucking heart attack, and then start that crap about your secret powers? I got a friend, Joey Fist, can open a Chubb lock with a single human hair, can walk through fucking walls, don't tell me about your special powers. You slept with a locksmith. You slept with a safecracker. When you weren't fucking or sucking them, they were giving you lessons how to be a thief."

She laughed at him as though she were indulging a child. "Whatever you say, babe. Whatever you say. I'll get a rag for that spill."

"Fuck it. I'll take care of it," he said, wiping the table with the hem of his bathrobe. "I don't want you prowling around my house, places I can't see you, putting aphrodisiacs in my Post Toasties, putting poison in my chicken soup, collecting Sharon's fingernail clippings for future use."

Eve was over at the wet bar pouring two fresh glasses of brandy. She came back and handed him one and then sat down with the other. Her coat opened up almost to her lap, and Hobby could see she was wearing the kind of buccaneer boots that flared out at the top and reached halfway up her thighs.

"I'm not mad at you, Paul. Have I ever gotten mad at you anytime over the years when you had this lady or that lady?"

"I'm marrying this lady. Maybe that's different for you."

"Everything's different for me. That's the point, sweetheart. I don't care who you fuck, who you marry. I've got your soul in the palm of my hand. I've got your damned soul right there."

She held out her cupped hand, fingers curled, blood-red nails pointing up, sharp enough to tear out a heart.

His hand tightened on the glass. She could see his hand tighten on the glass.

The grin on his face had shifted in a subtle way, had become a construction of wire pinned to his flesh.

"Will you stop with that shit, fachrissakes?" he asked. "You're like fucking Harry Stoller, all the time doing imitations of Clark Gable. Does the fucking imitation of Clark Gable all through lunch, for an hour, two hours. Won't drop it. Says, 'Frankly, my dear, I don't give a damn' when the waitress asks him does he want may-onnaise on his chicken sandwich. Half the people at the table don't even know who Clark Gable is anymore. You're like that with this fucking witch routine."

"Succubus," she said.

"What?"

"An evil spirit that takes the form of a woman to have inter-course with a man and drain him of his will."

"Shit. I know what's a succubus."

"I am your succubus, Paul."

"You're also a pain in my ass, creeping into my house without ringing the bell. How do you know Sharon's not here?"

"I know that Sharon's not here because I know Sharon's working late and won't even be home tonight."

"How do you know that?"

She smiled one of her mysterious smiles.

"Oh, fachrissakes," Hobby said, really frustrated and pissed off at the way she did that all the time. Pretending she knew things through unnatural means, it turned out she spoke to the person on the phone or saw them on the street. Something like that.

"What are you worried about?" she said. "Sharon knows we're old friends."

"Not old succubuddies," Hobby said, grinning a real grin.

Eve pulled down the lower lid of her right eye with a bloody forefinger, the old sign of truth.

"If you think she doesn't know we get it on, you're not very smart."

"Got it on," he said. "*Got* it on."

"What are you telling me, Paul, we're not succubuddies any-more?"

"She wouldn't like it."

"Sharon?"

"Well, yes, her, but I was thinking that Mae wouldn't like it," he said.

"Mae's a paid whore."

"Well, she's getting very touchy. This immune-deficiency thing."

"The plague," Eve said. "We are entering the plague years."

"You going to tell me you brought them on?"

"We all helped bring them on. We all helped."

She stared into her glass for a minute, the muscles of her face giving way to age and weariness, her body sagging as if the bones had turned to wax, counting up all the commonplace sins she'd committed, nothing but a lousy bit player in the game of evil.

"You're a real piece of work, you are, Paul," she said. "Worrying about what the mistress you share will say about any side dishes you care to taste, but not worrying a bit about the feelings of the wife-to-be."

"I didn't fucking say that. Sharon put it on the line when I asked her to marry me. Fidelity's not part of the bargain."

"Well, good for her, if she means it," Eve said wryly. "The Ice Maiden wants to do her bit to keep the plague years rolling. Maybe she and I can get it on someday soon . . ."

"I wouldn't like that," Hobby said.

". . . again."

"What the hell did you say?"

"Think about it," Eve said, smiling that goddam smile again.

Hobby had long since figured out the secret of Eve's power over people. She built up little webs of lies and promises and hints of secret pastimes, unsupported, outrageous, sometimes incredible. People were hungry for the little seeds of truth they believed must lie at the heart of her revelations, and they were willing to pet, persuade, and indulge her in hopes that she'd finally present them with real evidence and proofs. Evidence and proofs that probably didn't exist. But it still held people under a sort of spell. Curiosity really did kill cats.

And curiosity inevitably led to other things. To drunkenness and debauchery and drugs and foolish ceremonies that had a terrible way of becoming real.

"Are you fucking saying you and Sharon have done a trick or two?"

She put her glass down, shook her head, and took off her hat.

"No, no. We never have," she said, tired of the game all at once.

"Is that the truth? Are you telling me the truth now?"

"It's the truth."

"How come for the first time since I know you, you decide to tell me the truth?"

She got up and stood in front of the fire. She dragged the scarf off her neck. "I feel that we're in great danger."

"Will you cut the crap?" he said, but there was no conviction in it.

"You read the papers? You watch the six o'clock news last night? You have time to know what's happening in the world, or are you too busy with that cheap flick you're making?"

"I read the papers. I watch the news."

"Then you know that Younger's on the street."

"So what? He was dumb then and he's dumb now."

"He's had fifteen years to think about it."

"Why would he do that?"

"Because you went to see him in prison. You pretended to be his friend."

"I had to know did he have any idea."

She turned around to face him. "You never could leave well enough alone."

"You're the one dragged him into the goddam fun and games."

"You're the one invited him to the beach to slaughter the goat."

"Ah, fachrissakes, nothing's going to happen. It's all over," he said, and emptied the brandy glass.

She sighed the deep sigh of someone suddenly grown old and weary. "You want your wedding present now?"

"Jesus Christ," he blurted out, not having heard a word she'd said. "You've got me scared."

She opened up her coat. She was naked except for the boots riding halfway up her thighs. Her flesh, blocked by the wings of the coat from the light of the fire, looked bluish white. Her muff, below her belly, was very pale and thin, as though it had been worn away by too much use.

He'd never realized how thin she was, how unshapely, how unbeautiful. She'd always been able to conceal that. It was part of her art, her manipulation of reality, a manufactured illusion. He'd never known how old she was. Now he could see she was far older than he'd ever have believed. She saw in his eyes what he saw.

"I think maybe you ought to close that coat before you catch cold," Hobby said. "I think you ought to go home and get into your own bed."

"And that'll be that?" she asked, as though genuinely interested in his reply.

"I think you ought to go home."

She let the wings of the coat fall free as she walked toward him, but the coat still revealed her nakedness.

"There's a devil loose in the land," she said.

"I don't want anything more to do with devils."

"You can't help yourself." She went down on her knees and put her hands on his thighs. She pushed his legs apart. "I've got your damned soul in the palm of my hand."

24

Bitsy, sitting up on the roof, lifted his head and convinced himself that he smelled the ocean, even though it was many miles away. Maybe tomorrow he'd hitch a ride down to Santa Monica, maybe Malibu. Steal himself a pair of swim trunks from some shop.

All of a sudden his stomach cringed with hunger. It hit him like a rocket, the weakness charging up out of his belly like a wave. He could smell frying fish and meat, french fries and bananas, as if they were right there under his nose. His head was filling up with voices. One, he knew, was his father's, urging him to have more pork, more beans, more greens and gravy.

He closed his eyes and pictured his father. He'd know him if he saw him. He'd even know him if he heard him, even though he'd never actually heard his old man's voice in his whole life.

"You got any change?" a voice asked, kicking him out of the feast.

The wave of weakness passed but not the hunger. He opened one eye and squinted up at Hogan, standing there barefooted in his jeans and open shirt, his hair so blond it was almost white, his skin like buttered toast.

"I got no money. I got nothing."

"You want to go and get some?"

"I don't want to let some faggot fool around with me. It's too dangerous anymore."

"How do you mean dangerous?"

"You can get sick and die from something one of them faggots could give you."

"They got to be niggers or IV users."

"All they got to be is faggots that like to bugger you up the ass. God, you're dumb."

"So maybe we go steal a television out of somebody's apartment. Maybe we snatch somebody's pocketbook."

Bitsy closed his eye and tried to get back into his fantasy.

Hogan kicked his foot. "Hey, you falling asleep?"

"Go away. I'm thinking."

"What're you thinking?" Hogan asked, sitting down on a part of the rotting catwalk that hadn't collapsed altogether.

"I been thinking about maybe I get the hell out of this city and go someplace else."

"You want to go someplace else? Okay. How about we go up to San Francisco? Lots of action up there. How about New York? How about Miami? That's better. It's nice and hot down in Miami."

"How about you go where you want to go and I'll go where I want to go."

Hogan took no offense. "Where you want to go?"

"Some little town like the one I was raised up in."

"You going to tell me another lie?"

"What the fuck do you mean by that, you asshole?"

"I don't mind you tell me lies. I was just asking. I tell myself lies sometimes, too."

"Well..." Bitsy said, glad that Hogan hadn't taken offense at the "asshole" that'd just popped out. It showed that he was getting to respect him. Otherwise he'd get on his ass and start ragging him and making small of him. Then he thought that Hogan only made small of him when somebody else was around. When the girls were around especially. Maybe they could start being friends if they talked when the girls weren't around.

"You seen Sissy?" Bitsy asked.

"I don't know where is Sissy."

"How about Mimi and Moo?"

"Fuck Mimi and Moo. I ain't their mother. You want to be their mother, go ahead, be my guest."

So maybe they couldn't talk and get really friendly, Bitsy thought. He took a cigarette out of the pack in his shirt pocket and got his matchbox out of the side pocket of his jeans. He lit a cigarette and took a long drag, pointedly not offering one to Hogan. He put the matchbox back into his shirt pocket with the cigarettes.

Then he shifted his position and took a paperback out of his back pocket. It was so old it was falling apart. He went through an elaborate show of finding his place and leaned forward, giving his entire attention to the page, pretending to read in the fading light.

He wanted Hogan to go away. Then he could climb down off the roof and go over to a McDonald's and fill up—try to fill up—on hamburgers and fries.

"What the hell you doing now?" Hogan asked.

"What's it look like I'm doing?"

"Looking at a book. Looks like the same book you're looking at all the goddam time."

"I'm reading is what I'm doing."

"How long's it take you to read a book?" When Bitsy didn't answer, Hogan asked, "It got any pictures?"

"It's got some photographs in the middle but it ain't a comic book."

"So read some of it to me."

"Fachrissake, you'd think a person sees another person reading, that person would show a little good manners and shut up."

They were silent for a time. It wasn't a companionable silence. Not the comfortable silence of friends. It was more like that suffered by strangers trapped together on a plane or train, with nowhere to go.

"Did you ever do it to her?" Bitsy finally asked, wanting to try for some amiable relations again.

"What'd you say?" Hogan asked, startled out of his own thoughts, acting angry and defensive right off the bat.

"I said, did you ever do it to Mimi?"

"Oh, I thought that's what you said."

"So why did you jump like I stung you?"

"I was thinking."

"So, did you?"

"Once or twice."

"How about Moo?"

"Sure. Her too. What's the big deal? Don't you ever fuck 'em?"

"I don't feel like it. I could but I don't feel like it."

"How come?"

"I don't know."

The awkward silence descended on them again.

After a while Hogan said, "You ever been in jail?"

"What the fuck makes you ask a thing like that?"

"A thing like what? I asked a question. Was you ever in jail? Is that a big thing? It's no big thing."

"You been in jail?"

"Sure. Plenty of times."

"So I been in jail."

"Where?"

"Little Rock."

"When?"

"A couple of years ago."

"For what?"

"How the hell you expect me to remember for what? Something. Shoplifting. Car boosting. Something. I was supposed to go to trial in a week, maximum ten days. They kept me in there twenty-eight days. The judge had the flu. Something like that."

"Didn't nobody bail you?"

"Who was going to bail me? I didn't have nobody to bail me. They sent a social worker to see me one time. I begged him to get me the hell out of there. I mean I asked him what I was doing in there with all these old guys in the first place. Guys in their fifties, sixties, maybe seventies. Some of them shouldn't have been there any more than me. They should have been in a hospital. They was fucking crazy, you understand what I'm saying?"

"Take it easy," Hogan said. "Don't get your balls in an uproar."

"I mean they're all calling me pretty boy and son, and patting me on the ass every chance they get. I tell this social worker all what's going on and how I shouldn't be in there with these old guys but someplace with kids my own age. I'm only twelve, thirteen.

"There was queers in there. All over the goddam place. They'd be pulling their donkeys all night, beating their meat, whispering back and forth. This one guy comes at me with his cock in his hand. He looked like a fucking dwarf with this horse cock in his hand. I tell this social worker the reason they're keeping me in there is like these guys ain't got any women and that's why they got somebody like me with a tender ass in there. I got to fight them off all the time. I tell him even this one goddam guard tried to molest me. You understand what I'm saying?"

"The social worker do anything?"

"I never seen the fucker again. I seen him just the one time and never again."

"What happened?"

"What the fuck you think happened? I had to sleep, didn't I? I couldn't fight day and night, could I? I was in that fucking jail twenty-eight days before I appeared in court. Then they let me go out on probation."

"Sonofabitch," Hogan said. "So what's that? You protected yourself, didn't you? I bet you even got some favors. Whatever you had to do, it got you out alive."

"That why you sell your ass?" Bitsy asked. "So you can come out alive?"

Hogan stared at him for a long minute. "Well, fachrissakes, I got to eat, don't I? Besides, I don't do everything you think I might do."

Bitsy went back to his book.

"How can you read that thing over and over again?" Hogan asked.

"Who says I'm reading it over and over again?"

"That's the same book you been reading over and over again ever since I met you."

"You don't know what the fuck you're talking about."

Hogan snatched at the book but Bitsy hung on. Hogan stood up, still grabbing the book.

"Leave it alone, you sonofabitch!" Bitsy yelled, getting to his feet, too.

"You better let go the goddam book—you're going to tear it," Hogan warned.

Bitsy let go, tears of rage springing to his eyes, as Hogan turned his back and looked at the photographs in the middle of the paperback.

"Gimme back my fucking book!" Bitsy screamed, the tears streaming down his face.

"Fachrissakes, this the kind of stuff you look at? You sick or something? These is pictures of naked women all cut up. One's got her head cut off. Fachrissakes." He was sounding disgusted but still he was looking. "This the weird asshole what done that to them? Funny-looking fucker."

Bitsy let out another scream and threw himself at Hogan. The bigger boy, never expecting little Bitsy to attack him, went down. He hunched his back and tried to shake Bitsy off. It was like trying to shake off a cat. Bitsy was punching and scratching and biting.

Hogan started yelling and Bitsy was yelling. It sounded like a big fight—half a dozen people—not just two kids going at it.

Hogan managed to get himself turned around so he could shove Bitsy off him. He started to laugh but he couldn't. All of a sudden he felt as if he was fighting for his life.

He tossed Bitsy off over and over again, but Bitsy just kept on coming back, spit gathering at the corners of his mouth like dried-up salty foam on the rocks by the sea, his eyes burning in his head.

Fachrissakes, Hogan thought, Bitsy had eyes just like the fucking killer in the book.

He kicked out and caught Bitsy in the stomach with his boot. That took it out of him. Bitsy rolled over and puked all over the tar and the broken wooden walkway.

Hogan scrambled to his feet. He walked over to where the book had fallen and broken apart. The pages, stirred by the wind and scattered by their scuffling bodies, were all over the place. He went around and picked up all he could find, stuffing them back between the covers, not worrying about the order.

Bitsy was lying on his side, curled up around his belly, holding himself and crying.

Hogan squatted down and said, "Here's the book. Fachrissakes, how was I supposed to know a fucking beat-up old book like this was so important to you you'd start a fight over it? Go ahead, take it."

"Go fuck yourself," Bitsy said.

"You shut up or I'll smack you in the mouth again."

Bitsy rolled over on his back and stared a hole in Hogan's forehead. Hogan leaned over and put the book on Bitsy's chest.

"Shit fuck," Hogan said in derision, and walked away. He heard Bitsy scramble to his feet. He heard him running. When he finally turned, it was too late. Bitsy's hands hit him just below his collarbone. Hogan reached out and got one hand on Bitsy's shirt. The pocket tore away. His back slammed into the rotten railing. It gave way and Hogan pitched over into the central air shaft. He started to pinwheel before he smashed into the twisted, rusted iron rods and rubble.

Bitsy got down on his hands and knees and peered over the edge of the roof. Hogan was sprawled there, not moving. A pain started in Bitsy's neck and filled his head. He felt as if blood were coming out of his ears and nose. A fog as thick as black velvet slipped across his eyes. He scrambled back from the edge, afraid that he, too, would fall.

He climbed down off the roof, the hunger filling him up like a scream again.

25

It was six hours back to Johnson City and another thirty minutes into the Tri-State Airport.

Whistler slept practically all the way, waking up when they came within sight of the control tower and tarmac.

"You want a motel?" Hoke asked when he saw Whistler was sitting there with his eyes open, gazing around in the fuzzy way people do when they wake up in strange places.

"Where are we?"

"Just about at the airport. You want a motel?"

"I've got to wring out my sock pretty bad."

"Well, I asked you twice. Once when I stopped for gas and once when I stopped for a container of coffee at a drive-in."

"I didn't hear you."

"I figured. That's all right. So, you want a motel?"

"How many hours have I got to flight time out to Atlanta?"

"Let me think. Three, maybe four hours. They change the schedules."

Hoke pulled the cab up at the curb in front of the arrival-departure building.

"Go take your leak. I'll wait for you here."

Whistler got out of the cab, thought about it, and rapped on the glass on the passenger's side.

Hoke reached over and rolled it down.

"How do you know I won't take a walk, stiff you for the fare?"

"I got your luggage."

"That suitcase and what's in it isn't worth what I owe you.

Maybe I walk out another door, grab a cab to the Greyhound station."

"You see that cop over there?" Hoke said.

Whistler turned around and saw an airport cop looking their way. Hoke raised a hand and the cop raised his.

"I already gave Coolidge the sign to keep his eye on you."

Whistler grinned. "You funnin' me?"

Hoke grinned right back. "You'll never know unless you try to run out on me."

Whistler shook his head, pleased at the way Hoke's head worked, and went off to relieve himself.

When he came back he said, "I'm going to pass on the motel. By the time I get my clothes off, I'll be putting them right back on again. Give me the bad news."

Hoke handed him a slip of paper with the total charge already written on it. "That seem fair?"

Whistler was counting through his cash. "Hell, yes," he said, "but I don't have that much in cash. You take my check?"

"For some of it. Not for all of it."

Whistler handed over all the paper money he had. "You mind giving me back a twenty so I can get from the airport to Hollywood on the airport bus?"

Hoke handed him back a twenty. Then Whistler wrote out a check for the difference.

"I hope you don't sign that Gary Cooper," Hoke said.

Whistler handed him the check and Hoke looked at it.

"That your real name?" he asked.

"That's my real name."

Whistler got his bag out of the back, then stuck his hand through the window for Hoke to shake.

"It's been a pleasure, Hoke. One day maybe I'll come back here. You and me do a little hunting, a little fishing maybe?"

"You ever do any hunting and fishing?"

"No. I guess not."

"So don't make promises you can't keep and don't dream dreams that won't come true."

Whistler grinned, shook his head, walked away, and waved good-bye without looking back, thinking how there were people a lot like Bosco nearly everywhere.

Inside the terminal he put down his suitcase and sat down in a plastic chair. He tried to close his eyes but he was slept out. He got a local newspaper and read about farm prices and building starts.

There were a few people in the terminal and more arriving as morning came on.

A man and a woman came in with five kids. The man was wearing a work shirt and bib overalls, with a denim jacket slung over his arm. The woman was maybe ten years younger, thin and drawn, the skin tight on her cheekbones and around her wrists, as though it had been stretched and polished. Not a bad figure, considering, if all five children were her own, but there was a weariness to the curve of her back and the jut of her belly that spoke a lot about how soon she'd give way and start looking like a broken horse.

There was an older boy and a girl, maybe twelve and thirteen. Then three little ones, all girls, maybe four, five, and six. Six years between the oldest little one and the younger big one.

They sat down in the row of seats right across from Whistler. At first all five kids sat as still as stone, the father on one side and the mother on the other, like sheepdogs penning in a flock. The children stared at Whistler, as solemn as a crowd of deacons or belfry crows.

Whistler could see the children were all hers. They all had her pinched nose and pale blue eyes. The two oldest were dark-haired and the three little ones were blond. It was pretty plain there were two sets, the bigger children hers by another marriage and the little ones belonging to both of them.

You could tell that, too, by the way they'd arranged themselves. The little ones were sitting closer to their daddy. One of them was plucking at his jacket. After a while the littlest one climbed into his lap and whispered in his ear. He was gentle and patient with her.

The two big kids sat closest to the mother. The girl kept smoothing her skirt over her knees. The boy sat there brooding as only a teenaged kid can brood.

The father finally succumbed to the little girl's wheedling and went into his pocket. He came out with two dollars and handed them to the big girl.

"You go get the children a Coke, Phyllis, and one for yourself if you want."

"They're fifty cents," she said.

"Billy's got his own spending money."

The mother looked pained and uttered a soft sound of distress, but Billy didn't say a thing, just flicked a glance at the man out of the corner of his eyes like a snake striking.

Phyllis picked up the smallest girl and took the hand of the next smallest and went off saying, "Shirley, you stay close to me, you hear? I don't want to have to go chasing you." Playing the little mother.

The mother unsnapped her purse and her husband stiffened. The boy held his breath. For a minute there it looked as if she was going to give her son the money for a Coke that her husband wouldn't give him. For a minute there it looked as if she was going to defy the man who'd married her when she already had two children and take the side of the boy, who was having a bad time with his stepfather for one reason or another.

But she thought better of it and didn't dip into her purse. The boy smiled a bitter, ghostly smile, got up, and went over to the big window, where he could watch the planes being serviced on the tarmac. The woman got up and went off to the rest room.

The man's eyes caught Whistler's and didn't let go. Whistler could see how sad and confused he was about it all. How did you go about disciplining and raising and teaching a child not your own?

"My wife's boy by a former marriage," the man said, as though Whistler had asked the question. "Lost his father when he was very young. He's had a hard time of it."

He didn't say, a hard time accepting me or me him, but that was it.

Whistler thought about the boy he was trying to find, and how it would be if Faye and he were able to pick it up where they'd left it off, except there'd be a kid, not his own, around to discipline and raise and teach.

"Kids that age can make it hard on you," Whistler said.

The man nodded as though they'd settled something.

26

A wrap party is a Hollywood ritual.

At the beginning of a picture a whole bunch of people, some who know each other, some who've worked with each other once or twice before, some who've never met, get thrown together for thirty days, sixty days, ninety days—depending—in tight conditions, for ten, twelve, fourteen hours a day. It's like a big family confined to a cabin, breathing each other's breaths, getting into each other's pockets.

In the early days it used to be the wrap was pretty lavish, sit-down dinners at a local restaurant, the stars handing out presents to the crew, the crew chipping in to buy the stars and the director something expensive. One big happy family.

Then a little austerity set in, especially with the B's, and the wrap was held on the soundstage, plywood and sawhorse tables covered with paper, catered hot buffet, a couple of grips taking turns pouring the booze.

Like kids at a dance, where the boys stick together and the girls stick together except when forced to mingle, the people from the craft guilds tended to clump up, swapping dirty jokes and opinions about how they would have shot the last scene, given the opportunity. Except for the hairdressers, who tended to keep on kissing the asses of the stars because, after all, if they made a permanent connection with a big one it could make their careers, and others like the costume designers, who didn't consider themselves craftspeople but artists. The director moved between the two classes, impartial father to them all.

The only one who was a sore thumb as far as everybody was

concerned was the producer. Everybody figured the producer had screwed them one way or the other, on lousy food if on location, with deductions from their paychecks, on negotiations going in. Since Hobby was his own producer, he escaped that stigma. The actors and crew couldn't very well snub the man who'd just stopped being their father and who probably still owed them their last week's pay to boot.

Nowadays the wraps, though still held on the soundstages, had gone lavish again, with fancy catering, extras in opera hose and short skirts filling in as waitresses, and bartenders serving up the drinks.

Certain of the privileged and anointed were allowed to bring guests. Most of the cast and crew, also among the elite, wore their satin jackets embroidered with the name of the film or television series. It was the newest in thing. The newest mark of prestige and favor. The newest clever bit of advertising.

So here were maybe forty people, standing around or perched on stools or leaning against pieces of equipment, wearing black jackets with the name of Hobby's latest, *Witches in Heat,* and another forty still wearing the tools or the marks of the tools of their trade, and another forty dressed up for the occasion, all rubbing asses and elbows, positioning themselves for the next opportunity, the next job, the next roll in the feathers.

Hobby was standing at the end of one of the bars with a glass in his hand, listening to the bullshit being flung his way by his agent and his lawyer, Konski and Yibna, looking over their heads and wondering where the hell Sharon was. She'd promised to make an appearance, if only for half an hour. Was this the way it was going to be when he was married to her, some fucking merger taking first place when she should be standing by her husband, showing him a little support? Especially after the exhausting, nerve-racking labor of putting together a fucking motion picture?

If Monsignor Moynihan could take an hour from his busy day to show the flag of friendship, if Pig-Nose Dooley could take an hour for a friend even though he could be out there trailing his next victim, if the fucking witch queen, Eve Choyren—who was a monumental pain in the ass sometimes but gave great head—could leave her bubbling caldron to raise a glass and say well done, why couldn't Sharon make the effort?

So, because he was looking around and not really listening to what anybody was saying, he spotted Younger before anybody else did. Not that it mattered much, because the only other people in the room who would have recognized him right off the bat were Bolivia and Eve.

He looked for Bolivia, found him, and glanced toward the door. Bolivia took his meaning, moved his head, and saw Younger. He started moving away toward the exit, shaking his head, letting Hobby know he wasn't having anything to do with anything anymore.

"Fuck you," Hobby said under his breath.

Konski and Yibna were too busy bullshitting one another to notice.

Eve came from somewhere, materializing out of cigarette smoke the way she liked to do, and stood at his shoulder.

Konski and Yibna drifted off.

"I hope what I see isn't the shit hitting the fan," she murmured into Hobby's ear.

"What the hell does he want? What the hell's he doing here?" Hobby mumbled back.

"We'd better trot over there and see."

Hobby moved forward with his hand stuck out, a big smile plastered on his face.

Eve stepped around Hobby's outstretched arm and leaned up to give Younger a kiss on the cheek.

He flinched a little, as though the show of affection had taken him by surprise.

"Well, what the hell do you know about this?" Hobby crowed. "How the devil did you know I was wrapping up a picture?"

"I asked around," Younger said. "This town ain't much bigger than Dog Trot when it comes to gossip."

"Dog Trot. I love it," Hobby said, as though he thought Younger was some country comedian working his act.

"I came to thank you for offering to take care of my wife and baby," Younger said.

"Well, I tried. You understand I tried. But she disappeared on me."

"She disappeared on me, too."

"I'm sorry to hear that. I really am."

Hobby was still holding on to Younger's hand, giving him the old stand-by-me made famous by Lyndon Johnson, pumping good will through his fingertips.

"You were the only one showed me any friendship, Mr. Hobby."

Hobby threw an arm around Younger's shoulders and tossed a glance at Eve that said he was right and she was wrong. The asshole hadn't remembered a thing. He was just a dumb hillbilly paying his respects.

Eve laced her arm through Younger's on the other side. Together they walked him over to the food and refreshments.

"I don't want you to say any more about it," Hobby said with a smile that showed what a generous fellow he was.

"Well, I feel I got to. I had a lot of time to think about things when I was in prison."

Hobby stiffened slightly. A little shade of sarcasm there? A little hint of something not quite servile?

He looked around for Bolivia, wanting to give him a look that would tell him he couldn't walk away from it. If all of them couldn't walk away from the consequences of that night fifteen years ago, Bolivia sure as hell wasn't going to, as though he'd had no part in it. As though he hadn't been as stoned and furious and crazy as Hobby and Eve had been. As though he hadn't held the sacrifice down on the flat rock by the sea and even used the knife on her dying body.

"Look who Paul's got a love grip on," Yibna said to Monsignor Moynihan.

"Do I know him?"

"He's the Hog Wallow Killer just got out on parole after fifteen."

Hobby saw the group he'd left around the bar watching him as he approached with Younger in tow. Could see their lips moving, making speculations.

He saw Pig-Nose Dooley's eyes flicker.

"Come on up to the bar and have something," Hobby said, urging Younger along, feeling the arrogance in the man's stride.

"It's been a long time since I had a decent glass of whiskey," Younger said.

"Then make the first one a triple."

"I could use a job," Younger said, cutting, as they say, to the chase. It sounded fine, but Hobby could hear the threat in the statement, as heavy as a stone.

"We'll talk about it."

"Not odd jobs around one of your houses like you used to give me," Younger went on, his voice rising slightly, hitting his stride, ready to grab Hobby by the throat if he didn't get his promise.

"So, I said we'll talk about it," Hobby said.

"Not like one of those jobs I was doing for you when I lost my knife."

There it was. The threat. Laid right out so he couldn't ignore it. Couldn't pretend he never heard it.

"What knife?"

"You know I was drunk so much back then, I lost things all over the place and never knew what happened to them. But I had a long time to think. Fifteen years to think. I didn't remember where every goddamned little thing could've been lost, but I remembered about that linoleum knife."

27

It was a plain little house in a long row of plain little houses.

Most of the people who lived in them wouldn't be able to afford to buy them if they didn't already own them. They paid low mortgage rates on houses that had cost them fifteen or thirty thousand twenty years ago. Now they lived in houses worth a hundred and fifty, a hundred and seventy-five thousand dollars on paper and barely made it on Social Security.

The front door had a grille over a judas hole as big as a dinner plate. When the house had been built the judas hole was merely a convenient means to see who was at the door, not a peephole for the sake of security.

Whistler rang the bell and waited. He could hear footsteps on carpeting, then on bare wood, and then on carpeting again. The door in the judas hole opened up and a face like a nun's, eerily calm and composed, appeared in it.

"Yes?"

"Mrs. Charlotte Givern?"

"Miss."

"My name's Whistler."

"Yes?"

"You have a boy living with you?"

Her face went whiter. Whiter than it already was.

He remembered her and knew why the face of the woman in the photo he'd taken from Kate Trencher had looked familiar to him.

• • •

Fifteen years before, she'd sat in the witness box with her gloved hands clasping her purse on her knees, a plain-looking woman with mousy brown hair, frizzy whorls where it kinked up around her temples. A little hat sitting on top of her new permanent wave. It had a little veil, which was of no earthly use. She looked like a fugitive from the thirties. There was that about her, the drawn look of a farm woman driven from her home by the drought.

Her lashes were short and colorless, the eyebrows heavy but cut off so that they didn't really frame the wells of her pale eyes. It had given her the sad, quizzical look of a spaniel pup.

By the time she'd been sworn in and had identified herself as Charlotte Givern, nearly everybody in the court had forgotten her walk and the kind of figure she had. They remembered only that she wore a flowered print dress more than slightly out of style.

She was the fourth in a series of women called to witness the power Daniel Younger had over women of all ages, all classes.

She stood there, her face expressionless.

"There's no boy living here," she said.

"You mean John Younger from Dog Trot, Kentucky, doesn't live here?"

What color there was came back to her cheeks.

"May I come in?" Whistler asked.

"I don't know about that."

He looked up and down the street. "Do you have nosy neighbors?"

She opened the door and stepped back to let him pass into the small hallway, which led toward another door he expected led to the kitchen.

"In there," she said, gesturing toward the small living room. "Over there." She extended her arm, indicating a wing chair with a worn slipcover. Her movements were mechanical, as though she were a bad actress rehearsing the role of a maid.

When Whistler was seated, she sat down in a similar chair.

He remembered bits and pieces of her testimony, the lawyers' questions and her responses. Not accurately, not word for word, but the substance of it.

• • •

Listening to her tell how Younger had seduced and deceived her, got her to sell her house, leave her job, and follow him out to California from New Orleans without promise of marriage or a future, he'd had to wonder why, with all that going for him, Younger hadn't married rich or run a string of whores or got himself some education so he could've been one of the playboys of the Western world. But that, he supposed, was like asking why beautiful girls became whores, when conventional wisdom held that pretty women could do well for themselves just by being pretty.

He'd supposed it was with Younger's power to excite the lust of women the way it was with his own talent for attracting confidences. Whatever gifts a person had they just used and didn't much think about it. Otherwise the gifts would shatter and disappear—like a graceful dancer suddenly obsessed with watching his feet, so he couldn't dance anymore.

When Charlotte Givern had sworn on the Bible, it had been with a tight-lipped intensity that declared to one and all that she'd either been born with the fear of God in her skin or was reborn in Christ.

When she answered the questions put to her, it was in southern accents. Not the lilting velvet some possess but flat and twangy, with the trace of a whine in the upper register, as if fear or anger would result in tears. Her manner had the touchiness of the uneducated.

The lawyer'd got around to cost and loss and things like that. He'd asked her did she have an apartment in New Orleans and she'd said no, it was a house. She'd sold it because Younger'd told her to. And she'd given him the money for them to live on in California. And when the lawyer asked how come she'd do a thing like that, she'd said, "Because Inch Younger has the power of the Devil over women."

She sat there in her living room just as she'd sat in the courtroom fifteen years before, wearing a print dress.

Whistler knew it couldn't be the same one but it might just as well have been.

There was an urgency about her body, as though she were struggling with it to keep it from sending out invitations.

"I'm thinking back to the time of the trial," Whistler said.

"Were you there?"

"Yes."

"Then you know what I told them. But you don't know how I bore false witness against the man."

"What do you mean?"

"Inch didn't go back into that shack with that girl."

"Which girl is that?"

"The one who worked behind the bar without her top on."

"How do you know that?"

"Because I went looking for him that night."

"You were still seeing him after he was married?"

"Oh, yes." She said it defiantly, with a little lift to her chin.

"His wife was pregnant."

"That's why he came back to me. She couldn't..." She stopped and turned her head away. "I don't think this is any of your business."

"Are you saying you drove over to Buddy's Place in Malibu and..."

"He was supposed to come see me that night, and when he didn't I went looking for him, yes."

"How did you know where to look?"

"Because there was only so many places he liked to go, and he'd been doing some work for some moving picture producer down there."

"So what did you do?"

"I saw him coming out of the saloon and I got him and took him home."

"To your house?"

"No, to his own place."

"Why did you do that?"

"He was so drunk he didn't even know who I was. I got disgusted with him. A woman can only take so much."

"What else?"

"What do you mean?"

"There had to be something else. Otherwise why would you testify against him at the trial? Why would you let him go to prison for fifteen years when all you had to do was say you picked him up and he was with you when the barmaid was killed?"

She looked frightened for a second, as though Whistler could do something to her for having let Younger get convicted. Then she looked sly and said, "Who would've believed me? You know how they made me out to be."

She shifted in her chair and crossed her legs. Her appearance and manner seemed to change, as though she were a mimic who could enlarge her breasts and the span of her hips with a simple twist of her limbs. By moving an inch she seemed to thrust her pelvis at him and reveal more of her legs than a lady should, though her skirt hadn't crept up much above her knees.

"Besides, they had him for those other awful murders."

"But if the defense could've thrown some doubt on one of the murders, they could've cast doubt on all of them."

She didn't like hearing that. It made her guilt all the greater.

"Who are you anyway?" she asked.

"I'm a friend of Younger's ex-wife. I don't care if Younger was wrongly convicted or not. I'm looking for her boy."

"You want something to drink?" she said. "I haven't got anything hard. I've got some beer."

"I'd as soon have some coffee."

"I can do that," she said, and got up and left the room.

There was a large picture album on the coffee table. He leaned over and started turning pages.

He stopped at an eight-by-ten glossy of a woman with platinum curls, a red mouth, long black lashes, heavy theatrical make-up, and a beauty mark penciled in below the edge of her mouth.

It took him a minute to realize it was Charlotte Givern. Then he remembered that what she'd done for a living down in New Orleans and elsewhere had been brought up at the trial. They'd offended her greatly asking her about it.

The next glossy was a full figure of Charlotte showing a lot of flesh in a few pieces of glittery rags. There were others in which she wore even less and one in which she was altogether naked except for a pair of high-heeled shoes.

There were some leaflets announcing the appearance of Bebe Reboobza at a burlesque club on Basin Street.

He heard her heels on the wooden floor and quickly closed the cover of the album.

She came in and put down a tray with coffee cups already filled, a pitcher full of milk, and half a dozen packets of artificial sweetener.

"If you like sugar, I ain't got any more," she said.

She sat down, tore open a packet, poured it into her cup along with some milk, stirred it with a silver spoon, then picked it up, saucer and cup, and took a dainty sip.

"Do you know where Younger's boy is?" Whistler asked.

"I've got no idea," she said sharply.

"Your sister says she went to Dog Trot and got him from Younger's old man and that her husband, Bosley, drove the two of you back here."

"That's right."

"Bosley never went home."

"Well, my sister. You saw her, didn't you?"

"Then Bosley did drive you and the boy here to California and never went home?"

"I certainly haven't got him."

"Got who?"

"Bosley."

"How about the boy?"

"Not him either." She was frightened again. "He run away on me."

Whistler leaned in close, trying to show her as much sympathy as he could manage.

"Why'd you do it?"

"I kept tabs on Younger and all about him. That wife of his didn't want the child. She gave him away to that evil old man. I decided to get him and keep him until Inch got let out."

"And that way you'd get Inch back again?"

She nodded and tears came welling up in her eyes. She shook her head once or twice and then looked at the photo album, grabbing on to it for something to change the subject.

"How'd you like my pictures?"

"They were sitting there. I didn't realize they were personal."

"It's all right. It's all right. They're there to remind me of what I was once upon a time."

"Is that where Younger met you?"

"At a naked show? Oh, yes. That's what he wanted. He didn't know that wasn't truly me."

She lost hold of the cup and it fell off the saucer into her lap, the coffee that was left in it wetting her crotch. The saucer dropped from her hand, too, and bounced off her knee onto the rug. "He turned me into a whore," she said, making a wormy, sour fruit out of the word before she spit it out.

She turned her whole body away as though trying to flee. "He conjured me."

"Why did you maintain contact with him, then?"

"We are all redeemable in the Lord. I was going to give him his son when he got out, you see? I would show him all was forgiven and that a second chance in Christ could be his. We would be washed in the blood of the lamb together."

She raised her hands to the height of her shoulders, palms out, her fingers fluttering. "I was drowning in sin but I am on the shore. I was condemned to everlasting fire but now I am saved. I was as a corpse but now I am reborn. Sin no more. Sin no more."

Whistler put down his coffee cup and got to his feet.

"I was as an old tree ready to be felled," she moaned on. "I was like an old woman ready to lie down. Now I am like a child new risen from its bed. Sin no more. Sin no more."

"Miss Givern," Whistler said, but she clearly didn't hear him.

"Heed not the words and exhortations of the sinner, for he would drag you down into hell. I make my amends. Sin no more. Born in the Lord. Sin no more. Washed clean in the blood of Jesus."

As Whistler walked to the door to let himself out, Charlotte Givern began to speak gibberish, and he knew that the spirit was in her and she was speaking in tongues.

28

He didn't know how he got to where he was, sitting on the curb with his head between his legs, vomit all over his shoes, on the corner of Western and Hollywood Boulevard in Slant Side, where all the Asiatics gathered.

He remembered vaguely being offered more hard liquor than he'd had in years—the raisin snap he'd made in prison being strong but scarce—and he remembered grabbing at some pretty women, who'd laughed and brushed him off, except for one, who'd taken him into a corner and let him give her a feel. She'd told him that he had the strangest eyes and the softest hair, like animal fur. She'd just heard who and what he was. It gave her the shivers, she'd said, letting a man grab her tit who'd served time for murdering three women.

She'd given him a handful of pills and told him to pop a few and then meet her in dressing room A, where they'd do in privacy what they couldn't do in the middle of a celebration. But the pills had stunned his mind, making him forgetful of what she'd offered and even why he was there. To screw a job out of Hobby, because he'd finally figured out—sitting in prison for fifteen years—that Hobby hadn't come to see him or make him any offers because he felt friendly. He'd wanted something. For a long time Younger thought he'd wanted the story of what had happened for one of his moving pictures. But he'd really only wanted to know what Younger remembered about the knife or the orgies or the ceremonial mumbo jumbo they'd acted out that night.

He remembered telling Hobby that. He'd never meant to tell him that flat out, letting the truth just lay around like a sleeping dog you don't know for sure will bite or won't bite. Letting Hobby know he had a problem without saying he had a problem, so he wouldn't get to feeling there was only one way out for him, because the man who was blackmailing him might not really be blackmailing him. Doubt was always better than certainty, from the blackmailer's point of view.

The next thing he knew he was in a car with some character who called himself Milton, but who everybody else called Pig-Nose or Pig-Eye Dooley. The asshole was complaining about it.

"I can't help it I got little eyes and fat cheeks," Dooley'd been saying. "I been like this ever since I was a little kid. I come out here to be an actor. You know what I mean? You ever see Edward G. Robinson? There's a man who had a face like a frog, right? Still he was a big star. Nobody cared he looked like a frog. In fact it did him some good looking like a frog. So if I look a little bit like a porker, that could be good, too, right? That could be sympathetic. Everybody loves Porky Pig, you know what I mean? So how do you think I feel when they call me Pig-Nose but they don't offer me a part?

"So one day—I'm here from New York maybe a month, maybe two—I notice people act funny toward me. They act like they're afraid of me a little. Also a little respectful. A buddy of mine from New York, a practical joker by the name of Mike Rialto—you know him? Works as a private dick now and then? Got a glass eye he pops out one time in a bar and sticks it in his highball like it's a ice cube? Well, anyway, he tells me he spread the story around that I was a contract killer from New Jersey. At first I'm a little pissed off—it could ruin my chances for a part maybe if people are afraid of me—and then I think it's not so bad. The way people are treating me with respect, I mean. Wanting to be friendly with me. Inviting me to parties. Offering me jobs doing this and that.

"You know why I'm telling you all this?"

"I surely fuckin' don't," Younger said, so drunk he couldn't focus his eyes twelve inches in front of him, fighting down the urge to vomit.

"Well, I'm telling you because Paul Hobby just gave me a contract on your life."

"Wha'?"

"I said your friend Hobby, who was feeding you booze and keeping your mind occupied with that little twat, asked me to do you tonight."

"Where?"

"Well, how the hell do I know where? He left that up to me. The condition you're in I could find two inches of water laying in the gutter and fucking drown you. You got people who want to take your life, you shouldn't drink. You know what I'm saying?"

"I hear you."

"Well, so you're lucky I ain't a contract killer from New Jersey."

"I surely appreciate that."

"Sure."

After a little bit of silence Younger said, "I want to thank you kindly for not shooting me, if you was asked to shoot me."

"Well, Hobby left that up to me. I mean he didn't say should I shoot you or should I use a knife or should I choke you to death with a hunk of piano wire the way you read about."

"I thank you all the same."

"There any place special you want me to let you out?"

"Where are we?"

"Hollywood."

"So, if it's no trouble, you can let me off around Western and Hollywood Boulevard."

"That's Slant Side. You could get a Korean knife up your ass walking around there at night."

"They got me a room in a hotel there. I wouldn't know where else to go."

"So watch out for yourself."

Dooley cut a U in the middle of the block and headed for the corner of Western and Hollywood Boulevard.

Younger cracked the window and stuck his nose in the slipstream. After a while he said, "You mind if I ask you a question?"

"Go ahead."

"If you ain't a contract killer from New Jersey, how do you make your living?"

"I sell siding out in Downey and Covina, places like that. I got to stay out of Hollywood and other communities around here, you know what I'm saying? I mean what'd happen to me if I walked up to the door of somebody I knew and they found out I was going through their neighborhood selling siding? Christ, it'd ruin my reputation." Then he added, "You won't tell anybody I didn't shoot you, will you?"

"Hell, no. I wouldn't do that. What're you goin' to tell people though, in case they see me walkin' around?"

"I already figured that out. I'm going to tell them I took you behind a supermarket and tossed you in a Dumpster and put a pea in
your head. Only, because I had a couple or three belts myself, and
it being very dark, and the Dumpster being full of rotten cabbages, I
must've mistook one of them for your head and blew a vegetable
away."

"Why'd you put me in the Dumpster before you put the pea in
my head?"

"Because I shoot you first, it's a lot of trouble lifting you up into
the garbage bin. You know what I'm saying?"

"I never thought about that."

"Well, see, I thought about it. If I wanted to be a contract killer I
think I could be pretty good at it."

"Looks that way."

"Except I wouldn't know where to go to try out for the job." He
pulled up at the curb. "Here's the corner. You want me to drive you
up to your hotel?"

"No, thanks. It's just up the block. The air'll do me good."

Younger got out of the car and Dooley called him back. He
handed him some folded bills.

"What's this?" Younger asked.

"Hobby paid me a thousand on account."

"He walk around with a thousand in his pocket?"

"I don't know. Took it out of petty cash, out of his pocket, out of
somebody else's pocket. How do I know? So there's a couple
hundred."

"What for?"

"Well, I figure it's only right you should make a little. Fair is
fair."

Younger thanked him and stood at the curb, watching Dooley
drive off. He put the money into his pocket, his fingers touching
the extra pills he'd stashed. Then he sat down in the gutter and
threw up on his shoes.

That made him feel better.

He decided he'd better stand up and walk home; otherwise a cop
car could go cruising by and arrest him for drunk and vagrant.
Besides, he was very tired all of a sudden.

He started walking. After two blocks he realized he was going the
wrong way on the wrong street. He was going to turn around, when

he saw a gas station sign sticking up in the sky about two blocks ahead. He decided it would be a good idea to wash off his shoes.

When he got to the station and used the hose to get the crap off his feet, his head was clearing up pretty good, but he was all turned around. He went over and asked the two attendants, who were lounging around the office, which way was Western, and they pointed it out to him.

He heard them laughing behind him when he started down the boulevard, but he figured they were laughing at a joke and not because they'd decided to have a little fun with the yokel and send him on a wild-goose chase.

It took him five blocks before he knew he was walking away from the hotel. That made him mad, and for a minute he thought about going back and beating the shit out of the two assholes. Maybe he'd even grab a cab so he could get back quicker. Then he thought about how that would surely get his ass tossed back in the slam, so he decided to go on up ahead into the bright lights and get himself a soda pop to wash the bad taste out of his mouth. He checked the street sign. He was on Santa Monica Boulevard.

Mimi and Moo were hanging on the corner, having walked that far because it was a very slow night and they thought maybe they could get away from the competition, and also they'd be closer to home when they decided to give it up, if they decided to give it up.

They saw Younger walking down the street toward them.

"You think this one's got any money on him?" Mimi asked.

"He looks drunk to me," Moo replied.

"So that's good."

"Anybody on foot in this town couldn't have much money."

"Would it hurt to ask?"

"Never hurts to ask."

When Younger reached them, Mimi stepped forward and said, "How'd you like to have a lot of fun for a little money?"

Younger grinned and took the two hundred in crumpled bills out of his pocket. "This enough?"

29

So, what with his empty belly always giving him hell and his family shitting in the corner and leaving the food out for the rats and going up on the roof when he warned them not to, his life was very hard and full of irritations. It troubled his sleep. It made him dream.

In Bitsy's dream his father was grinning at him with a bloody knife in his hand and at first Bitsy was afraid. Then his father asked him how come he wasn't eating all the good roast pig he'd just gone to the trouble of slaughtering and cooking. Fresh pork stuffed with bread and apples. Nothing better. Beans out of the field behind old man Younger's house. Potatoes out of the root cellar. Let the good times roll, his father said. Dive in! You know, Pa, Bitsy said in the dream, when I grow up I'm going to be a pig butcher just like you. Well, his father replied, my pappy taught me, so it's only right that your pappy should teach you. Here! Grab ahold of this knife!

He woke up—it was around two in the morning, maybe two-thirty—reached for a cigarette, and found that he didn't have a cigarette. He didn't even have the pocket in his shirt where he kept his cigarettes. It'd been torn right off. An image, like the head of a rat, peeked around a corner of his brain. He tapped his back pocket. He had the paperback—what was left of it—but the matchbox was gone, along with his cigarettes. So his cigarettes were gone and so was the matchbox with a folded fiver in it. He'd carried that matchbox around since he'd been a kid. It'd been his only possession. That and the paperback book that sonofabitch Hogan had ripped apart.

They could be up on the roof or they could be down in the bottom of the air shaft.

The rat crept forth and Bitsy started to tremble and shake as if he'd taken a fever all of a sudden. It was like a curtain of smoke lifting away. All of a sudden he remembered having the argument with Hogan and running toward him with his arms outstretched. But he didn't remember anything after that. Didn't remember climbing down off the roof, or having something to eat—if he'd had anything to eat—or going to sleep, or anything.

He searched the rooms to see if there was anybody else around. Usually there'd be somebody asleep or just going to bed or hanging around scratching their nuts this time of the night, but the rooms were empty except for himself. Even Dipper was gone and Dipper hardly went anywhere without checking with him first.

He went over to a window by the air shaft and looked out and down. It was as black as pitch but he knew Hogan's body was lying there.

Bitsy started to tremble even worse. He put his hand on top of his head and calmed himself as though he were shutting off a valve. He didn't want to do it, but he knew he had to do it. Somebody else could look out the window and see Hogan lying there.

He felt for the little flashlight he'd copped from the drugstore and went downstairs to the basement and through the door to the air shaft. It was choked with garbage a couple of feet thick. Clouds of flies rose up when he kicked his way over to Hogan, who was staring at him with his eyes wide open.

Hogan had been impaled on several pieces of rusty iron reinforcement rod. They stuck up through his neck and chest and belly.

Bitsy stood there, not stirring the garbage up any more. The flies settled, drinking from Hogan's eyes and mouth. Bitsy tried to spot the colors of the tarnished foil. There were so many bits and pieces of iridescent color in the rotting mess, how could he spot a piece as small as a matchbox?

After half an hour of poking around, the flies making a terrible buzz when he disturbed them again, he gave it up. What'd he need with an old matchbox anyway?

He found a piece of cardboard big enough to use for a shovel and started covering up Hogan's body. He didn't know what else to do. When he got to the head he looked away and finally tossed the cardboard over the face.

As he was about to go look for breakfast he thought that maybe the matchbox and his cigarettes could've landed on the roof when Hogan tore his pocket. He climbed back up to the top floor.

He heard somebody crying up above when he reached the next to last landing.

Moo was sitting in the corner rubbing her eyes. Her hair was hanging around her face like seaweed and her blouse was so far off one shoulder her breast was hanging out.

Bitsy stooped down and asked her what she was crying about, but she wouldn't stop rubbing her face so he could see her. He took her wrists and pulled her hands away.

She laughed and said, "Hi there, Bitsy, how's it going?"

The pupils of her eyes were like pinpoints.

"What're you crying about? What's the matter?"

She started to moan and tore her hands out of his grip and covered her face again.

"What're you on?" Bitsy asked. "Where'd you get the stuff? Where you been all night? Where's Mimi?"

Her wails grew higher and thinner.

"The terrible things he did to her," Moo whined.

"Who did?"

"My God, the awful things he did."

"Who did?"

"I don't know. I don't know. Somebody."

"Well, who? Can't you remember who?"

She shook her head no, her hair flying all around, strands of it trailing along her cheek, her eyes still unfocused from the drugs in her system or the shock to her brain. Her eyes rolled back and up. For a minute Bitsy thought she was going to faint, but then he realized she was only trying to look up the stairwell to the roof.

Going up on the roof was a risk and an adventure. The side plate that held the iron steps to the wall was all twisted and bent away. Part of the railing was gone. The top landing tilted and you had to push against the metal-clad door very carefully, otherwise you got the feeling that you were going to push the staircase, with yourself on it, right out into space, where you'd fall eight stories or maybe forever.

He made it up along the twisted planes of the steps, picking his way in the dark, throwing the little pencil beam of light ahead of him. He reached out and pushed against the door. It gave an inch, screaming on its rusted springs and hinges like an angry cat that had just got stepped on. He took another step up and got his elbow against it, then his shoulder, and then he was on the roof with the California sky filled with city-shine above his head.

He stood there for a second, looking at the light through squinted eyes and listening to the sounds of the restless city whispering like the wind through trees. He took a sniff and the air smelled good for a change. He wondered if just maybe they were going to get a stretch of three or four days without rain or Santa Ana winds or smog that could cut your lungs into ribbons. He was starting to fog out in his thoughts. He thought he heard cows mooing.

When he snapped himself out of it, the cows kept on mooing. But there weren't any cows, just Mimi lying on her back with her clothes half torn off her. Some of them thrown aside. Some of them under her and some of them stirring in the night breeze as if she were breathing heavily.

His belly clenched like a fist. He felt a burning in his scrotum and his heart started to beat so hard it rocked him a little. He crouched down to keep from falling and duck-waddled over to her, reaching out a hand to touch her breast and see if she was alive.

Her mouth was bruised and battered, the red of her lipstick all mixed up with the red-brown of dried blood. A couple of teeth were broken, the jagged ends showing in an ugly smile. The flesh around her eyes was puffed and stained a terrible blue-black.

Whoever had killed her had bitten her breasts until they'd bled. There were bite marks on her belly and the inside of her thighs. Somebody had shoved a broken bottle up into her between her legs.

The goddam cows wouldn't stop mooing. The sound was coming from behind a parapet decorating the corner of the building. He went to look and saw Dipper huddling there, hugging his knees. He kept his eyes closed, figuring, as a child would do, that if he couldn't see anybody, nobody could see him.

"Hey, Dipper," Bitsy said, reaching out very slowly to touch him, because he didn't want to spook Dipper and scare him over the edge. He talked soft and low, telling Dipper not to be scared.

Dipper looked up at him, his face all swollen from crying, his grief and terror laying tracks on his cheeks, his mouth starting to twist up, ready to start wailing again. "Where was you? Where did you go?"

"I'm right here. It's okay, Dipper. What the hell you doing up here on the roof?"

"I came up to watch Mimi and Moo do it with the man. I didn't do it. I didn't hurt nobody."

"I know you didn't. I know that. Give me your hand."

Bitsy held on to Dipper's hand as Dipper slid on his rump along the edge of the roof to safety.

Dipper hugged him and Bitsy hugged Dipper back.

30

He swung through the door of Vickie's Victorian Parlor Pub off Western Avenue, out of the heat into the cold of the air-conditioning. The sign outside said "Topless," as though the beer joint was caught in a time warp and still thought it was the sixties or seventies.

That was all right with Inch Younger. It made him feel right at home, as if fifteen years hadn't gone by without him.

He was three days out of prison and it no longer felt like a miracle.

Going in, he'd been told by the authority, "There's always a chance for parole. Do good time."

"Work the system slow and easy. Talk to the chaplain. When the time's right, come to Jesus," the cons had said.

"I been washed in the blood of the lamb. I am like a infant, reborn."

That turned the trick.

"Here's your suit and tie. Report to your parole officer every week. Get a job. Get a fixed address. Stay away from criminal companions. Stay out of saloons and bars. Don't get into any trouble."

He took a bite out of the refrigerated air, it felt so good.

The wooden bar was sitting right there inside the door. Walking in out of the bright sunlight, he knocked his leg on a stool first thing and for a minute or so could hardly see to sit down.

There were a couple of animated beer signs over the back bar. One was a scene of a mountain glen, with a stream running through it to a lake in which a fisherman stood knee-deep with his pole in his hand, while a stag stood in the background watching him.

The barmaid, a big-titted, skinny-hipped, slightly pop-eyed sweetheart with a beehive hairdo dragged out of the fifties, clip-clopped across the duckboards in a pair of feathered mules. Her thirty-eights were slung in hammocks of see-through gauze, and the panties she wore were no more than three strings and a patch of blue.

"I feel like a beer," he said.

"That helps," she said, "because that's what we got."

"I feel like a cold beer."

"What kind?"

"What kind you got on draft?"

"We got Coors on draft."

"That all you got on draft? You don' have no Heineken's on draft?"

"We got Coors on draft. We got Heineken's in bottles."

"How about them signs? That one says Heineken's on draft."

"You always believe everything you read?"

"Well, I believe a lot of what I see."

"So?"

"I'll have a draft."

"That's Coors."

"I gotcha."

She clip-clopped off to pull the beer. Drained a half inch off the head and brought it up to the rim again. Walked it over and set it down. Picked up his buck and said, "Buck and a quarter."

"Buck and a quarter for eight ounces?"

"That includes the floor show. What do you think?"

She walked away into the gloom at the other end of the bar, tightening up and rolling her ass cheeks, giving him a buck and a quarter's worth.

She stood there with her arms folded across her belly, watching two men playing a game of pool on the table underneath a hanging light, but Younger could tell she was watching him with the back of her head. Every once in a while she'd shift her weight, bouncing her buns, giving him a little encore.

He drank three quarters of the beer in one go, then sat up close to the bar, the glass standing on the wood between his cupped hands, a cigarette in the corner of his mouth sending up a plume of smoke that clipped his nose and spiraled up and out across one squinting eye on its way to the stained pressed-tin ceiling. Checking her out. Checking out the legs and ass.

Her flesh, so white it was tinged with blue, reminded Younger of one of the baby hookers he'd tasted last night. Good-for-nothing little twats trying to clip him for his roll.

The barmaid got bored teasing him with her back. She came trotting over across the duckboards ready to push it a little.

"You all right?" she asked.

The air conditioner was blowing hard, raising her skin around each hair so she looked as if she were all broken out in colorless pimples.

"Ain' you cold in that getup?" Younger asked, all oil and sympathy, yet somehow putting a little leer into it, as though her cold body was making his body very hot.

"I could get pneumonia."

"Ain' you got a apron, maybe a sweater, you could throw on?" he asked, looking first at her belly button and then at the valley between her breasts, as if he'd be very sorry not to have her to look at if she did what he suggested, even though his tender nature had urged him to make the suggestion.

"I put a sweater around me, and the first thing you know, Harry walks in and sees me and throws a fit."

"Harry's the boss?"

"He's the owner. Also my boyfriend."

"Well, that makes up my mind, then," he said.

"About what?"

"I was on my way out of town when I see this place and thought I'd have a cold beer for the road. Then I see you and for a minute there I almost changed my mind and decided to hang around."

"Hang around for what?"

"Well, you know."

"You got a nerve, haven't you?"

"What's the matter? What did I say?"

"You know what you said."

"I said I got a look at you and thought maybe it'd be worthwhile gettin' to know you better. That's what I said. What'd you think I said?"

"Well, I think that's pretty much what you *said* but I don't think that's what you meant."

He stretched his arms across the bar and grasped the inside edge with slender brown hands which a lot of women had told him were a nice feature. She took a step back as though she thought he was reaching for her.

"How's that?" he asked.

"You said 'you know.'"

"Well, what's so bad about 'you know'?"

"You know," she said. When she smiled she had a very attractive dimple at each corner of her mouth.

"I don't think it's nice of you to think I meant somethin' I didn' actually say," he said. "I mean you could think I *meant* all kinds of terrible things, when I wasn't even thinkin' terrible things."

"I didn't say anything about terrible," she said, flirting, showing her dimples again. "You want me to freshen up your beer?" She moved forward, coming a lot closer than she needed to to pick up his glass, leaning her breasts against the backs of his hands.

"My God," he said.

"What's the matter?"

"You must be really cold."

"What makes you say that?"

"Your buds is as hard as two frozen huckleberries."

"That's not why they're hard," she said, moving away with the glass in her hands to top off his beer at the pump.

The two guys at the pool table finished up and racked their cues. They walked down the long aisle along the bar toward the door, looking once at Younger, then at the barmaid standing there measuring the glass of beer with her eye as if it were a matter of great importance.

"Hey, Fran, take it easy," one of them said.

"You, too, Mackie."

"Don't do anything I wouldn't do," the other one said. He laughed and cut his eyes toward Inch, then looked her in the eyes as he passed as if to say there was nothing much she could put over on him.

"That's like giving me permission to rob a bank," she said, and walked over to set the fresh beer down in front of Younger.

"You Vickie?" Younger asked.

"Am I who?"

"The sign outside says Vickie's Parlor."

"Harry made that up."

"So what do I call you?"

"Frances. Fran. Ain't you got ears? Didn't you hear Mackie say 'So long, Fran'?"

"He said 'Take it easy.'"

"Whatever."

"So, Fran, it looks like we're all alone."

She looked at the watch on her wrist and said, "What do I call you?"

"Everybody calls me Inch."

"What does that tell me? I mean is it the opposite?"

"What do you mean, the opposite?"

"You know. Like they call a fella what's five feet two Stretch, and a fella what's got white hair Blackie. You know"—her eyes fell to his crotch—"the opposite."

He laughed. "I've been told," he said.

"Told what?"

"Me and a Missouri mule."

"Never met a man who wasn't a bragger. Never met one who wasn't a liar."

He made a serious face and dropped his hands to the buttons on his fly. "I could show you."

She put out her hands with her fingers spread and backed off until she bumped into the backbar, as if she thought he was going to leap over the wood and shove it in her face. Warding him off. "Oh, no, never mind."

"It wouldn' be no trouble."

She shivered.

He got up off the stool and walked over to the pass-through while his fingers undid the fly on his jeans. She stood there as if she couldn't move, as if she were stuck there, a bug on a pin. He reached in and pulled himself out. Her eyes dropped to his crotch. He wasn't lying after all about him and a Missouri mule. He pressed himself against her. His hands went around her ass and his fingers plucked at the strings on the bikini bottom.

"Hey, fachrissake, you crazy? This is a place of public business." She was laughing.

"This's only going to take a minute."

She twisted her hips and pushed him away hard. "Hey, Harry could walk in here any time. Right this minute. Harry could walk in here and then there'd be hell to pay."

"Fuck Harry."

She managed to find a little space, pushing herself along the backbar, her elbow sending a line of eight-ounce glasses crashing to the duckboards.

"Look what you're doing, goddammit," she said. "I said no, and no is no!" She slapped him on the shoulder, her hand sliding off and catching him alongside the neck and jaw.

The look on his face made her stop laughing fast. He snaked out a hand and grabbed her wrist. With the other hand he reached behind her and took an empty display bottle off the counter and busted it off so he had just the jagged neck.

He held it to her throat. "You can't do like that. You can't tease a man with your tits and ass, makin' smart remarks, lickin' your lips and starin' at his crotch. You're gonna ride the fuckin' mule. Oh, yes, you are."

She jerked away and ducked under his arm, cutting hers on the bottle he threatened her with. She screamed as if her lungs would burst and ran away from him across the duckboards, stumbling in her ridiculous feathered mules.

"Cut it out, fachrissakes, cut it out," Younger said, tossing the bottle aside. "I ain' touchin' you. Just stop yellin'. I'm goin' out that door and you ain't never goin' to see me again."

The door swung open at his back, letting in the light from outside.

"What the fuck?" somebody said.

"This goddam maniac's trying to rape me!" Fran yelled.

Younger turned around fast, his hand going into his pocket for a knife, thumb popping the blade.

One of the pool players, the one she called Mackie, was standing there.

"I come back for my sunglasses," he said, staring stupidly at the knife in Younger's hand, then at Fran, who was cowering against the backbar, clutching her arm, blood seeping between her fingers.

"Hey, you sonofabitch," Mackie said.

"You just back off," Younger said. "You just back off you don't want me to cut your fuckin' throat."

Mackie picked up an ashtray from the bar and swung at Younger's head. He did it so suddenly that Younger didn't even duck. The sharp edge cut him right at the hairline and he started to bleed.

He circled around Mackie—who turned in place, making sure Younger didn't take a swipe at him—until the way to the door was clear.

Younger was out and away.

"Call the cops," Mackie said.

"Harry'll have a fit," Fran said, starting to cry because she was bleeding and because she was afraid that if the nut who cut her was picked up, he'd say what happened and Harry'd believe she caused the trouble shaking her tits and ass at the sonofabitch.

Which, of course, was what she was told to do, paid to do. So if Harry didn't want men glomming on to her treasures, why did he have her prancing around in nearly nothing at all, catching pneumonia?

"Call the cops," Mackie said again, going over and putting his arm around Fran, letting his hand wander down and giving one cheek of her ass a little squeeze.

"Jesus Christ, Mackie, what do you think you're doing?" she asked.

"Well, I was just trying to give you a little comfort after I saved you from getting raped and all."

"You want a reward, you'll have to take a free beer, fachrissake. You keep doing what you're doing, what's the difference that prick rapes me or you rape me, except he's got a dong like a baseball bat?"

31

Whistler lay on the bed in his rickety house hanging out over the pass. The wind was kicking up through the canyon and creeping under the house, rattling its floorboards and threatening the poles that pinned it to the hillside.

He was tired but he was also stalling. He didn't want to have to tell Faye he hadn't been able to keep hold of the string that led to her boy.

Some things you could walk away from.

Like he'd walked away from being Sam. Sam the Sad Man, the Sandman.

He'd never wanted to be a clown.

He'd come to Hollywood like hundreds of thousands of others down the years, looking for fame and fortune, drawn by the glitter and swank, the evil allure of it. Not really knowing what to do. Ready to do just about anything and everything for that elusive thing—more avidly sought than Arthur's Grail or Jason's fleece—called the break. The chance to be somebody. A screenwriter of fabled drunkenness. A director of mythic rage. A movie star of godliness.

Armies of nobodies wanting to be somebodies, knowing nothing, willing to try anything, asking what do I got to do, when do I got to do it, how do you want it, straight up or on the rocks.

He got into the clown suit by lucky chance, the way Fred Mac-Murray was said to have made the movies because he was wearing a trench coat a certain director admired, or Lana Turner got noticed wearing a sweater.

He'd been looking for work, any kind of work. He was hanging around a local television studio out in Burbank. Somebody got sick just before airtime.

"You think you could wear a clown suit?" somebody asked him.

"What does it pay?"

"Scale."

"What do I have to do?"

"Just read the idiot cards. Say a few words before the kiddie cartoons. Half an hour five times a week. Saturday and Sunday mornings. Just until Bobbity Boo gets over the flu."

"Show me what I have to wear."

"Go to wardrobe over there."

He was pointed to a room where a fat gray-haired lady with a cigarette dangling from a lip like a shovel was crushed in a closet they called the wardrobe department. When she heard what was wanted she said, "You can't use Bobbity's gear. A clown's makeup and gear belong to him exclusive. A clown'll kill to protect his face and his gear. I'm tellin' you. I used to be with the circus. So what-taya got?"

"Nothing."

"I'll make you pair of pants and a jacket out of some scraps. You go make yourself a face."

What did he know about inventing the face of a clown? He knew Ronald McDonald. He knew Emmett Kelly. He knew Marcel Mar-ceau's Mr. Bip. That's all he knew.

He applied whiteface. He made a mouth that turned down in-stead of up. He wanted something a little classy, a little classical. He could draw a bit, and he drew a tear underneath one eye and a flower on the bottom of that cheek, so it looked as though the flower was growing because he was watering it with his tears.

The trousers the wardrobe lady made out of bits and pieces came just below the calves of his legs, so she gave him a pair of white stockings and red ballet slippers to put on. The jacket was cut bo-lero length, so he put on a long-sleeved white blouse that puffed out of the too short sleeves. The old circus woman tied a white satin sash around his neck under the shirt collar and spread it out to make an absurdly oversize bow tie. He refused a hat and wore a black bathing cap instead.

He worked out okay, reading the idiot cards. Not trying to do anything on his own.

When Bobbity Boo got over the flu it was too late for him. Bobbity Boo wouldn't work for scale but Sam the Sad Man would.

It paid the rent and put food on the table and could be glorified as a foot in the door to stardom or on the ladder to fame.

One evening, when a piece of film didn't arrive, he ad-libbed a fairy tale. They liked it enough to ask him to do one every night. They gave him a raise in pay, pushed the show to an hour, and moved it from before supper to just before bedtime.

They did a series of promos drawing the attention of parents to this new storyteller and keeping the connection to the old show. He was Sam the Sad Man, your Channel 8 Sandman. "Let the Sandman put the kiddies to bed."

There was something odd about the stories he told. Some of them were touched with little horrors. A couple of mothers wrote in complaining that the Sandman was giving their kids nightmares. Some viewers called in asking what the stories meant.

Sometimes he talked with them over the air, giving them a little simple advice like "Hang in there," "It's always darkest before dawn," and "Every cloud has a silver lining." That sort of thing. The management took note.

They dropped the kiddie show because *Sesame Street* was hammering it into the ground.

The Sandman went late, late night. A call-in show that drew the ratings and the advertisers.

"I'm a pop psychologist," he told Faye the first time they met.

He didn't really counsel anybody. He was smart enough not to do that. Smart enough to know people just wanted somebody to listen. Somebody without a human face that could disapprove. Who was better to confess your sins to than an image on a seventeen-inch screen? Who better than a clown? A clown was even better than a priest.

Then the woman called in and said she was going to take her life, and he hadn't been able to do a thing about it. He'd just jabbered at her, signaling the engineer to call the cops, while he frantically tried to hold her on the line, trick her address out of her, waiting for help to arrive. Listening to her slip through his fingers. Hearing her say good-bye.

Now he hadn't been able to do a thing about finding Faye's Johnny.

He lay there staring at the ceiling. Then he sat up and called Faye.

Some kid answered and said that she was out of Magdalene House working the streets, making it sound as though she were whoring, not trying to rescue whores. He told the girl to tell Faye, when she checked in, that Whistler had called and would be at Gentry's coffee shop.

32

His name was Houlihan but they called him Hooligan. He didn't mind. He thought all monikers were compliments. He prided himself on being as tough, as cruel, as unforgiving as any pimp, macgimper, child stealer, cutthroat, or ball breaker on the street.

His partners lasted nine months, a year. They said he had body odor like a moose. The real reason they asked for a new partner was that they just couldn't stand his lousy personality. He wouldn't give a blind man a piece of string for his guide dog. He wouldn't give a hooker the benefit of a doubt. He was the best goddam homicide dick working out of Hollywood Division—maybe in the whole city—and everybody knew it.

When he held his chin in his big hand, his thumb and knuckles left whitish marks that took a long time to fade away.

He was holding his chin in his hand at that minute, being obviously patient with the street turds who were sitting on two wooden chairs in front of him, because anybody with half an eye could tell that neither one of them had the understanding of a fart or could think any faster than you could piss in a bowl.

The one who'd given his name as Kentucky was rattling on. The one called Dipper was squirming, looking at Hooligan as though he feared him greatly. He leaned toward his friend, trying to get his mouth to his ear, and for a minute there Hooligan thought he was going to topple over into the other kid's lap.

"Bitsy, I got to go pee-pee," Dipper said.

"Can I take him to the toilet?" Bitsy asked.

"Can't he go by himself?" Hooligan replied in a voice that was very intimidating.

"Sure he can go by himself, but in a strange place like this he could get lost."

"We don't want him to get lost, do we?"

Bitsy knew he was being badgered but he didn't know why. Didn't know that Hooligan had no patience or sympathy for the lost or strayed.

"If I went with him, he wouldn't get lost."

"Maybe you'd both get lost."

"I wouldn't get lost."

"Suppose, say, you wanted to get lost?"

"Why would I want to do that?"

"Because maybe, now that you're here and you see me looking at you, maybe you decided it wasn't such a great idea calling the cops."

"Why would I think that? One of my family was done. You think I would just walk away?"

"Well, that'd depend, wouldn't it?"

Bitsy knew exactly what the big, ugly cop was going to say if he asked him depend on what, but he asked him anyway.

"Depend on if her death occurred as a result of a domestic quarrel," Hooligan said.

He meant that Bitsy and Mimi'd had an argument and he'd killed her, but Hooligan was being cute putting it the way he did.

"If it was me done her I never would've called the cops at all."

"That's what I'm saying. At first you thought it was a good idea because who'd think the murderer would call in the police. Then, like I say, you got a look at me and now maybe you don't think it was such a hot idea."

"Oh, Jesus, Bitsy, please," Dipper wailed. He was squirming so badly on the seat it looked as if he was going to fall off. He was clutching his pecker to keep it from letting go, his face all twisted up in a peculiar kind of anguish.

Hooligan looked around for somebody. He saw Isaac Canaan at his desk, hat square on his head the way old rabbis wore their hats, hunched over a plate of something Hooligan didn't want to guess what it was.

"Isaac. You want to take this kid to the toilet, he should take a pee before he lets go in his pants?"

"Take care of your own prisoners, Hooligan," Canaan said.

"He ain't a prisoner. He's just a kid what's got to take a pee."

"Why does he need an escort, then?"

"His friend don't think he can find his way back."

"So let his friend take him."

"I'm in the middle of an interrogation here."

"What's the beef?"

"Homicide."

"Him?"

"I don't know if he done it. But he called it in."

"Who's the victim?"

"A baby hooker. Street name's Mimi."

Canaan put the plastic lid on his meal and came over, shuffling along as if it was more than his feet could bear to step on the floor, as if he was so tired he might fall asleep before he ever got across the room.

Street wisdom had it that Isaac Canaan, the kiddie-vice cop, never slept but only catnapped. Hadn't slept for years, since some pervert abducted, raped, mutilated, and murdered his only niece, a child of seven. It was also said that he never took off his hat because he had a deforming wound on his head, or because he wanted to be reminded of his pledge to one day find his niece's murderer, or because he believed with a belief that amounted to a religion that a man could catch cold and die if he went around with his head uncovered.

For a minute it looked as though he was going to walk right on past the suffering Dipper, but as he went by he held out his hand as he would toward a child.

Dipper took it, and together, lurching and shuffling along with their queer gaits, they made their way across the squad room toward the toilets.

"Back to you," Hooligan said. "Where you get them cuts and abrasions on your hands?"

"What?" Bitsy said as though stung by a bee. He looked at his hands as though he'd just that second discovered them there at the end of his arms.

"They look like the kinds of wounds a person'd get punching somebody around the head and face."

"Oh, no," Bitsy said. "My hands is always cut up. They get cut going through garbage cans and Dumpsters. Sometimes I got to fight to protect myself."

"So why don't you just tell me what Mimi said that made you mad enough to beat her to death?"

Bitsy started to tremble, even though he knew the bastard didn't really believe what he was saying but was only trying to scare the shit out of him.

Canaan came shuffling back with Dipper, who still clung to his hand as if he was afraid to let go. The retarded boy looked at Bitsy, then at Hooligan, then looked away as though afraid to draw attention to himself by staring at the big man threatening to eat his friend alive.

Hooligan had no mercy. He watched Bitsy as if he were nothing but a bug under a microscope or a dog turd on the bottom of his shoe.

"All you got to do is ask Moo," Bitsy said.

Hooligan leaned forward and said very softly, "You know what, you little prick? I could hang it on you no matter what this fucking Moo has to say."

"Well, she'll tell you it wasn't me. I wasn't even there when it happened."

"So maybe I hang it on your friend what can't hold his water."

"Dipper wouldn't hurt a fly."

"So who else you got hiding out in that building?"

"Nobody's hiding out. Some people live there because they got no other place."

"You got regulars?"

"We got regulars but we also got plenty of people passing through. Drunks and crazies. All kinds of people passing through."

"Tell me who's the regulars."

Bitsy hesitated for a second, trying to work it through in his head. Everybody knew you weren't supposed to help the cops. You start helping the cops and the first thing you knew they were asking names and addresses, tricking telephone numbers out of you, and calling the places you ran away from.

"None of the regulars would've hurt Mimi."

"Maybe one of them saw the person who did it. You ever think of that? Just give me some names and we'll go and ask some questions."

Bitsy flashed on the idea that if he left Hogan's name out of it they'd find out that he was one of the regulars from somebody else, and the next thing you know, they'd be out looking for him, thinking maybe that he was the one who'd done it, and when they couldn't find him they'd think that he was the killer for sure. Then somebody—this big asshole with the red face—would remember that he'd left Hogan's name off the list and they'd start wondering why. Or maybe they'd kick around and find Hogan lying under the garbage and then...

"Don't fucking think about it so much," Hooligan said. "You'll give yourself a headache. Just answer my question."

Bitsy rattled off the street names of twenty people, some of them members of his family, some of them casuals he knew around from here and there. He mentioned Hogan but didn't single him out by his tone of voice or in any other way.

Hooligan wrote the names down, making Bitsy slow down once or twice so he could get them all.

All of a sudden Hooligan said, "How old are you?"

"What difference?" Bitsy asked.

"Don't ask me what fucking difference. I just told you, I ask you a question you answer the question. What do you think you are, a fucking lawyer?"

"You want a lawyer, sonny?" Canaan asked.

Hooligan and Bitsy both said "What?" at the same time, only Bitsy was just asking and Hooligan was letting Canaan know he should butt out.

"You're the kid they call Bitsy, ain't you?" Canaan asked.

"My name's Kentucky."

"So, okay, that's a street name you use here or there. What's your real name?"

Bitsy hesitated. "John," he finally said.

"But everybody calls you Bitsy. That right?"

Bitsy nodded, suddenly wanting to cry because this tired old hound of a cop was being nice to him.

"So, Bitsy, I asked you did you want a lawyer?" Canaan said.

Hooligan got up off his chair like somebody'd shoved a spike up his ass, grabbed Canaan by the arm, and walked him off several feet. "Why don't you keep your nose out of this?"

"Did you ask me to come over or did you ask me to come over?"

"I asked you take the dummy for a pee."

"I don't want to have a fight with you, Hooligan," Canaan said wearily.

"So do like I tell you. Butt the fuck out."

"What you're doing here's not right. You're harassing that kid—he's hardly out of his diapers—and there's no lawyer present. There isn't even somebody from juvenile."

"This is a homicide."

"I understand that, but he's still a minor—anybody can see that—and if you keep on questioning him without somebody's here to represent his interests, whatever you get won't be worth the paper you use to wipe your ass."

"Who's going to say?"

"Well, the kid's going to say, for one. And I'm going to say, for another."

Hooligan gave way grudgingly. "You want to take a chair, so take a chair. But I don't think we need lawyers and social workers putting their hands over his mouth right at the minute."

"Okay, I'll take a chair," Canaan said.

They went back to Bitsy and Dipper. Canaan looked around and pulled the chair over from the next desk. He placed it between the two kids. Dipper looked grateful.

"Sergeant Canaan here's from kiddie vice," Hooligan said. "He spends his life trying to protect kids like you even when you don't want to be protected. He won't let you answer any questions that could incriminate you."

Bitsy looked at Canaan sidelong, suspicious that they were going to play the good-cop-bad-cop game on him.

"You can still have a lawyer here if you want one," Canaan said.

Bitsy thought a minute, then said it was okay, he'd answer what he could. "I got nothing to hide."

You got plenty to hide, kid, Canaan thought. We all got plenty to hide and we damn sure better hide it or the world'll crush our bones and drink our blood.

33

It was crowded in Gentry's. Mike Rialto, the sometime private detective and all-the-time procurer, with his dress-up blue glass eye staring at his plate, was sitting in a booth having the seafood special. Bosco sat on the other side of the Formica, his hand resting on a copy of the *Book of Kells*.

"Whistler back from wherever?" Rialto asked.

"If he is I don't know it."

"You used to always know where Whistler was."

"That was before," Bosco said, with a little twist to his mouth.

"Before what?"

"Before this Faye walked back into his life."

"It's happened before, a woman's caught Whistler's attention."

"It's happened many times before. But this is different."

"How different?" Rialto asked.

"I think what we got here is a case of"—Bosco spoke the last words with some hesitation, as if they were strangers to him—"true love."

"What're you talking, true love?"

"I'm talking Whistler wants to find out if his all-time tender squeeze truly loves him. He's ready to give her guarantees that he truly loves her, so he goes off to look for a kid he ain't got the slightest chance of finding unless God loves him a lot."

"So, if he can't find the kid, what does that get him?"

"It gives him the assurance that she loves him truly if he fails do her the only big favor she'll ever ask him for in her life and she still kisses him on the nose."

"That's crazy, he goes to all that trouble to fail."

"Hey," Bosco said, "there's love and there's love. I had my lost child and Canaan's got his and Whistler's got his." He made a sound of disgust and waved his hand in the air, chasing away his bad feelings as if they were flies. "Ahhhg! Let him walk the streets. Let him waste his fortune on air travel. Let him run the string."

"Who's saying otherwise? I ain't the one whose nose's out of joint."

"Just leave it alone."

"I never touched it. But now that the subject's on the table it's hard not to speculate about the cost of such a quest. It's going to cost a lot. One way or another it's going to cost a lot."

"You know anybody who gets home free?"

"Shush, shush, shush," Rialto said. "Look who just walked in."

Whistler walked the length of the shop and took a seat next to Bosco.

"So, what's happened while I've been gone?" he asked.

"A baby hooker was raped with a busted bottle. They collected her from a roof," Bosco said.

"That why it's so quiet out there on the stroll?"

"Something like that gives the children pause. It don't stop the old-timers, walking around with razors in their shoes, from enjoying the temporary reduction in competition though."

"I tapped a long shot out to the races day before yesterday," Rialto said. "Forty to one. Had a hundred riding on her nose. Finally got a little luck."

"You had any luck, Bosco?"

"Well, my house ain't burnt down and my van's still running and it ain't raining, so my stump don't hurt."

"You've been lucky, too," Whistler said.

"I won't ask," Bosco said.

Whistler shook his head.

Shirley Hightower came over and asked Whistler if he wanted anything. He ordered pie and coffee and she went away.

"Finding a lost or runaway kid is very hard," Rialto said judiciously, one private license to another. "Finding one after two, three years, you can forget it."

"Well, maybe I can forget it," Whistler said, "but I don't know about the lady who asked me to go looking."

Shirley came back with his pie and coffee and they all fell silent, each one deep in his own thoughts.

By the time Faye came through the door, Whistler had finished the pie, a hamburger, and some soup. Rialto had asked him how come he ate his dinner backwards. Then he'd left and Bosco had gone back to work the counter, leaving Whistler alone.

So it was only Whistler who saw the way her face changed expressions as she walked toward him down the aisle—going from sunny and full of expectation to sad—until the last one stuck. She read it all in the time it took her to make the distance from the door.

The booth across the aisle, next to the window, had just been vacated and Whistler moved her over there. It was the booth where he conducted business. Where he could look out on his neighborhood and its citizens.

"How far did you get?" she asked.

"I got from Dog Trot to Johnson City to Moodyville in Pickett County to Charlotte Givern's house in the Valley."

"Charlotte Givern?" she said, the name as familiar as her own hand but still vague, the way things are vague when you don't want to remember them.

"She testified at the trial. She was the woman who sold her house and—"

"I know, I know," Faye said sharply, almost harshly, angry at him for reminding her. "I remember. What took you to see Charlotte Givern?"

"She'd gone to get John from old man Younger."

She was quiet for a minute, digesting that, doing the equation.

"They never told me."

"She and her sister and her brother-in-law bought him from the old man. Then the brother-in-law drove her and the boy to California."

She waited for the worst, which she knew was yet to come.

"But he ran away," Whistler said.

He expected her to cry, but she didn't cry. She just sighed and looked out into the street, where the soldiers in an army of lost and runaway children paraded up and down.

"He could be right out there and I might not even know it. I could've touched him, offered him a cup of hot chocolate."

"You would've known him."

"Maybe a good mother would know her child after ten years, but I wouldn't make any bets on me."

34

Moo, looking sullen and scared, was delivered to Hooligan from the hospital, where they'd given her a checkup. Aggie Schirra, the policewoman, had the paperwork in her fist.

"Give her your chair," Hooligan said to Bitsy.

Bitsy started to scramble to his feet but Canaan tapped him on the arm and told him to sit down. He gave Moo his own chair and leaned his hip on the corner of Hooligan's desk.

"Watch it," Hooligan said, "I can't reach my cigar."

"Never mind your cigar," Canaan said quietly.

Dipper reached over, took Moo's hand, and kissed it. She ignored it and so did everyone else.

"They give her a clean bill, Aggie?" Hooligan asked the matron.

"She made it as hard on the doctors as she could."

"You mean she ain't grateful for all we're doing for her?"

"Keep your hand on your wallet," Aggie said.

"I ain't a thief," Moo flashed.

"So I'll keep my hand on my pecker instead," Hooligan said.

"You hear what he said?" Moo protested to the policewoman. "You hear him talk dirty to me? I ain't a perpetrator, you know. I'm a victim."

"You're a *little* victim. Your girlfriend was a *big* victim," Hooligan said.

Moo's face started to crumple up. She bit her lip to stop herself from breaking down.

"You want to cry, go ahead and cry," Canaan said.

"She don't want to cry. She's tough," Hooligan said, making her reserve seem contemptible.

"For chrissake, she's only a kid, Hooligan," Aggie said, taking her cue for kindness from Canaan.

"She's a hundred years older than you," Hooligan said. "So, good-bye, Aggie. You done good." When Aggie walked away, Hooligan slouched back, put one hand between his belt and his stomach, and looked the paperwork over, glancing up at Moo for a couple of seconds every now and then. "What was the arrangement?" he asked.

She looked at him directly, not knowing exactly what he meant.

"Where'd you pick the bastard up?" Hooligan said.

"On the boulevard."

"Sunset? Hollywood? What?"

"Santa Monica."

"Jeeesus, why can't you people stay in one place?" Hooligan mumbled.

"Mimi and me wanted to see something different."

"Just taking a stroll?"

"That's right."

"Just walking around, two girls on your own? What time was this?"

"Maybe one o'clock."

"One o'clock in the A.M. you're walking along a deserted boulevard?"

"It wasn't deserted. There was cars and some people."

"I'll bet there was crowds of goddam people walking around Santa Monica Boulevard that time of the morning. Whereabouts on Santa Monica?"

"Between Western and the cemetery."

He happened to look up right then and she happened to be staring at him, and a little exchange that was almost human passed between them at the sound of the word.

"The cemetery," Hooligan said. He looked at Canaan but Canaan didn't look back. Hollywood Cemetery was where the body of Canaan's little niece had been found, lying broken, bent backward over a tombstone.

"You want something to drink?" Canaan asked Moo.

"No, thank you," she replied, half smiling at him, folding her hands in her lap as though she were a little girl at a tea party being as polite as she knew how to be.

"How did this man approach you?"

"He asked us what two pretty young things were doing walking around alone that time of night, and we said we was coming home from work."

"You mean you was looking for work, don't you?" Hooligan said.

"We wasn't soliciting."

Canaan leaned forward. "Look, I want to tell you something, Moo. Nobody here's trying to get you to say something that'll incriminate you. We don't care if you were out there soliciting. We're trying to get a handle on this man who killed your friend."

"I admit to soliciting and you'll toss me in juvenile."

"We're going to have to keep you anyway, Moo. You're underage, for one thing. For another thing you were witness to a murder, and we don't know what the killer might decide to do about that if we let you out there to wander the streets, do we?"

"So you're going to protect me down in juvenile?" she said, sarcasm coloring her words like rust on a blade.

"You cooperate and I'll see what I can do. I'll get you into a halfway house or a shelter if I can. I'll speak for you in front of the judge."

Bitsy wanted to tip her the wink not to fall for the cop's hound-dog kisser and his soft voice, but he couldn't catch Moo's eye. She was staring at Canaan like he was her grandfather. She was ready to climb into his goddam lap.

"So what did this man say?" Canaan asked.

"He went along with the gag and asked us where we worked and we said in a cocktail lounge and he said doing what and we said serving drinks and he said too bad he didn't like cocktails, all he drank was beer and maybe a little whiskey when he was feeling poorly. And pills when he wanted to get high. It was quicker than likker, he said."

"He said 'poorly' like that? When he was feeling 'poorly'?" Canaan asked.

"That's right."

"He have an accent like he was from the South or Texas or someplace like that?"

"He could've. He talked slow. He talked around his smile like he was chewing on something, you know what I mean?"

"When did you drop the act about being cocktail waitresses coming home from work?" Hooligan asked.

"When Mimi decided he wasn't vice."

"Who made the offer?"

"He did. He asked us where a stranger in town could get a little."

"A little what?"

"That's just what he said. 'A little.'"

"So you told him he already found the right place?"

"We told him if he wanted to walk with us we could maybe take him somewhere he could get what he wanted. He said we looked like what he wanted and we said that was okay with us but we didn't do it in the gutter or in doorways. So he came with us."

"Back to the building where you was camping out?"

"Yes."

"Didn't he act nervous? Didn't he start acting a little fly, two girls want him to go into an empty building with them?"

"He said he knew all the tricks. He said he knew how the Murphy game was worked. How girls lured a john up into a building where some pimp was waiting to beat him up and take his money."

"So how come he ended up doing the two-step with you up on the roof?"

"He said somebody'd tried to pull the Murphy game on him down in Washington, D.C., once and he'd kneecapped the pimp with an iron bar and busted the whore's nose with his fist."

"Didn't that make you nervous?"

"Ain't you heard? Things ain't the same as they was when you was young. You got to take your chances."

"They ain't the same as when you was young either, sis. Ain't you heard, fucking can kill you?"

Moo looked at Canaan and then at Bitsy, asking them to bear witness to the fact that this big bull of a cop was talking dirty to her again.

Bitsy was looking at her practically openmouthed. He could hardly believe the dumb twit who used to follow Mimi around like a dog could take care of herself the way she was doing, giving tit for tat, slugging it out with the mean bastard.

"So look at me while I'm talking to you," Hooligan said. "After he picked you two up and romanced you a little, you took him up on the roof so you could get to be better friends?"

"That's right."

"Getting up on that roof is like walking a wire, I been told."

"We do it all the time. There's nothing to be afraid of."

"Maybe not for you, but maybe it is for somebody else. Maybe you were figuring this john'd fall off it and break his neck. Then you could pick his pocket without any worries."

"I'm not a thief," she said again.

"Or maybe you figure you get him trapped up there on the roof with some of the wolf pack you live with in that building."

She didn't answer; she just stared at Hooligan for a second, then looked away when he started studying the fistful of papers.

"When did this man give you the drugs?"

"What drugs?"

"The yellow jackets. The bennies. Whatever. The speedballs. Don't jerk my chain, I told you."

"We took a couple."

"So you were flying high?"

Her face broke up as if she was going to laugh and then as if she was going to cry.

"Who did this john fuck first?" Hooligan went on.

For a second Bitsy thought Moo was going to clam up to teach this lousy cop you could catch more flies with honey than you could with vinegar. Then it became pretty clear that she couldn't remember.

"He have sex with your friend first?" Canaan asked softly, leaning closer as if she were just having a conversation with him and nobody else.

"No, with me. I think."

"And then with your girlfriend?"

She nodded again and then shook her head.

"Is that a yes or a no?"

"He tried to have sex with Mimi but he couldn't."

"So he couldn't make it twice?"

"Well, it looked like he was having trouble, and she did something dumb."

"You mean dumber than usual?" Hooligan said.

"She said something about his thing," Moo told Canaan, ignoring Hooligan altogether.

"Don't go all girlish on us," Hooligan said, making sure she didn't leave him out. "What did she say about his pecker?"

"She said it wasn't working too good, was it."

"Like that she said it? Very polite? 'Mister, you have a pecker there what don't work'?" Hooligan said in mincing tones.

"She said his cock was all wore out. He'd been bragging about what a hose he had. He kept telling us we should pay him instead of him paying us."

"How come you're talking dirty to me?"

"I'm not talking dirty. I'm telling you what he said. That's what he said."

"So Mimi made the mistake and joked about this man not being able to do what he'd been bragging about he could do," Canaan said, "and that made him mad?"

Suddenly her expression went blank. She looked at Bitsy as though she expected him to tell her what to say. Her mouth went slack and she shook her head hard.

"I don't know," she said. "I don't remember."

"Did he hit her?" Canaan asked.

"I think so."

"Did he hit her more than once?"

"I think so."

"Did he bite her?"

"Did he what?"

"Did he bite her breasts and thighs?" Canaan asked, wincing as though he was ashamed to be speaking to a girl young enough to be his granddaughter—or his niece—the way he was.

She shook her head and shrugged.

"Where did he get the bottle? Did he bring it up on the roof with him? Was it already there? Did he bust it or was it already busted?"

"I don't remember."

"What the fuck do you mean you don't remember?" Hooligan suddenly roared, his face getting redder than it usually was, leaning forward into her face as if he meant to tear her throat out with his teeth.

Canaan was on his feet, putting himself between Hooligan and the girl, going down on his haunches and taking her hands, making her look into his face.

She twisted her head away, trying to look over his shoulder so she could see Bitsy, as though he could help, her pretty face twisted up like a child's, trying to remember something she'd forgotten, afraid of punishment. Afraid of something.

"Hey," Canaan said. "You knew Bitsy here and some of the other kids were downstairs in the building, didn't you?"

She nodded.

"So why didn't you start yelling for help when he started beating up on your friend?"

"I did. When he got mad and started shouting at Mimi I went downstairs looking for Hogan and whoever else was around."

"Hogan?"

"He's the biggest one of us. He's like the head of the family."

Bitsy frowned.

"If I didn't go down looking for somebody, maybe he wouldn't've done what he done. I could've helped Mimi get away from him," Moo said.

"Did you find Hogan?"

"No, he wasn't nowhere around. A couple of the girls was there but they wouldn't come up on the roof with me."

"How about your friend Bitsy over there?"

"I couldn't find him either. I went back by myself but the man was gone and Mimi..." She started to cry and shake all over.

"You sure you got that right? You sure you went looking for your friends? I mean, you were high on whatever that john gave you. You sure you actually got down off that roof on that rickety stairway and actually climbed back up again?"

She ducked her head until her chin was resting on her chest.

"Look at me, honey," Canaan said very gently, as he used to do when his little niece pouted and ducked because she thought her Uncle Isaac was going to scold her. "I'm not going to yell at you. Nobody's going to yell at you. I mean, I just want to get it straight. What you remember."

"I don't remember," she murmured.

"You sure that man left while you were downstairs looking for your friends?"

Canaan moved a hand as though he meant to cup her cheek, but Hooligan grabbed him by the shoulder to pull him back so he could get in closer. His mouth was open, ready to bellow at her, his patience all torn away.

Canaan twisted around, still in a crouch, and pushed Hooligan back.

"Back the hell off. They never should've let this kid out of the hospital. They should've kept her for the night."

"Get the fuck out of my way," Hooligan said.

"This kid's still in shock," Canaan said.

"I don't give a shit you say she's in shock."

They were both standing up now, belly to belly, toe to toe, and nose to nose.

"She can't remember."

"Probably still coming down off her speedball high. Maybe a little LSD trip. Maybe a needle."

"It doesn't matter. Give her a little room."

Hooligan sat down and leaned back in the chair.

"Ah, fachrissake, Canaan, you ain't even a Catholic, so why're you working so hard to be a saint?"

35

The bleeding wouldn't stop. Everybody knew a scalp wound bled a lot and looked worse than it really was, but it wouldn't goddam stop. It kept running into his eyes every time he took the wadded handkerchief away.

It hurt like hell, too. He felt in his pockets for some of the pills the woman at Hobby's wrap party had given him, but he didn't have any left. He'd given them all to those two baby whores the night before.

He shouldn't even be walking down a main drag like Western Avenue the way he was, because some squad car could go breezing by, maybe get a gander at his bleeding kisser, and pick him up because it was a slow day.

He'd get the hell off it as soon as he found the industrial emergency hospital he remembered seeing someplace along here. Maybe they could clean him up, put a plaster on the cut. Maybe they'd even have to stitch it up. He couldn't go on walking around bleeding.

He didn't hear the car come up behind him and stop. He knew something was up when he heard the door slam. Then the squad car moved past him and stopped again about twenty feet in front of him. He turned around and saw one cop walking toward him. He turned around again and the driver was out of the vehicle and coming toward him, too.

"Good morning, sir. Are you going to tell us you cut yourself shaving?"

"Somebody jumped me from an alley back there."

"Are you a visitor to our city?"

"What makes you ask that?"

"I thought I detected an accent. Southern maybe?"

"Kentucky."

"Well, good for me. Just passing through?"

"I been thinkin' about settlin'."

"I hope this unfortunate event doesn't sour you on our fair city. Would you mind coming over here to the police vehicle and placing your hands on the roof?"

"I don' see why I should. A man gets mugged, and this is how you California police take care of him?"

"We intend to take care of you, sir. I want you to know that. What we're going to do here is take reasonable precautions. You can understand that, can't you?"

"I put my hands on the roof, I'll bleed all over myself again."

"You just hold your head back, sir, and my partner, Officer Shalley, will stanch the flow of blood while I save you the trouble of looking for your credentials."

The second cop put his hand on Younger's arm and said, "Please don't argue about it, sir. Just do like Officer Crump asks. It'll only take a minute and then we'll take you someplace where you can get that wound looked at."

Younger walked over to the car and put his hands on the roof, holding his head back as the blood started dripping down his face again. The second cop took a clean handkerchief out of his own pocket and applied it to Younger's forehead.

"Why'd you stop?" Younger asked. "Lookin' at the back of me, you couldn't see I was cut."

"You were walking like a man in some distress, sir."

"What's this you've got here?" Crump said as he pulled the switchblade from Younger's pocket.

"That's a knife," Younger said.

"Well, I can see it's a knife. Maybe I should've asked what you're doing with it."

"Where I come from everybody carries a knife."

"For what reason?"

"To cut rope, skin rabbit, whittle a whistle, clean your nails. What the hell?"

"What the hell, indeed. It may be the custom to carry a knife in your part of the country, but we look at switchblades as illegal weapons around here."

Younger knew they were ragging him with the polite talk and the fancy language. There was nobody so prejudiced against outsiders as policemen. They hated outsiders with a passion, because new-comers usually caused more trouble than established citizens. Since Los Angeles was a city of immigrants, the cops hated nearly everybody.

The car radio started squawking. The flat, strangely inhuman voice of the police dispatcher announced an assault with a deadly weapon at Vickie's Parlor. Crump, grinning, reached in and got the mike off the hook.

"This is unit three twenty-one. Officer Crump. What kind of weapon?"

"A broken bottle and a knife were in evidence. Will you respond?"

"I think we've got cause to believe we have the perpetrator in custody."

Another car cut in and said they'd take the call at Vickie's Parlor, get a statement, and bring in the complaining party for an I.D.

Officer Crump reached for the cuffs on his belt.

"You going to cuff him?" Shalley asked.

"According to the book."

"You cuff him, he keeps on bleeding all over himself. Next thing you know..."

Shalley didn't have to finish it. Crump knew all about suspects and perpetrators claiming police brutality.

"You're going to just have to sit in back with him," Crump said.

"You don't mind I sit in the back with you, do you, sir?" Shalley asked.

"Go fuck yourself," Younger said, defiant now that he could smell the odor of cooked goose.

"Isn't it a wonder how quickly strangers learn the language?" Shalley said, as he put his hand on Younger's head to make certain he sustained no further injury getting into the squad car.

36

"*Take* a break?" Hooligan said. He got up and went over to the shelf where the coffeepot and a collection of stained mugs were lined up. Canaan shuffled along after him.

"What do you think?" Hooligan asked, pouring himself half a cup. "You think that little cunt's telling us the truth?"

"I don't think she knows what's the truth."

"You think she's lying to us?" Hooligan asked, wetting his lips with the coffee.

"I didn't say lying."

"Shit. Cold."

"I said she maybe doesn't know the truth. Maybe she can't remember how things happened."

"So you don't think she's lying?"

"I didn't say that either. What I said was she maybe don't know what's the truth, what's not the truth."

"You don't think she'd lie about some asshole what did her girlfriend like he did?" Hooligan said, putting down the offending cup.

"Maybe it's easier for her to do that than to trust us. But I'm saying maybe she doesn't even remember."

"Drugged out?"

"Maybe that and maybe something's blocking her memory."

"You believe that shit?"

"Where've you been? You never heard of selective amnesia? You never heard of shock?"

"So what do we do?"

"We run her through it again. Maybe we jar something loose,

maybe not. If that don't work we get the police psychiatrist in, have a look at her."

They started back to Moo, Bitsy, and Dipper.

Crump and Shalley came in with Inch Younger between them, looking as if they held a trophy of the hunt. A gauze pad was taped just at the top of his forehead, and his hair flopped over and almost covered it.

They passed Moo no more than ten feet away. She looked at Younger but acted as though all she saw was an injured man in custody.

Dipper was looking, too, and Dipper, with little except the moment ever occupying his mind, stood up and pointed at Younger's back.

"You got to go take another pee?" Hooligan asked harshly, beside himself with annoyance over how the day was going.

"He done it to Moo," Dipper said, the words tumbling muffled and wet out of his flaccid mouth.

"What'd he say?" Hooligan asked.

"That man hurt Mimi and done it to Moo," Dipper said. Then, scared to death, he turned and ran away.

Canaan was on his feet, going after Dipper to bring him back and shut him up before he said anything more.

"Hey, Crump, just a minute," Hooligan said. "Turn that sonofabitch around."

"Jesus Christ, no!" Canaan yelled, giving up on Dipper and turning back.

Crump said, "What?" and wheeled around, still holding on to Younger's arm, so that Younger and Shalley on the other side were brought up short.

Hooligan was looking at Moo, who was standing up and staring at Younger with a look of dreadful fear on her face.

"Is this the sonofabitch? Is the dipsy right? Is this the cocksucker what done your friend?"

The significance of what was going down did not go unremarked by Elmore Balfry, public defender, who was standing on one leg making like a water bird while sucking on a can of Nehi orange and shooting the shit with his fellow defender, Bill Giovinne, there to protect the rights of Benny the Dip.

When you're the second student from the bottom in the first

class graduated after certification from the smallest and newest law
school in the city, you've not only got to grab your opportunities by
the throat but you've got to move like a bat out of hell—the anal-
ogy being well taken, since Elmore was often called Bats by his
fellow public defenders. When he'd gotten his job with the city,
he'd considered himself lucky, not because he'd been given the
chance to do some good for the underprivileged but because he
knew that a clever man could turn the defense of the poor and
downtrodden into a stepping stone to greater things through the
proper cultivation and exploitation of the press.

Grabbing Giovinne by the elbow to make certain of his attention,
he said, "You see and hear that?"

"See and hear what?"

"Hooligan just ran a *showup* on that sucker with the bandage on
his head."

"Is that a bandage?" Benny the Dip said. "I thought he was a
A-rab."

"That's no Arab," Balfry said. "That's my chance to stick it up
Hooligan's ass. So, you saw the directed identification, Giovinne?
What about you, Benny?"

"I saw what you saw. Do you think you can cut me a deal on this
little beef they stuck me with?"

"Public defenders can't cut you a deal, Benny, for Christ's sake,
what do you think? It's the prosecutor makes deals."

"You can use some influence."

"We use everything we got to save your ass, Benny, don't you
know that by now?"

"I mean you could call in an extra favor, use a little extra mus-
cle."

"Do I look like some kind of asshole? You think I'm going to put
you on the stand as a collaborating witness and the D.A. asks you
did we offer you a deal and you say yes, we did, so where does that
leave us anywhere except high and dry?"

Benny stood there looking thoughtful.

"You decide to trade baseball cards with the D.A.," Balfry said,
"I'll see to it some friends of mine out on the street break your arms
and legs. So what did you witness?"

"I saw Hooligan clamp his meat hook on that A-rab's arm and ask
the Baby Jane did she identify the fucker as the prick what done
her friend."

"You got a memory, Benny."

"The best."

"What did you see, Giovinne?"

"The same thing."

"So I've got my witness and I've got my corroborating. Take care of my man, Giovinne, while I go over and introduce myself to my client."

He walked away, leaving Giovinne openmouthed, as Giovinne finally realized that he'd seen the chance the same time Bats had, only Bats was copping it and leaving him with Benny the Dip.

He wondered how long Bats would let the cops go on shitting on their own parade before he flushed them down the toilet.

Balfry was known among the city-desk reporters as "Old Tit for Tat" or "Young Quid Pro Quo," quick to leak a confidential tidbit, eager to cooperate, making it very clear that payment was to come in future when a case of sufficient interest might reasonably call for a seven-column feature story or three pages in the Sunday supplement.

He'd let it run until he'd squeezed every drop of blood out of it, if they'd let him.

He plowed through the gathering riot—the cops and morning gonifs, vagrants, and prostitutes with their tits half falling out, past the baby whore and Hooligan, who was still clamped on to the bandaged man, fighting with the uniformed cops for possession like dogs over a leg of lamb—and headed straight for his prize, his reward, his ladder. And got there just as Captain Leech, summoned by Isaac Canaan, put his beefy body between Balfry and Inch Younger, one hand outstretched as if he meant to straight-arm the public defender out of the play.

"Back off, Mr. Balfry," Leech said.

Balfry didn't bother looking at him. He just walked around and under his arm and put his face up as close as he could get it to the scared, beleaguered Younger, who appeared to think he was about to be the star of a lynching right on the spot.

"What's your name?"

"Inch Younger."

"That your real name?"

"Daniel Younger."

"I know you?"

"I never saw you before in my life."

"And I never saw you either, Younger, but I know you because I read the papers and, even though it was only a two-column photo on page three, I know you're the Hog Wallow Killer, who just walked out of prison."

Younger frowned at the rush of comment which sounded like the surly roar of a pack of wolves ready to break his leg bones and bring him down where they could chew on this throat.

"About that I don't give a shit," Balfry said. "Daniel Younger, did anybody Mirandize you?"

"No, sir."

"Can you afford a lawyer?"

"No, sir, I can't."

"Well, then, you got me. I'm the public defender." He didn't say anything about being *a* public defender. He made it sound as if he were the one and only. "I'm authorized to assume the conduct of your case as of this very moment, giving you the advantage of having advice and counsel right from the git-go."

"I didn' do nothin'," Younger said.

"That goes without saying. But it's what I can do for you that counts. Do you accept me as your attorney of record?"

"Yes, sir."

"Good. First off, Sergeant Houlihan, get your meat hook off my client. There are no photographers here, so it gets you nothing. Next, Captain Leech, I'd like to have an interrogation room where I can confer with my client."

"He hasn't even been booked yet," Leech said.

"So book him and let me have my hour with him."

"Go ahead, process Mr. Younger."

"Who's supposed to be the arresting officer?" Crump said, seeing his lucky collar slipping out of his grasp and off his record.

"You and Shalley sign him in for suspicion, vagrancy, and violation of parole."

"You've got a long reach, Captain," Balfry said.

"I smell beer on his breath," Leech said. "You book him in, officers." He looked at Hooligan. "Then, Houlihan, you get the young woman to sign the complaint and you sign it, too." He turned to Balfry. "In my office, counselor?"

Balfry tossed Younger a reassuring smile and followed the captain.

After he closed the door, Leech said, "You want to declare yourself as Mr. Younger's attorney, it's all right with me, Mr. Balfry, but I'll need confirmation from your office. You want to use my phone to call in, you're welcome."

"I think that can wait, Captain Leech," Balfry said, giving back elaborate courtesy for courtesy. "Right now, I'd like to walk Mr. Younger through the booking process. Just to see everything's done by the rules. Unless you'd like to have a conference first so we'll have an idea of what charges will be brought against my client."

"I think I'll decide after talking to the district attorney's office."

"So, until then, okay, Captain? I'll just go walk my client through and then I'll have my little talk with him."

Leech was leaning against the desk, staring at Balfry as though wondering what kind of man he was.

"You named him," he said. "You recognized him as a killer the parole board dumped back on the street. He's not out a week and he's got himself in some kind of trouble."

"Well, he's been accused. That doesn't make him guilty."

"We'd all be better off if we could dump him back."

"That's not the way it works, Captain."

"I know how it works, Balfry. I'm just saying you got to think about what you do and why you do it."

He glanced over Balfry's shoulder at the growing commotion outside.

Hooligan's desk had become a magnet, drawing people in from all over the room, from outside the station house, from the Police Building downtown, the offices of the public prosecutor and the public defender, the newspapers and the television stations.

The word had gone out that one of the lost children of the night, working a hookers' stroll in Hollywood, a disadvantaged child of sorrow, had met up with her final tragedy in the person of a sadistic pervert, a man of Appalachia, raw and uncivilized, who first fucked her with a dick the size of a corncob and then did the deed again with a broken beer bottle, murdering her in the process.

To sweeten the pie for the media, there was a Down's syndrome youngster and another pretty, underage whore, dressed like a rock star and beginning to enjoy the notoriety so suddenly showered on her.

The cops were high on the news because here was one of those times when alert officers had stopped and apprehended a suspicious person who turned out to be a goddam rapist-killer, the fact of which would put to rest for at least a week all complaints about the inefficiency and impotence of the police establishment.

Balfry had walked Younger through booking. They had had their talk. Now he stood next to him for the photo opportunity which he'd allowed.

"Let me get this straight," the man from the *Times* said to the lady from Channel 9. "This character by the name of Younger picked up two teenaged doxies from a Hollywood stroll. Took them up on a roof. Had carnal knowledge of the one and killed the other with a broken bottle."

"Because she laughed at him," the lady said.

"Why'd she laugh at him?"

"Because he had a small tool."

"I just heard the sonofabitch's hung like a stallion."

"Well, that's not what I heard," she said, eyeing the reporter as though she doubted his innocence in the whole affair, all men clearly suffering great troubles with penis inadequacy and ready to abuse any woman who dared to let loose a little snicker instead of falling on her knees in ready worship.

"Maybe he told her a joke," the reporter said.

"What he was holding in his hand was a joke."

"But he'd already had a go with the first hooker and she didn't laugh."

"We're not all the same, Charlie. Everybody has a different sense of humor."

Benny the Dip watched Giovinne watching, with pure greed and envy, Balfry at Younger's side.

"Shouldn't we be discussing my case, Mr. Giovinne?"

"You figure it's fair, Benny? You figure it's fair that fucking Bats Balfry gets a rapist-killer for a client and I get a pickpocket? What kind of justice is that? I'm here and he's here and that fucking Bats Balfry runs over there like he's wearing track shoes and cops a rapist-killer for a client. That Bats could fall into a barrel of horseshit and come up with a gold horseshoe in each fist."

"I got a couple of bruises."

"It's the kind of case," Giovinne went on, not even hearing Benny, "makes reputations. Win or lose. There are such opportunities. Negotiations on venue alone could give a person twenty inches, three thirty-second sound bites a day for a week."

"What are we talking inches and bites here?"

"Column inches in the newspaper and thirty-second takes on the six o'clock news," Giovinne explained. "And when they get down to the plea bargain it could mean a feature in the Sunday paper and on the air."

"Talking plea bargains, Mr. Giovinne, what about you walk over there and see if you can make me a deal while their attention is elsewhere? Who the hell cares about a pocketbook booster when a peckerman has gone berserk?"

Just then Mackie, his friend, and two uniforms escorted Fran, her nakedness half covered by a hastily donned short jacket, feather mules still on her feet, through the door and into the squad room, where other cops were just about to take Younger to the holding cells downstairs.

She screamed, and then yelled, "There's the sonofabitch tried to rape me!"

Leech reached for the phone. "Get me the name of the parole officer who's got a gazoony by the name of Daniel Younger in his caseload."

37

Whistler felt as though he were trapped inside a glass bowl with Faye. Whatever they said to start a conversation seemed to hit the sides, slide around, and disappear somewhere around their feet.

"I'm sorry to bring you bad news," he said.

"Oh, don't be. I'm not going to shoot the messenger."

"Somebody wants you, I think," he said, gesturing out the window.

Jojo stood there trying to get Faye's attention. She waved him in. After a little hesitation he came into the coffee shop and down the aisle to their booth.

Faye introduced them.

"Sit down and have something?" Whistler asked.

"No, nothing," Jojo said. "I just came to tell Faye she was needed."

"I'll go back with you," she said, starting to slide out of the booth.

"Not over to Magdalene House," Jojo said. "Down to the courts."

"What's the matter?" Faye asked.

"You know those kids, those two white girls dress the same? Call themselves Mimi and Moo?"

"Yes, I know who you mean."

"Well, one of them's dead and the other one's coming up before the court on a solicitation charge."

"Let's go," Faye said, pushing herself out to the edge of the bench.

Whistler put out a hand. "What're you going to do?"

"Keep the kid from going to Sybil Brand or some other facility where she could come to harm."

"You want me to come along?"

"No sense showing up in a crowd," she said, getting to her feet. "This is what I know how to do."

"I hope you do a better job than I did."

"You know what's your trouble, Whistler?" she said, putting her hand on his. "You'll always be Sam the Sad Man, taking the world on your shoulders."

Then she walked out, leaving him there with the *Enquirer* for company.

38

Judge Phillip Esposito didn't want to be in court. Especially this court.

He'd been appointed to the civil court and was only on loan to juvenile because of their case overload and his own good nature.

After two weeks of hulking youngsters charged with rape, sodomy, assault, and murder, who couldn't be indicted, arraigned, or, in some cases, even tried, and frightened children, scarcely more than babies, being tossed from one authority or jurisdiction to another, he was fed up with the queer management of justice in family court.

He'd learned soon enough that there'd be no verdicts or sentences. If a defendant—not to be called a defendant but a respondent—was found to have committed the crime for which he or she stood accused, a petition was filed, first at a brief hearing and then at a fact-finding hearing, before a court that was admonished to think first and foremost of the minor's welfare. Even if that minor had taken a lead pipe and beaten the brains out of an old lady who wouldn't let go of her purse.

Should a finding be made against the respondent, there'd be a dispositional hearing before the same judge who found him or her at fault—at which time a juvenile could be locked away for years.

Juveniles appearing on complaints of truancy or mischief-making were given similar treatment, and there were even cases known where single mothers, desperate for a weekend of relief from the burden of child care, turned a son or daughter in for being unmanageable, not realizing that those weekends at Juvenile Hall appeared on the record and branded their kids as bad numbers.

He hated the sloppy law applied to juvenile cases. He hated the nitpicking private and civil-rights lawyers who often appeared without a clue about the peculiarities and vagaries of the system under which he was forced to operate.

He hated the prosecutors and legal-aid attorneys who, for the most part, were just putting in their time. And perhaps he hated most of all the overzealous law guardians who were out to save the world and every rotten, raping, sodomizing, sniffing, snorting, needling, murdering bastard in it.

He hated his lousy chambers, which smelled of old socks and rotting orange rind, and he hated the watery crap he'd had that morning.

Today he was listening to all those who had a claim on the court's time and was ready to discharge his three principal responsibilities to each and every one of them, fairly and squarely.

He would assign counsel to those who lacked the means to provide it for themselves, if counsel had not already been assigned. He would schedule hearings according to the calendar availability of each of the Parts of the Court. In cases of children accused of offenses he would, with the help of the probation officer, decide whether they were to be paroled to their homes while awaiting hearing, remanded to Juvenile Hall, or placed in some other city institution or shelter.

"All right," he said, picking up a police department complaint against Moo, true name unknown; fixed residence unknown; employment, prostitute, signed by Detective Francis Houlihan, Hollywood Division. "Who's representing this young woman?"

"Helen Dunne," Fargo from the city attorney's office said.

"Where is she?"

"I've got no idea, Your Honor."

"Is the complaining officer present?" Esposito asked.

"Right here, Your Honor," Hooligan said, getting to his feet. "Detective First Grade Houlihan."

"Okay, Mr. Fargo, Detective Houlihan, would you approach the bench."

When they were standing before him, Esposito bent forward over his folded hands and said to Houlihan, "Do you know the drill concerning prostitutes?"

"Yes, Your Honor."

"The drill for prostitutes is you book them, give them an appearance date, and let them go on their own recognizance."

"She's underage."

"We don't know that for sure."

"All you got to do is take a look."

Esposito glanced at Moo sitting there and noted that she had a sweet face once you got past the paint and powder. She looked pitiful, like a child dressed up in her mother's discarded underwear and nightclothes.

"What I'm saying is we can't be sure, so we take the quicker route as long as it does no damage. So, you see, I'm not clear about the reason behind this complaint. Is this juvenile brought here under special circumstances, or just charged for simple soliciting?"

"Murder, Your Honor."

"That changes the lyrics. But I don't see anything about murder in the complaint."

"We're not charging her with the murder. We want to hold her as a material witness," Fargo said.

"So why this complaint?"

"This person lives on the streets, Your Honor. If we don't hold her she'll disappear," Houlihan said.

"You know that?"

"That's what these kids do best, Your Honor, disappear."

Esposito looked at Moo again and noted the gloves she wore.

"Are you cold, young lady?" he asked.

"No, sir, I'm not cold," Moo said, getting to her feet.

"You're wearing gloves."

"They got no fingers."

"So why are you wearing them?"

"It's what everybody's wearing."

"Everybody?"

"Well, a lot of the girls."

"I wouldn't know about it. I've got no daughters. What would an old fuddy-duddy like me know about fashions of young women?"

"You don't look old to me, Your Honor."

"Who told you to call me Your Honor?"

"I seen it in the movies. Everybody's supposed to call the man Your Honor."

"So I'm the man, am I?"

"You look like the man around here."

"More people should show your good sense," Esposito said,

glancing one way and the other, taking in clerk, stenographer, lawyers, Houlihan, and some spectators.

"Why did you choose this way of going, Mr. Fargo?" Esposito murmured.

"Well, you know, Your Honor, we try to hold her for appearances, the law guardian lets out a yell. This way we can hold for a hearing. Take maybe two or three weeks. By that time we have first discovery, maybe even a grand jury brings down a finding in this homicide."

"Why do it the easy way when you can do it the hard way? Right?"

"The detective's correct when he talks about these kids doing a vanishing act."

"Well, I don't like giving the court a bad name, tossing kids into custody for the convenience of the police and prosecutor."

"She could be in peril," Fargo said.

"Okay, step back. You return to your seat, too, Detective," Esposito said.

There was a minor disturbance at the back of the courtroom as a slender woman in a three-piece beige suit, struggling with a shoulder bag and briefcase, poking at a loose strand of hair, came hurrying down the aisle.

"Ms. Dunne," Esposito said, "are you representing this young person in this matter?"

After she unloaded the bag on the floor and the briefcase on the table, Dunne held up a finger.

Moo sat down as Dunne snapped open the briefcase with both hands, took out a sheaf of papers with one, and held up the finger of the other again. She scanned the top sheet, nodded her head, walked over to Moo, bent over, and held a quick consultation.

Faye moved from a seat farther back to one in the first row, right behind the place where Moo was sitting, and bent forward as though wanting to get Dunne's attention. But Dunne ignored her.

"Are you planning to respond to my inquiry any time soon, Ms. Dunne?" Esposito asked.

"Yes, I'm representing Ms. Smith."

Esposito looked at Moo and said, "You notice Ms. Dunne doesn't have your good manners? She doesn't address me as Your Honor."

Moo giggled.

Esposito liked that. He started to feel better.

"I call her Ms. Dunne," he went on, playing for the laughs. "You notice I show her that courtesy? But she doesn't address me as Your Honor."

Dunne was ignoring him, too.

Faye said, "I might be able to help, Ms. Dunne."

"How help?"

"I'm a volunteer at Magdalene House."

Dunne regarded Faye closely for a moment and then turned to the judge as he said, "This case began five minutes ago."

"I didn't know it had been called."

"You're supposed to know."

"I was unavoidably detained."

"Had trouble getting out of bed?"

"Trouble with my car."

"Get a new car."

"I would if I could afford one."

"Get the old one repaired."

"I will, Your Honor."

"Now you call me Your Honor."

"May I have a few minutes to confer with my client?"

"Confer."

"You can stick your head in here, too," Dunne said to Faye. "What's your real name, Moo?"

"Everybody calls me Moo."

"All right. If you won't tell me. Moo? Your name's probably Maureen. So, Maureen, were you soliciting?"

"Even if we was, nobody saw us. I mean no cop saw us."

"The soliciting charge is just a convenience," Faye said.

"What do you mean?"

"They want to hold Moo in custody so they can get her when they need her as a material witness in a homicide."

"So, we make them petition for guardianship and put her in protective custody."

"Protective custody'd probably mean Sybil Brand. I'd like you to offer Magdalene House as an alternative."

"How does that sound to you, Maureen?" Dunne asked.

"I don't want to go nowhere," Moo said, "except out."

"I don't blame you."

"Just a second," Faye said. "You can't put her back on the streets."

"You may be right, but I'm going to try to fulfill the wishes of my client. If she wants to seek haven with you afterwards, that's up to her." Dunne got to her feet. "I move for dismissal of the charge. There are no witnesses to an act of solicitation."

Hooligan got wearily to his feet. "Your Honor?"

"Yes, Detective Houlihan?" Esposito inquired.

"I can testify before the court to witnessing the respondent soliciting acts of sexual commerce on the public thoroughfare. I was in the process of searching for the respondent in order to press a complaint when she was taken into custody on this matter."

"Wait a minute!" Dunne said, practically jumping out of her skirt. "Which act of solicitation is she being charged with, the one this officer is now claiming, or the one he claimed he witnessed before?"

"Motion for dismissal denied," Esposito declared.

"Would the court expound the reasons for denial?" Dunne said, in tones of total disbelief. "The complaint against my client stands revealed as spurious out of the mouth of the complaining officer himself. Convenient acts of solicitation drop from his lips like plums."

"The purpose of the juvenile court is not to reconcile the anomalies of the law but to consider the welfare of the minor brought before it," Esposito said. "For whatever the reason. No matter what the circumstances. We must decide if this young woman is to be allowed to leave, no doubt to return to the streets, perhaps to leave the city and the state, in any case to be exposed to the possible threats and dangers of retaliation from someone who may have strong reasons to wish her silent. The welfare, not always the rights, of the minor is paramount in our deliberations, and so I must deny motion for dismissal and remand the respondent to a place of protective custody."

Dunne was red-faced and sweating with bottled-up anger and frustration. Esposito was aware of her discomfiture and was enjoying it.

"Will the court set a limit?" she asked.

"Until she is called to testify or the danger is past."

"I beg to inform the court that I intend to file a writ of mandamus."

"Noted." He motioned to the welfare worker, a heavyset black woman wearing a print dress and shoes a size too small for her feet.

She minced up to the bench and waited for the judge to start the dialogue, her eyelids lowered as though she was prepared to suffer patiently all the foolishness she was about to hear and all the ineffectual solutions she was about to be part of.

The two attorneys went up to the bench to join the consultation. Dunne turned around and looked at Faye. Esposito eyed her, too. Dunne went over and asked her, "Are you licensed?"

"Pending."

"That'll have to do. You mind stepping up with the crowd?"

They approached the bench together.

"Will you identify yourself, please." Esposito said.

"My name is Faye Chaney, Your Honor. I'm here to offer my help."

"Ms. Dunne informs me you help run a facility called Magdalene House. I'm sorry but I've never heard of it."

"It hasn't been open long."

"Are you official?"

"License pending, Your Honor," Dunne said.

"If your facility's not officially authorized, I don't see how this court can take advantage of it. We can't remand a minor into the custody of anybody who walks in off the street claiming to run a shelter."

"I didn't know this was a question of remand or even of custody," Faye said. "As I understand what's been said here—as much as I've heard—it's been decided that Moo, being without fixed abode, is being deprived of her freedom and certain rights simply because she has no fixed abode."

"And to protect her from possible harm."

"But if she had a fixed abode, would you send her to Sybil Brand or any other public facility?"

"As long as there was a responsible adult to watch over her, probably not."

"I'm a responsible adult."

"It will save us all a mandamus proceeding," Dunne said.

Fargo shrugged and nodded.

The welfare worker blinked and nodded.

"Our facility is open to the court's inspection," Faye said. She dug into her shoulder bag and handed up some documents.

"We have letters from the mayor and other city officials."

"Your Honor," Dunne said, "I strongly recommend placing the respondent into Ms. Chaney's shelter."

"All right. Step back and let's get on with it."

When they'd all moved away from the bench, Esposito looked at Moo, putting a benevolent expression on his face.

"Young lady, here in open court and in the public view, where coercion or undue persuasion is clearly out of the question, and on a purely voluntary basis, I ask you if you accept the temporary guardianship of Ms. Chaney."

"Yes, Your Honor," Moo said.

"Will you agree to accept and abide by the rules of her establishment and not run away first chance you get?"

"Yes, Your Honor."

"You understand we ask this promise of you in order to ensure your safety and welfare?"

"Yes, Your Honor."

Esposito looked at Hooligan.

"We're going to want a little police cooperation on this. A little surveillance. A watchful presence."

"Yes, Your Honor."

"Everybody satisfied?" he asked, looking at Dunne.

"Yes, Your Honor."

"I should be so lucky."

39

Balfry was leaning on the first desk he'd been able to find close to Leech's half-glassed office. By rights he should have been inside, sitting in with Leech and Sharkey Gore, Younger's parole officer.

He'd been asked to give them a minute. In a minute they could cut a deal and conspire to thwart the law. He didn't think about accusing them of thwarting justice, because, as far as he was concerned, if they tossed the hillbilly back into the slam to serve out his time and then some, it would only be right. It would only be fair.

But what he was dealing with here wasn't a question of rights or fairness or justice. It was a question of the law in its many fascinating and outrageous twists and turns.

Legislators were mostly lawyers, and the writers of laws, ordinances, and regulations were mostly lawyers who should've been writing instruction manuals for Japanese consumers, and the judges who interpreted and adjudicated the law were mostly lawyers—so was it any wonder there were so many nooks and crannies a smart attorney could slip in and out of in the body of the law?

He didn't mind the cops using every angle they could find to get the hoodlums, rapists, and murderers off the street, but they shouldn't manipulate the system behind his back—in front of his face, behind plate glass—the way they were probably doing.

Sharkey Gore was a man on a short fuse. But when the spark hit the powder there'd be no explosion, just another burned-out case.

He'd been at the parole-officer racket seven years. Six and three-quarter years too long. He hadn't been in the job three months when he realized that most of the assholes and gazoonies who passed through under his supervision were irredeemable. There might have been a few who could be saved from a life of crime, but he didn't have the knowledge to identify them or the time to give to them if he could.

They were balls in a pinball machine, bouncing off the bumpers, dropping down the holes, slamming around like crazed animals, ringing up the score against a world of innocents without the guts to pull the switch on the ones who should have been blanked out the first time they maimed or killed, rolling to the bottom and into the well where dead balls landed when their trip was over.

"What I'd like you to do here," Leech said for the third or fourth time, "is keep this perpetrator off the streets until he comes up for hearing."

"I hear what you're saying," Gore replied, "but you got to hear what I'm saying. What I'm saying is, this charge you want to put against Younger is pussy. You're telling me he goes into a beer joint where this barmaid's shaking her booty under his nose, and he reaches out for a pat maybe, and she panics and cuts her arm on a busted bottle, and all of a sudden Younger's trying to get the hell out of there but this trucker as big as a tank is blocking his way and making like he's going to tear off his head."

"For chrissake, where'd you get all that?"

"I read the report. I read the deposition from the topless barmaid with her tits hanging out. Teasing the animals. Ought to be a law against it. I mean these women give it a shake but won't give you a taste, what the hell do they expect?"

"I don't want to argue that. What I'm saying is, even if the assault on the barmaid's nothing but two conflicting points of view over the same incident, why do we take a chance on this perpetrator when we've got the possibility he might've been up to his old habits the very night before?"

"Well, like right there, see?" Gore said, like a man catching a train out of a bad situation. "You're jumping to the conclusion that somebody murders somebody once, they're going to murder somebody again. You bring that into court, the defense attorney argues they can't use that prior conviction because it'll prejudice the jury against the defendant in the current action before the court. The judge says he's right. Fachrissake, we don't want the jury to know that this sonofabitch sitting there accused of one crime was convicted of the same crime before. He decides the other way and it goes to appeal."

"I just want you to question his parole suitability," Leech said, ready to reach across his desk and break Gore's nose.

"You want me to revoke his freedom and call him up on parole violation. So I do that and the commission looks bad. I mean here these people have listened to his story, what a good prisoner he's been, how he's been reborn in Christ and all. Never got any tickets —maybe only a few tickets—for infractions. Not a week later his parole officer's tossing him back, after they said what a good fish he was, just because the asshole had one beer too many and reached for a barmaid's tit."

"Could've killed a fucking child!" Leech shouted.

"Hey. We're talking here. Ain't we talking here? What's with the yelling? You trying to intimidate me?"

"I didn't mean to yell. This shit is getting on my nerves. Balfry, sitting out there with a release in his hands that he got from some asshole judge didn't even have a hearing, gets on my nerves."

"I understand what you're saying. You got to understand what I'm saying. You say he could've killed this baby hooker. You don't know that."

"That's right, I don't know that," Leech said, holding on to himself with an effort, speaking very softly, very reasonably. "Forensics isn't finished yet. The investigation's just started."

"You got a bad identification. What you've got there is you've got the old poisoned fruit."

"I agree. I'm not even going to charge him on suspicion of committing the larger crime. I'm not even charging him with assault on the barmaid. I'm just acting on her complaint."

"See? What you want to hit him with is a drunk and disorderly. I take away his parole for a drunk and disorderly and the commission accuses me of prejudice and harassment."

"Fuck the commission."

"Get the judge to set the bail so high Younger can't make it."

"Fuck the judge. He already set it for ten thousand. You'd figure somebody like Younger don't make the ten thousand. But he don't have to make the ten thousand. All he's got to do is get a bondsman to put up a thousand cash."

"What bondsman's going to put up a thousand cash for a paroled killer accused of another homicide?"

"That's right, a bondsman's got more sense than the law and the courts. He don't worry about prejudicing his wallet if a perpetrator's loaded with priors. But I just told you the charge I was trying to hold him on isn't murder. It isn't even assault. He's already got somebody to pledge ten thousand surety to a bondsman. That's why Balfry's out there with a release in his fucking hand."

"That's right, it's a drunk and disorderly," Gore said, as though he hadn't heard or said a word after that one remark about the D and D. "You want me to pull the plug on him on a D and D? You want me to look like I'm a hard-nose? In my office, you got a hard nose you better stick it up the right asses or you'll be out on the street."

"You ever talked to this Younger? You ever looked into the fucker's eyes? I've got to tell you, he's a piece of work, he is."

"He wasn't due for the first report until next Friday."

"You mean you didn't have him in to give him any warnings?"

"I like to give them a week on their own."

"So nobody'll think you're a hard-nose."

Leech stood up.

"I got to ask you. What are you supposed to do being a parole officer? You supposed to keep them from going back, or are you supposed to see that the commission don't make a bad mistake and put some fucking criminal back out on the streets to do it again?"

"I'm there to listen to their beefs, keep the tight spots greased, work it slow and easy until I get my retirement, if I last that long. Just like you."

40

"*You* see this kid around?" Whistler asked, shoving the photograph he'd taken from Kate Trencher into Isaac Canaan's hand.

"I just had a look."

"Take another look. Take a closer look."

Canaan put the photo almost on the tip of his nose. "I don't know. What you got here is a face smaller than the nail on my pinkie. What can I tell from a picture like this? All I see is a kid squinting his eyes against the sun. I'm no magician."

He handed the photo to Bosco, who also took a second look.

"You're a wizard," Whistler insisted. "Everybody on the street says you're a wizard picking out kids you've seen on the missing circulars and the milk cartons. Memory like an elephant."

"Maybe if you blew it up. Better yet, maybe if you forgot all about it."

"All about the kid?"

"All about it," Canaan said, meaning the photo and the kid and Faye and foolish hopes.

"I can't do that."

"Okay. Then you better keep an eye on her."

"I am keeping an eye on her."

"I mean a special eye. Her ex—old man's out of Q."

"I didn't know that."

"It was in the paper."

"I must've missed it. It must've been in the paper when I was out of town. How come they let that gazoony out, he chopped up three women?"

"Only chopped up two. Murdered the third."

"I'll apologize to him when I see him."

"Don't get starchy with me, Whistler. I'm not getting starchy with you. That ain't all."

"There's more?"

"He was picked up yesterday for assault, maybe attempted rape, on a barmaid in a topless joint."

"What topless joint?" Bosco wanted to know. "I didn't think there was any topless joints left."

Canaan ignored the interruption. Whistler didn't even bother glancing Bosco's way.

"Seems like he went into this topless joint for a beer. Here's the barmaid prancing around in a string up her crack and her treasures hanging out for all to see. Must've been a terrible temptation for a cocksman like Younger, so long deprived. Anyway, he claims she sent him an invitation and when he tried to start the party she called it off. That was all. She called it off and he was ready to leave, when a couple of customers came in, heard the woman screaming, saw she was cut—"

"Younger cut her?"

"There was a broken bottle. She claims it was in Younger's hand. He claims not. Anyway, she was cut. One of the customers hit Younger on the head with an ashtray. Cut his scalp. Bled like a pig. That's how come the cops picked him up walking down the boulevard. Younger says he was just trying to get out of the place." He paused, letting that much sink in, and then he added, "But that ain't all."

"There's more?" Bosco said, just by way of priming Canaan's pump.

"There's these three kids, a girl and two boys, down at Hollywood station. Hooligan's questioning them about a girl—was a friend of theirs—found dead on the roof of this condemned building where they live. Ought to make the owners fix those buildings or knock them the hell down. The girl was coming down off a high, shaky as a hooker with six-inch heels walking into a high wind. One of the boys was retarded. The other one's okay. Shalley and Crump—these two uniforms—bring in Younger. It looks like a parole violation. Maybe he'll be sent back for violation, maybe not. Depending."

"Depending on what?" Bosco asked.

"Depending on how full the goddam jails are. You push them in the front door, somebody's got to fall out the back. That's how come, Whistler—you asked the question before—they let a killer like Younger take a walk. He did good time. They don't take a chance on him, they got to take the chance on somebody else."

"So they bring him into the station," Bosco said, finding Canaan's place for him.

"The retarded kid stands up and points the finger. Next thing you know, Hooligan's got his hand on Younger and he's turning him around so the girl can have a look. I try to stop it but I'm too late because I'm off trying to catch the retard, who was so scared when he sees the gazoony he thinks did the dirty to the girl on the roof that he's trying to fly. As it turned out, he got away from me anyway.

"The girl who just missed getting killed herself has her look at Younger. She says he's the perpetrator. Bats Balfry—you know Bats Balfry, the defender?"

"I heard about him," Bosco said, as Whistler nodded his head.

"Bats Balfry jumps into the act, accusing Hooligan of having a showup instead of a lineup. So what we got is a released felon, picked up on suspicion,. identified by a retarded kid and a drugged-out baby hooker, standing there with a cop fingering him for a murder and practically pulling an identification out of the baby hooker with a pair of pliers. Any judge in the county'd have to be crazy to remand on that kind of information."

"So he walks again?" Whistler said as if he already knew the answer.

"Oh, we book him for having beer on his breath or something else just as lame, hoping we can figure something out before Balfry starts making demands in front of the press, who're gathering like flies around a dead cat. Then the barmaid with the tits comes prancing in and *she* points the finger and that's enough to hold him. But how long's it going to hold him? That's another question."

"All they got on him is what you already told us?" Whistler asked.

"Except one other thing. The dead girl up on the roof? Her attacker left teeth marks on her breasts and thighs, shoved a broken bottle into her vagina. Also scratched some marks on her chest. They're not all that clear but you got to figure he was in a hurry."

"What was the marks?" Bosco asked, irritated because Canaan was nursing it along the way he was.

"Six sixty-six."

"Sonofabitch. The mark of the beast."

"Just like one of the mutilated bodies was marked for which Younger took the fall," Canaan said.

He put his head down and worked on his soup, his hat riding square on his head.

"Marks or no marks," he said, "I don't think they're going to hold him. That's why I'm telling you, keep your eye on Faye."

"Yooo, Bosco," the cook called from the pass-through into the kitchen.

Bosco turned around and said, "What do you want?"

"Telephone for the lieut."

"I ain't a lieut," Canaan said.

"Harold wants to promote you," Bosco said.

Canaan slid out of the booth. "Well, he's the only one."

"You'd think a man goes around cutting up young women, cutting numbers on their chests, would never get through the walls again," Whistler said.

"They was hookers, Whistler," Bosco said. "A lower form of animal life to these people sitting on boards and commissions. They wouldn't admit any prejudice. Probably don't even know they got it. But they got it and it makes a difference. Animals killing animals, cutting down the predator population? What the hell."

Canaan came shuffling back, looking sad but maybe no sadder than usual. He slid over in front of the remains of his soup.

"That was Hooligan Houlihan. I asked him to keep me current. Younger's on the pavement."

"How the hell did he do that?" Whistler asked, his agitation showing in how thin his voice sounded.

"Hey, don't lose it," Bosco said, trying to remember the last time Whistler had given up his pose of lofty resignation.

"Well, they had nothing on the murdered girl, because a showup's tainted. It wasn't enough to hold."

"How about the goddam scratches on her chest? How about the mark of the beast?"

"It only looked like six-six-six if you wanted it to look like six-six-six. At least, the technician on the scene made no special mention of it. Just said scratches. I mean the girl had a bottle shoved up in her. Who's looking at a few scratches on her chest?"

"How about the barmaid identifying him as the man who assaulted her and cut her?"

"Similar situation. She's trotted into the station house, and here's
this gazoony standing there with everybody pointing the finger at
him. You'd have to be blind not to see that Younger was the man on
the spot. On top of which she could've heard somebody say he was
the Hog Wallow Killer, just got out of prison. A celebrity. You understand what I'm saying? How could she resist joining the parade
of people accusing him? Get a little of the spotlight? Balfry grabbed
that ball and ran with it."

"Let him out on his own recognizance?" Whistler asked, still ap-
palled at the way the system had put a killer back out in the crowd
with hardly any hesitation.

"Oh, no, the judge set bail."

"How much?"

"Ten thousand."

"Well, for chrissake, where would Younger get that kind of
money?"

"It only takes ten percent for a bondsman."

"Where'd he get a bondsman?"

"He made a call. Some woman by the name of Eve Choyren came
down with the cash."

"Who the hell's this Eve Choyren?" Bosco asked.

"You don't know?"

"If I knew I wouldn't ask."

Canaan scooped up the last spoonful of soup and put it in his
mouth. "Cold," he said.

"So, I'll give you seconds. Who's this Choyren?"

"She says she's a witch," Canaan said.

"The Wicked Witch of the West?" Whistler remarked, making a
lame joke of it.

"Fachrissake, I always knew it. We're living in Oz," Bosco said.

41

Taking a new girl home was always a chancy time. Nervous-making. Sometimes bad chemistry flared up right off the bat between the new girl and the ones already there, who thought the house was theirs and Faye their mother.

Sometimes there was a show of arrogance, a refusal to fit in, even if the other girls tried to make it easy. The new girl wouldn't do her share of housework. Drove her roommate crazy with irritating habits, deliberately offensive.

She introduced Moo to Sheryl and it seemed to go all right.

Every time one of the other girls came home from work, Faye would introduce her to Moo: Ivy and Helen and Brenda. By the time they got to Arlene, Moo said, "I won't remember," as though afraid that failing to remember everybody's name would be a mark against her. By the time they sat down for supper, the girls of Magdalene House had sized her up and decided Moo was just dumb enough and sweet enough to pose no threat to anybody.

"Moo's got a special circumstance," Faye said. "She saw her friend beaten up and murdered."

The girls all looked at Moo. She blushed and shook her head.

"Well, she didn't actually see her friend die but she saw everything that led up to it," Faye said, taking a little of the shine off Moo's celebrity.

Still the girls, streetwise as they were, made mouths and eyes of sympathy, because violent death was something to think about, even at second hand.

"The police wanted to put her in Sybil Brand..."

There was a chorus of disapproving ooohs.

"...but they agreed to let her stay with us until she's called to testify. As far as I'm concerned, she can stay on as long as she likes after that, but that's up to her. So what this means is we should keep our eyes open."

"For what?" Brenda asked.

"For anything. For everything."

After supper, while those on the rotation cleared the table and washed the dishes, the rest of them went into the living room to watch television.

It was all over the six o'clock news.

It hit Faye like a slap in the mouth. It drove her back into the cushions of her easy chair. The sight of Younger in custody again. His soft hair blowing around his head like the fur of some mountain animal. His eyes slanted and narrowed like those of an animal at bay.

Nobody'd told her he was getting out, she thought. How *could* they have told her? Nobody knew where she was. Nobody knew Faye Chaney was the Faye Younger who'd sat in the courtroom listening to the horrors committed by her husband.

They'd dug up archive footage of the old trial and conviction. Faye figured prominently, looking abused and deathly ill, carrying her big belly around like a badge of shame through the curious crowds. Looking, thank God, nothing like she looked now.

It was a one-minute bite on the network.

The local channel announced a one-hour special at eleven which would examine in depth the multiple-mutilation slayer who, having escaped death row, had been unthinkingly, foolishly paroled after only fifteen years in San Quentin. That wasn't the worst of it. Now, only a few days after his release, the depraved killer had been arrested for the attempted rape of another barmaid in a Hollywood tavern and was the principal suspect in the perverted mutilation killing of a child prostitute. In spite of eyewitnesses and three identifications the killer had been released on bail. Legal technicalities, the machinations of an ambitious public defender, and the failure of a fatally flawed criminal-justice system had put yet another killer back into a helpless and terrified population.

Faye couldn't feel her hands. They were lumps of lead at the end of arms made of straw. Her head felt alien to her, as though it were on a stalk ten feet tall.

She looked at Moo. There was the beginning of real fear in the girl's eyes. She looked back at Faye and somehow knew they were tied into a common fate.

"That's what we've got to watch out for," Faye said.

42

Bitsy was out on the streets looking for Dipper. Ever since he'd been chased out of the police station with his mind on other things —like whether Moo, confronted with that asshole who was up there on the roof partying with her and Mimi, was going to have her dope-fogged memory shaken, for instance—he'd been trying to find Dipper, who'd just gone wandering off when nobody was looking. He knew that Moo'd been taken to the shelter called Magdalene House run by that blond woman and that nigger with the candy bars, but he didn't have a clue about where Dipper might have run off to after he'd escaped from the police station.

He could be out there wandering around, getting himself into trouble, doing who the hell knew what? Remembering things he shouldn't be remembering. Talking to people he shouldn't be talking to.

Bitsy felt he was invisible walking through the crowds of shies and shines, sex pistols and spicks, trash ofays and nickel merchants. He wrapped the reverie around himself like a mantle of invisibility. He walked among the thieves and trolls, the bitches and witches, the gonifs and gyrfalcons, and not a soul could see him as he searched the boulevard.

"Why you walking so funny?" a voice asked him.

He turned around fast to see Dipper standing there staring at him, with Duckie on one side and Roach on the other.

Bitsy straightened up and wiped his face with his hand. "I been looking for you, Dipper. Where the hell you been?"

"I was looking for Hogan."

"You find him?"

"I don't know where he is."

"So we found Dipper," Duckie said.

"Well, you could've told somebody. I don't see you in the building, how do I know something ain't happened to you? How do I know somebody ain't picked you up in a car?"

"Why'd anybody want to do that?" Roach asked.

"Take you down to Mexico. Take you to the dogfights. Feed you to the winners."

Dipper started to cry.

"What are you trying to do," Roach asked, "scare the shit out of old Dipper?"

"I was only making up a story," Bitsy said, reaching out to touch Dipper's hand. "I'd never let anybody do that to you."

Dipper recoiled from his touch, moving behind Roach as though seeking protection there, and Bitsy realized he didn't even have the loyalty of Dipper the dummy anymore.

"What's the matter with you? Why're you looking at me like that?"

"Like what?" Roach asked.

"Like I don't know what."

"So if you don't know what, how are we supposed to know what?"

"Like you know something I don't know."

"What would we know that you don't know?"

He got it then. They were putting him on. They were challenging him. They were trying to make him feel foolish because, with Hogan gone, one of them wanted to be the leader. Or maybe Dipper had told them things. So what? A half-wit tells you things, who's going to believe what he says?

Fuck 'em.

He wouldn't stand there playing games with them. He'd just put on his cloak of invisibility and go over to that Magdalene House and see Moo. Maybe she'd be grateful for the way he stood up for her, the way he stood by her. Maybe she'd be so grateful she'd give him a little. If she wouldn't give him a little, maybe she'd get him something to eat from the refrigerator.

43

Canaan had given him all he knew about Eve Choyren but, for a change, it wasn't all there was to know.

If Whistler knew the town and Bosco knew its alleys and Canaan knew its underworld, Mike Rialto, the one-eyed procurer who called himself a private detective, knew the secret vices of the upper crust.

Now the upper crust of La-La Land isn't the same kind of crust as the crust in New York, Chicago, or San Francisco. It's made of money, sure, but it's also made of fame, notoriety, and the ability to flourish in the glare of neon and the burning heart of kliegs.

Whores can pull themselves up by their garter belts and become movie queens. Two-bit gonifs can scratch up thirty grand and parlay it into a five-million-dollar flick with a little luck and the right connections. Country CPA's become managers for rock groups grossing tens of millions and buy castles in the hills. All you've got to do is jump aboard the wheel and pray that fate doesn't give you the finger.

"Eve Choyren's a very scary person," Rialto said. "I don't know does she have the evil eye, but I seen her talk people into things you wouldn't believe. She'll take on men or women—maybe large dogs and ponies—it don't matter. But the thing is, I've seen her talk respectable women into doing the same."

"How's she do that?" Whistler asked.

"How should I know? All I can swear to is I seen her one time at the drugstore go over and chat up this lady I knew was happily married with three kids. They keep on looking over at Billy Durban, who was sitting in the booth with Choyren."

"Billy Durban, the dwarf who lived with Mary Willibald, the movie star, after she stuck a fork in his pecker, thinking it was a sausage, at that party they tell about?"

"That's the one. Billy Durban, who had a horse cock like Man o' War. So this was before the incident with the fork and what came after. This is when Durban was just selling papers and hanging around the drugstore."

"So?"

"So the next thing I know, this cool blond lady's trotting off with Choyren and Durban. Half an hour later I get a call from Choyren asking me can I deliver a couple of hookers over to her apartment, which was in that pink stucco building down on Crescent Heights. You know the one?"

"With the plastic palms around the pool?"

"That's the one."

"Choyren still live there?"

"Last I heard."

"Which was when?"

"Two years, maybe three."

"She drop out of sight?"

"No, she's around, but the drugstore's closed and I don't know where practically anybody from those days is hanging. But she's around. I hear about her now and then."

"How hear about her?"

"Well, she's still running these what she calls sabbats up in the canyons around Calabasas."

"The police know about them?"

"Sheriff's department knows. So what? Witchcraft ain't illegal. Just a lot of screwballs jumping bare-assed over swords and fire, kissing the master's bunghole. Doing this and that."

"There's been some killings."

"Oh, sure. But I mean there's been some killings by Democrats but you can't ban the party. You know what I mean?"

"There's been some really nasty killings."

"Murder's murder. I don't know if it's any worse just because somebody draws stars on the ground in goat's blood and so forth. What are we debating here?"

"You made the delivery that time?"

"Oh, yes. I rustled up a couple of hustlers—they weren't out on the streets like melons on a grocery stand back then, but I had my sources—and took them over to Choyren's place. I figured maybe I'd get a peek, see if she'd really talked this woman into what I thought she'd talked her into."

"Did she?"

"The woman was laying inside a nest of pillows, naked as a jaybird—only her shoes on—waiting for all comers. Choyren even asked me if I'd like a taste. I said I'd do without."

"Maybe she had an angle on the lady. Maybe she had facts you didn't have."

"Always possible."

"And maybe the lady had a habit."

"More than likely," Rialto agreed. "Where you got cults and covens and sabbats and all like that, you can be absolutely certain you got drugs. You on a case? You running down a deal on some donkey dust? What's your interest?"

"She just put down a thousand to get a paroled killer back on the streets after he broke parole."

"A thousand?" Rialto repeated, his eyes brightening at the thought that somewhere in this conversation could maybe be a nugget for him.

"You think she's got that kind of money to throw away?"

"She ain't got a pot or a window. She lives on what she can scratch."

"She got any rich friends?"

Rialto thought about that. "Jesus, Whistler, what we got here is a case of valuable information."

"I'm asking a favor."

"I understand that. You've been asking me little favors and I've been giving you little favors for ten minutes now."

"Conversation. You've been giving me conversation."

"And happy to do it. But now you're asking for valuable information."

"Who came to see you in the hospital when that gazoony put a knife in your neck?"

"Well, you did, Whistler. You did. But that was then, and now is now. What you're asking for here is valuable information, my stock and trade."

"You remember how you gouged me for fifty and there I was on a mission of mercy?"

"I sold you some information. See? That's all I'm doing now. You want some valuable information, it's got to have a price. After all."

Whistler reached into his pocket and peeled off two twenty-dollar bills.

Rialto didn't look bowled over but he took the double sawbucks and tucked them in his pocket.

"You know Paul Hobby?"

"Not personally."

"But you know he's getting married."

"I read about it in the trades."

"So he's getting married and he has a bachelor party for hisself down to the beach at Malibu. Got a hundred people, maybe more, down there to celebrate with him. He don't invite me. I can't understand that. There was a time when he used to call on my services..." He waved a hand as if he were brushing the flies off a dead friendship. "Well, the hell with that. He has this bachelor party. All men except for the pussy act and twenty hookers. Except for Eve Choyren, who was the only lady guest. What do you think of that?"

"What do you think of it?"

"I think maybe she's not going to be too happy about him getting married. And if he goes through with it—like it looks like he's going to do—I think maybe she'll try to get a little something for old times' sake. They was thick as thieves fifteen, sixteen years ago. She was the technical adviser on a lot of those flicks about satanic cults he made. There was talk he spent a lot of time in Calabasas."

"Where she put on her act?"

"That's right."

"Is that what I paid forty bucks to hear?"

"The point I'm making—use your head—is that if Choyren was bailing anybody out with one large, Hobby could be about the only fool she knows would give it to her. What I don't see is the connection. I wonder if this paroled killer's an old boyfriend or something like that. What's his name?"

"Don't you keep up? How many paroled killers you think we got hitting the pavement at one time?"

"Sometimes it's a fucking flood."

"His name's Younger."

"That was the Hog Wallow Killer, right?"

"That's right."

"That's your interest?"

Whistler nodded. "I want the connection. Can you help me reach out and put my hand on this Eve Choyren?"

"You want to put me on your payroll, I should go look around?"

"I can't afford you," Whistler said, standing up. "Just point my nose."

"Why don't you try Hobby's place on the beach or his house in Brentwood?" Rialto went into his pocket and got out his address book and a pencil. He wrote down a couple of addresses on a napkin. "Here's his addresses. No charge. You could try Choyren's apartment house first. She could still be living there. She could be home. Maybe she's retired and stays at home with her cat. Even witches get old, you know."

44

"**You** keeping a watchful presence on that halfway house like the judge said?" Canaan asked.

"You the captain?" Hooligan replied, pissed off at Canaan because Canaan was the one who'd yelled no when he'd put his hand on Younger and asked for an identification from that dippy kid and the baby hooker, thereby announcing to one and all that he was running a showdown that would get tossed out just as it did get tossed out, so that a killer was put back on the streets.

Now he was afraid that, sooner or later, Canaan would remind him of what an asshole he'd been. So the best thing to do, Hooligan figured, would be to cut the old prick off at the pass. "You taking over command?"

"I'm asking you if anybody's keeping an eye on that girl."

"The little whore, you mean?"

"I mean the girl who maybe can *really* identify the man who raped, mutilated, and killed her girlfriend *if* and when it's done the right way. *If* it's not too late."

"This ain't your case, Canaan," Hooligan said.

Canaan stared at him with eyes as flat as sheets of lead.

"You going to tell me, ain't you going to tell me, are you watching that goddam house?"

"I put in a request for six uniforms, three shifts."

"What'd they give you?"

"They give me two uniforms, one to a shift, two shifts. Also frequent drive-bys. They start first shift tomorrow."

"Sonofabitch. It looks like everybody wants to do it the wrong way."

"Leech made the point this Younger's hardly going to go after the baby hooker in the light of day. If he's going to go after her at all."

"What makes you say that?"

The color started rising up past Hooligan's collar, flooding his face. "Balfry already told the fucker that the hooker's identification wasn't worth diddly-dick."

"How's that?" Canaan said, enjoying the moment.

Hooligan's face looked like a side of beef. The sonofabitch rabbi prick had worked it so he'd have to point the finger at himself.

"Because the I.D. was tainted."

"Oh," Canaan said, as though he hadn't even thought about that before, and took a walk.

Magdalene House was in a building so old it had a cellar, not a common thing in La-La Land.

Bitsy couldn't find his way in through the front door or the back door—they didn't have the kind of locks you could slip with a piece of plastic—and he didn't want to ring the bell.

The cellar door was five steps down into the ground. It was secured with a padlock through the swivel eye of the hasp. Not a very good padlock. A dollar-twenty-nine padlock. He busted it off after working on the old wood of the door with his pocket knife for twenty minutes.

The cellar smelled of coal, though the bins probably hadn't been used to hold any coal in forty years.

The farther back he walked away from what light came through the pane of glass set in the cellar door, the darker it got. It brought back memories of his childhood when he was bad and his damned old grandfather would put him down in the root cellar and close the door. He knew the old man was sittng on the slanted doors and wouldn't get the hell off until he was good and ready. He felt the familiar panic rising up in his throat as he got closer to the stairs leading up to the first floor.

Maybe Moo wouldn't even be in the house. Or if she was in the house, maybe there'd be people all over the place, like that big nigger, who'd no doubt grab him by the neck and throw him out the door.

He found the bottom steps and climbed them one careful step at a time. He turned the knob on the door at the top and pushed. It wasn't locked. It opened into the kitchen.

The kitchen smelled of pine soap. Everything was very clean— so clean it surprised him. That's how long it was since he'd been in an ordinary home.

He could hear a radio playing rock music somewhere deeper in the house. When he started down the hallway toward the front of the house it got louder, and he could hear somebody going *doppa doppa doppa doppa* with the beat.

There was a desk under the staircase leading to the upper floor, with an open book on it. The pages he could see were half filled with names, most of them repeated over and over. There was a rack with a lot of keys on hooks behind it. It was like the desk in a hotel. He figured the guests—the inmates—in this particular hotel had to check in and out. Take a key to the front door and sign out. Come back, sign in, and put the key back. He wondered how many of the girls forgot and how often. He went around the desk and took a key from the hook labeled "front door" and put it in his pocket. Who knew? Maybe he could use it sometime.

He checked the pages of the book more carefully. He saw Moo's name, put there when she'd come in. It wasn't written down again. Whoever was singing with the music kept it up. He realized—from when Mimi and Moo would sing together, making like rock stars— that it was Moo.

She was in the living room, writing or drawing in a notebook. There was a bowl of apples on the coffee table. She didn't hear him come in, what with the radio blaring, but she sensed another presence and looked up quickly.

"Jesus Christ, Bitsy, you give me a scare," she said.

She talked so softly it seemed to him she was opening and closing her mouth but hardly anything came out. She tilted her head as if she was puzzled about him being there.

"You all alone in the house?" he asked.

"The rest of the girls got jobs. The ones that got night jobs are out working. The ones got day jobs are in bed."

"How come there's nobody at the desk watching the door?"

"This ain't a jail, what do you think? If I wanted to walk out, all I got to do is walk out."

"So why don't you?"

"I don't know. You want a apple? Go ahead and have a apple."

Bitsy picked one and took a bite.

"I wouldn't hang around here if I didn't have to," he said, looking around the room with something close to envy in his nearly
expressionless eyes.

The hunger came over him like a sucking wind. It sucked the
feeling out of his hands and the brains out of his head. He thought
of pork freshly killed and roasted. He thought of apple cider and
yams. He thought of all the things that he'd so rarely had. That he'd
dreamed his father would one day give him. He shivered with the
desire.

"Bitsy?" Moo said.

"What?"

"You was fogging out."

"Oh. Why ain't you in bed?"

"I got permission to stay up, this being my second night and all. I
got a lot to think about."

"Is that what you're doing?"

"Well, no, I'm drawing. Can't you see?"

"What are you drawing?"

"Pictures."

"What kind of pictures? Can I see?"

She hesitated. "Well," she said, doubtfully, "these ain't pictures
you draw for fun."

Bitsy frowned and pointed at the couch where she was sitting.
"Can I at least sit down?"

"You're not supposed to be here."

He took another bite of the apple.

"What's the matter? Men not allowed?" he said around his chew.

She laughed and said, "Men?" as though Bitsy was trying to
make a joke.

He let her get away with making fun of him. "That big nigger
must come in and out of here."

"Jesus, you don't have to call him that."

"Call him what?"

"What you called him. Nobody nice says that about a person
anymore."

"Where I come from a nigger's a nigger."

"Don't."

"All right. Come on, let me see what you're drawing."

"Oh, all right. Here."

She thrust the notebook at him. He laid it open on his lap and found the first drawing, then turned the pages, looking very carefully at each one. "They're almost the same. What are they supposed to be."

"Can't you tell?"

"Well, this looks like somebody in a white dress with red polka dots laying on the ground."

"That's Mimi. That's blood and that's the roof."

"Oh. So these sticks is the railing?"

"That's right."

"And this is like the whatchamacallit in the corner of the roof?"

"That's right." Moo seemed pleased that he recognized it.

"Who's this?"

"That's somebody hiding behind that whatchamacallit. I just remembered that. I remembered that while that sonofabitch was doing it to me, I saw somebody's head looking around the corner."

"That must've been Dipper."

"I guess so."

"So how come they all look the same?"

"They're like therapy."

"What do you mean?"

"If I draw the scene over and over again they say that I won't be so afraid."

"You afraid?" Bitsy asked, looking at her with his fey eyes filled with pity.

She'd never noticed before what strange, nice, pretty eyes Bitsy had. He was really very cute. She felt teary all of a sudden. "It was very nice of you to stick with me down to the police station and all."

"I couldn't let you do it on your own, could I?"

"You want to come upstairs?" she asked.

His heart was beating hard and fast. He could read things in her eyes. He couldn't remember when a girl had ever looked at him the way Moo was looking at him. "What for?" His voice sounded funny.

"You want to see my room?"

"Okay." He put the half-eaten apple on the table and stood up.

She walked up the stairs first and he realized she was wearing a nightshirt with nothing at all on underneath. If he'd leaned up and forward real fast he could've kissed her on the ass. He wanted to touch her, could hardly wait.

"You know what else they said?"

"What else?"

"They said maybe I could remember more of what happened if I drew it over and over again."

He pulled his hand back and reached into his pocket to see if his knife was there.

45

The sea was a bowl of gray-green poison under a cover of cloud so low it fingered the beach. The waves scarcely swelled. Somewhere a storm was drinking the ocean's blood. It was on its way and would probably shatter the silence within the hour. The fog lay on the cold sand like a shroud.

Hobby had gone in for a swim all the same. Maybe he'd thought, without knowing he was thinking it, that lightning might flash out of the threatening sky and strike him—the highest thing by inches bobbing on the sea—on top of the head and split him down the middle.

He'd thought, and knew he was thinking it, that it wasn't fair for a man at his time of life to be punished for something that the foolish young man he'd been fifteen years before had done. The booze, drugs, women, pornography, adventures, excitements, crazy parties, and novel ceremonies—of which at least one had gotten out of hand and caused a string of unintended consequences—had all been the product of swollen balls and hormones run riot. A clear case of diminished capacity brought on by natural causes.

For God's sake! How was a man supposed to be responsible for tricks played on him by Mother Nature? Weren't hormones just as powerful an instrument of aggressive, violent behavior as alcohol and sugar? Didn't that ex-politician up in San Francisco get away with murder just by claiming he'd been eating too many Twinkies? Didn't wife beaters, wife murderers, get away with it every day of the week just by saying they'd been drunk or strung out on this or that?

And all that business of black cats, pentacles, Aquarius, Lucifage

Rofocale, prime minister of the infernal spirits, slaughtered goats, kissing assholes, diabolic pacts, and naked women spread out on flat altar stones was nothing but a lot of playacting, a lot of bullshit. Nothing you could really believe in, fachrissakes. Nothing *real*.

His hair was wet. He was wearing his tatty robe. His legs looked blue, corpselike in the light of the mercury lamps that illuminated the patio and washd into the living room.

Eve Choyren was sitting on a huge leather pouf beside the mirror-topped coffee table. She was taking vials and pillboxes and candles from a canvas carryall. There was a small iron incense burner in the shape of a toad. There was a dagger and a copy of the *Grimoire of Honorius*, prescribing steps for summoning the Devil, slaughtering a goat, beheading a black cock, and tearing out the eyes of a cat.

Hobby watched her. He claimed to believe none of it but still his anxiety level was very high, his heart beating fast, his breath quickening.

"I don't know if this is such a dandy idea," he said.

"When will Bolivia get here?"

"He won't get here. I called him up and told him to come down for a little conference about this problem and he says he's got no problem and he doesn't want to sit in on any shit about summoning the Devil."

"He said that?"

"I just told you."

"I mean he said exactly that? He called it shit?"

"So who gives a rat's ass what he called it? He ain't coming."

"But he is the *hungan*. He even taught me things."

"He says he's a head grip and making good money, and all that other shit was just shit to lure the suckers when he was nothing but a raggedy-ass illegal up from Mexico. Just the come-on for the sideshow. Besides, he says he's a reborn Christian and won't have anything to do with that other shit ever again."

There was the sound of distant thunder. It came rolling in off the sea, the conversation of sea monsters.

"Your friends desert you," she said, as though she saw that a heavy curse had been put upon him.

"What the hell're you talking about?"

"Bolivia refuses to lend us his power. Pig-Nose Dooley's hand loses its skill when on a mission in your behalf."

"It was dark and he mistook a cabbage for Younger's head. It can happen."

"That's what I'm saying. It can happen. But it doesn't happen just because it happens. It happens because it's made to happen. Because it is part of a plan." She made a gesture as if to sweep smoke away from her eyes. "Let it pass."

She continued with her arrangements, laying out the necessities for a conjuration as carefully as a master chef lays out the ingredients for a famous dish. Laying out lines of cocaine and syringes for the injection of speed, putting Quaaludes in a candy dish and preparing pipes for the smoking of crack as well.

> "He who forges the image, he who enchants—
> The spiteful face, the evil eye,
> The mischievous mouth, the mischievous tongue,
> The mischievous lips, the mischievous words,
> Spirit of the—"

"Why'd you bring all that shit?" Hobby asked.

"You don't like this shit?"

"I mean, what's the use of it? That asshole doesn't like anything except liquor. If you got plans to steal his senses, you should've brought a jug of white lightning. Never mind all this coke and speed. A gallon of home brew'd do the trick."

"This isn't for him," Eve said.

"Who the hell's it for then?"

"For you. For me. To get us up for what we've got to do."

"I don't believe in this crap," Hobby said. "I never believed in this crap. I went along with it for the kicks. For the crazy broads and the kicks," Hobby said. He sounded desperate, as if he hoped telling her of his skepticism would move her to release him from any obligation. "How the hell I let you drag me into this sick shit with all your mumbo jumbo is beyond me. I can't believe I fell for it."

"You didn't fall for it. You wanted it. You embraced it. You were hungry for it." She sounded as though she was tired of it all. Tired of laying down the con. Tired of selling bullshit by the ton.

"Don't start a sermon. You're not going to start with one of your fucked-up sermons, are you? Because I want you to know—I already told you years ago—I don't believe in all your shit. I never believed in all your shit."

Eve smiled. "Ah, well, sure. I understand. So you don't believe. You joined in for the women and the thrills."

"And for the tricks. You know, the tricks I could put in my films. All the goat shit. Killing those goddam goats."

"The naked actresses lying down, allowing you to use their bodies as altars?"

"That's right."

"The candle wax and flames, the blood and fat in the chalice, the throat of the goat ready for slitting."

"Cut it out."

"The throats of the whores ready for slitting," she said in a conversational tone.

"Jesus Christ," Hobby said, as though she'd just that minute reminded him of something he'd tried so hard to forget.

"Don't call on him," Eve said. "You don't believe in him either. Isn't that what you've always said? Don't believe in Christ. Don't believe in God. Don't believe in anything except kicks and thrills and running down to your grave a mile a minute. Who cares what you believe? Who cares what anybody worships? A goddess with the trunk of an elephant and thirty arms. A god with the head of a hawk. An old man with a white beard chipping away at blocks of stone. A poor tortured sonofabitch hung up on a cross. A creature with the wings of a bat and a tongue of fire."

She held her arms straight out at her sides and threw her head back.

"Astaroth, Asmodeus, I beg you to accept the sacrifice which we now offer to you, so that we may receive the thanks we ask."

"If we're going to do him, let's do him without the playacting," he said angrily.

Eve laughed out loud and dropped her arms.

"Suppose he doesn't come?" Hobby asked.

"He'll come."

"How's he going to even get here?"

"I gave him my car to use."

"What?"

"I got here by taxi. I had the driver let me off a mile down the highway. I told him I was going to sit on the beach and have a glass of wine by myself."

"He must've thought you were loony. A day like this."

"This is the land of loonies."

"Why'd you go to all the trouble? Why didn't you just pick Younger up and bring him with you?"

She was cutting some lines on the mirrored tabletop with a common single-edged razor blade.

"I didn't want to take the slightest chance that anybody'd see us together. He arrives in my car and I drive away in my car. If any of your neighbors notice, they'll see nothing strange. My car was here, so I was here. And then my car is gone, which means I went away. But they never saw me with anyone."

"Fachrissakes," he said, his face clenching up like a fist, as though he was about to scream or break out weeping. "Somebody could see him getting out of your car. I don't know if we've thought this out."

"I've thought it out. He remembered the knife. He'll remember the rest. He'll remember we were there. He'll remember the ceremony and the sacrifices, and he'll know he spent fifteen years in a cage for crimes he didn't commit."

She handed him a thin silver tube, fancier than a rolled-up dollar bill. Hobby slipped off the couch to his knees, stuck one end of the tube in his right nostril, closed the left with his thumb, and snuffed up a line of coke. Then he held the right nostril closed and snorted another line up the left.

He shivered as the charge burst through his head. He felt his balls swell and his cock engorge. The magic of the white powder convinced him that he possessed powers he didn't possess.

"Hooooo!" he yelled.

She walked over to the glass doors and threw the switch that turned out the lights around the pool. The approaching storm grumbled at her.

The chimes above the front door announced someone.

"There he is," Eve said, turning around and going over to the bar.

While Hobby went to the door, she mixed a large glass of undiluted brandy, rum, and vodka. "White lightning," she said, smiling.

Younger came into the room like the cock of the walk, like a gambler with all the aces hidden in his sleeve. He was wearing a

faded work shirt and jeans with a sleeveless quilted vest. The boots
he wore made him look even taller than he was.

"My God, but you're looking good," Eve said, approaching him
with the glass. "Lean and mean."

"Prison's no place to get fat," he drawled.

"Here you go. First one of the night."

He looked at the glass, then sniffed it. She took it back from him
and drank from it.

"Did you think I'd want to give you the poisoned cup?"

She was laughing at him. She knew she had the power. He'd
known witch women in the hills but they were nothing like Eve
Choyren. He hadn't been afraid of them but he was a little afraid of
her.

"No, I didn't think that," he said. "I just think you people got me
drunk last night."

"Didn't get into any trouble, did you?" Hobby asked.

"Woke up in a Dumpster full of rotten vegetables."

Eve and Hobby glanced at one another.

"You got me drunk before we got a chance to talk about what we
were going to do for each other," Younger said.

"Whatever you want," Eve said. "Isn't that right, Paul? You're
ready to give Inch whatever he wants, aren't you?"

Hobby was walking around above the floor, ten feet tall, his
fingers made of willow wands, the dust of blasted stars swimming
on the edges of his vision.

"Well, I don't know. You know what they say: 'You give an Inch a
job and he'll smile for a mile.'" He laughed, thinking himself the
funniest man he'd come across in a long time.

Rain started to fall on the patio beyond the glass doors, into the
pool lying still as lead under the lights.

Manny Shiner was Hobby's neighbor to the south.

They weren't exactly friends. They weren't exactly good neighbors. There'd been times when they'd been very social and times
when they'd passed on the beach and not even spoken.

There'd been one time, fifteen, sixteen years before, when
Shiner'd had great hopes for a relationship with Hobby. That was
when he'd been in love with the brash, up-coming young producer.

He'd invited Hobby over to his house for little suppers and the use of his steam room

Hobby had reciprocated, inviting Shiner to his beach roasts and picnics. There were always a lot of pretty, hopeful girls at Hobby's parties. Hobby had always tried to fix Shiner up with one or more of them, as if he hadn't known Shiner's persuasion and preference. It might have been an ironic gesture or it might have been a discreet nod toward the closet in which Shiner kept at least half his life.

He remembered the first goat roast Hobby'd thrown, the smell of meat bursting into his face when he helped uncover the carcass and cut away the burlap and the palm leaves. That had been the highlight of that year—of many years—kneeling there, naked to the waist, cutting into the roasted flesh with a butcher's knife as sharp as a sword-edged blade of grass.

He remembered the next time he'd been asked to another such feast and celebration. It had been held farther north along a stretch of dunes. There'd been fewer guests. He'd felt priviledged to be invited.

This time the goat hadn't been already slaughtered and dressed. It had been dragged into the circle of the fire alive. Eve Choyren, naked under silver-and-black robes, had chanted incantations in a tongue he didn't understand, had never heard. It was all a kind of foolishness that frightened him. The foolishness of cruel children who invented rituals before impaling cats or plucking the wings from butterflies. The worst kind of foolishness, which could lead to all sorts of horrors.

He'd watched in fascinated disgust as a man with a hillbilly accent grabbed the goat's chin in the crook of his arm and stretched its neck back and cut its throat with a hooked knife.

There'd been a naked woman laid faceup on a mound of sand roughly shaped like a block of stone. An altar. She was drunk or drugged. He saw the look on Hobby's face and the faces of the big, dark-skinned man they called Bolivia and the white-fleshed priestess called Eve.

He'd never been so terrified in his life.

So he'd run away, the sound of the chanting chasing him down the sands.

He and Hobby hadn't spoken for a long time after that, and when

the case of the mutilated women set the community to talking,
Shiner had never said a word. It had been better to forget or pretend that it had all been a dream.

Now he heard the chanting coming from next door, and looking
out the window, he saw the firelight from Hobby's living room
splashing on the deck. He closed the sliding doors to his patio,
shutting off the sound of the sea and all but the highest, thinnest
notes of Eve's conjuration.

Eve Choyren knew all about the hypnotic power of incantations
and conjurations. She knew all about the effects of alcohol upon
the brain and of drugs upon human behavior. She was aware of and
had a supply of the drug employed by Haitian witch doctors to
produce zombies—those victims they claimed were animated
corpses, who were nothing more than ordinary people with their
minds and wills stolen from them.

She knew about all of it and talked about all of it and threatened
to use all she knew, but in truth she was as foolishly afraid of the
powers she toyed with as any of the foolish seekers who'd ever
placed themselves in her hands.

The Reverend Jim Jones had led five hundred people into suicide
with a garbage can full of Kool-Aid punch. Manson had pointed
the finger and people had been murdered. Less dramatic, television
preachers, weeping buckets of crocodile tears on the public air-
waves, had continued to harvest the pockets of America even after
confessing their carnal sins. And a disc jockey somewhere or other
had asked people to send in twenty bucks, without offering anything in return, and had collected more than a quarter of a million
dollars.

Her ceremonies had led to ritual murder once, fifteen years before. Bolivia and Hobby had gone mad, out of control. And she'd
even joined in, while Younger was lying back against the dunes in
a drunken stupor.

Now she was hard at it, trying to prove to herself that she could
con, twist, seduce, and motivate the ignorant mountain man into
committing suicide, erasing any suspicion that might fall on her or
Hobby once and forever.

Steal his mind. Turn him into a zombie. Send him out into the
storm, far down the beach to the sacrificial cove. Send him down

there with a knife. Have him cut his own throat. Have the bastard kill himself, and prove to Hobby that she still had the power, that she'd never set him free altogether, that she wouldn't be tossed aside to grow old alone.

"I conjure you, O Spirit, to appear within the minute," Eve said, her arms upraised, head thrown back, silver-and-black metallic robe opened all along the front, her naked body shining through. Suddenly desirable. No longer weak but powerful. "By the power of the great Adonai, by Eloim, by Ariel, Johavam, Agla, Mathon, Parios, Almouzin, Arios, Membrot, Tagla, Oarios..."

Younger was slouched back against the cushions of the suede couch, watchng it all with the uncomprehending innocence of a woodland creature, fey eyes glittering in his brown face, soft hair standing out from his head like the scorched floss of milkweed. He lurched forward and gained his feet.

Hobby stared at him, wondering why the man wasn't already on his knees, on his back, stoned out, blacked out from the quantity of drug-laced booze he'd consumed. Knowing what he'd have to do, what he and Eve had agreed upon in case the zombie caper didn't work. All this mumbo-jumbo crap. What was the use, stunning Younger's brain? What was the use, making him commit suicide? Take the gun out of the drawer of the coffee table. Shoot the son-ofabitch between the eyes. Bury him in the Hog Wallow. Who'd ever look there again for a missing person? Who'd ever look for this particular missing person anyway? Good riddance to bad rubbish, they'd say. Just who in the world would give a good goddam if Inch Younger disappeared? Get the gun out and use it. Just to shut Eve up if nothing else.

"...Tabost, Gnomus, Terraea, Coelia, Godens, Aqua, Gungua, Anua, Etituamus, Zariatnitmik!"

"Well, bulllllshit!" Younger said, reaching into his pocket.

"O Oualbpaga!" Eve cried.

"You're playin' those fuckin' games again," Younger said.

"O Kammara!"

"Look what I got."

"O Kamalo!"

"I got me another linoleum knife!"

46

Moo's room was at the very top of the house, under the eaves. She went in first and turned on the little lamp on a table beside the bed. She put a finger to her lips.

"You got to be quiet," she whispered.

"How come you got a room by yourself?"

"That's the way it works. The newest girl gets a room by herself. Later on, if you want to stay, you got to share."

"Are you going to stay?"

"I don't think so." She looked at him as though seeing him for the first time. "I'm glad you come to visit me."

"My pleasure," he said, not knowing how to handle somebody being so glad to see him.

"Whooosh," she sighed, sitting down on the bed. "I've been really scared."

"About what?"

"It was on the news. That person I I.D.'d was let out of jail. Come sit over here by me."

He took the few steps to the bed and half crouched there. "How come they left you alone?"

"There's cops watching the house. The judge told them to be sure to keep an eye out."

"I didn't see no cops."

"Sit down. Sit down. You think I'm going to bite you?"

He sat down and she put her arm around his thin shoulders. It made him shiver.

"You cold?" she asked.

"No. Did you hear what I just said? I didn't see no cops."

"Well, you wouldn't, would you? I mean if cops was watching a place they wouldn't be standing out on the street shining flashlights on their badges, would they?"

"If I couldn't see them and they saw me break in here through the cellar, how come they ain't kicking the door down?"

She grew still and listened, as though she expected to hear the crash of a foot on the door right then and there. She put her hand on his thigh, still holding on to his shoulder with the other.

"Hey," she said.

"What?"

"You're scaring me. You ain't cold, I'm cold. You promise to be good, we can get under the covers."

"I don't want to do that."

"Oh? Why not?"

"I don't think I could be good," he said, making it sound very bold, very experienced.

She giggled softly. "I don't think I can be good either."

When she kissed him and pushed her tongue into his mouth, it surprised him. She started pulling at his shirt, getting it up out of his pants.

He reached down between them and struggled to get his belt undone and zipper pulled down. He could feel her pubic hair as coarse as wire wool on the back of his hand. The excitement was so strong in him that he could hear the pumping of his blood hissing in his ears until they ached.

Moo fell back on the bed and pushed him away as he fell on top of her, his mouth still glued to hers, struggling to free himself with one hand and hold on to her with the other.

"What are you doing?" he asked, anger rising in his voice.

Why was she pushing him away? Was she just teasing him? Was she just getting him all hot and bothered so she could squirm away and laugh in his face?

"It's all right," she whispered. "I'm trying to get my shirt off."

She raised her legs and pulled the cloth out from under her buttocks. A smell of musk, warm and bittersweet, filled Bitsy's nose and mouth.

His belly was churning. There was a sweet stinging sensation all along the inner parts of his thighs. His scrotum cringed as though he'd stepped into a cold bath.

She pulled him back on top of her, her legs thrown wide apart, open to him. She fumbled between them and took his cock in her hand, trying to insert it.

He couldn't control himself. He came with a shudder.

She looked at him with something like surprise. She started to laugh. Then she remembered.

What else could you do? Canaan wondered.

There weren't enough cops. And even where there were enough cops, mistakes were made all the time. People didn't show up where they were supposed to show up. Too few people were assigned, and too late. The sea of drugs rose higher and higher. The stray children gathered from everywhere. They died in the streets and alleys.

You had to do what you could to stop it. It was like that book somebody'd written when he was young, in which this youngster thought it was up to him to stand in the fields of rye and keep children from running off the edge of the cliff.

You had to do what you could, even if it meant not having a life and rarely sleeping.

He pulled up to the curb across the street from Magdalene House. He could see the light on in the vestibule and behind the living room curtains. There was another light in a little window high up under the eaves. Somebody was awake. Was it the girl?

The van belonging to the halfway house pulled up into the driveway. The black man, Jojo, and Faye Chaney got out. They stood at the curb and looked straight at his car. Canaan raised his hand as if to tell them the police were watching. They didn't seem to take any notice. Jojo went around to the driver's side and got in again behind the wheel.

Faye turned toward the house and looked up at the lighted window of the attic room. Then she went to the door and used her key.

Faye climbed the stairs. She went all the way to the top. She wanted to see if Moo was all right. Or if she was afraid and sleepless and in need of comfort. She put her ear against the door and listened. There was no sound. She tapped lightly on the panel. Moo had probably fallen asleep with the light on.

She opened the door and, in the light of the table lamp, saw a humped tangle on the bed. A charge of fear chopped at her chest. She hit the switch for the overhead and saw that a half-naked man was sprawled on top of Moo.

Then, in the moment it took for Bitsy to twist around and face the intruder, Faye saw the birthmark shaped like the foot of a toad on the side of his narrow chest, underneath his armpit.

"Oh, my God!" she said.

Bitsy was off the bed, the front of him covered in blood, his knife in his hand.

"I couldn't do it. I was so excited I couldn't do it and she laughed at me," he said, as though that was all the explanation she needed.

Faye didn't even throw up her hands. She stood there, waiting for her fate as if it was only fair.

47

The rain had moved inland from the sea.

It spattered the dusty sides of the apartment building, which was ready to be torn down. The peeling stucco was like the hide falling off the flanks of a pink elephant. It was a stage set gone to mold and mildew.

The hinges on the gate were rusty. One of them had broken through the keeper, and the gate hung there wired back permanently, never to open and close again.

Some of the mailboxes had been jimmied and their doors stood open like a bunch of gaping mouths. He checked the nameplates and found the one for E. Choyren.

The smell of chlorine coming from the pool, blackened by the rain, was so heavy it stung Whistler's nose. The plastic palm trees had developed leprosy. They were gray and corpselike.

He climbed up to the second floor, nearly slipping on the top step where the industrial surfacing had worn away. There was a light on behind the drapes that covered the picture window, but no one answered when he first rang the bell and then pounded on the door with the side of his fist.

After two or three minutes he was ready to leave.

A man in a black plastic slicker and a crushed Irish hat appeared at the top of the staircase at the other end of the balcony. When he got closer he said, "Looking for somebody?"

"Eve Choyren doesn't seem to be home."

"Isn't home."

"You happen to know where she is?"

"Who wants to know?"

"Never mind."

"Hey, don't get touchy. I just want to know are you a friend, an enemy, a cop, or a creditor."

"She have so many visitors she needs a social secretary to sort them out?"

"She used to have hundreds of friends. Well, people she knew or who wanted to know her. Had her share of enemies, too, in her glory days, when they'd have her on television explaining witch-craft and all that other nonsense."

"You're not a believer?"

"I gave up believing in such things when my momma told me there was no Santa Claus."

"You said cops."

"Cops used to come around like clockwork every time somebody showed up dead with scratches on them or some black candle wax under their nails, or when they found a cat with its eyes gouged out. Hazard of the trade, she used to call such attention."

"And lately?"

"Not so much lately. Just people dunning her for money lately. Eve's fallen on hard times. She puts on a brave front when she goes out in her slicks and satins, but she's having her troubles making ends meet. It's the town, you know."

"How's that?"

"You're not young, you're not anything in this town. Look around. Even witches. You'd think the older the witch the more she'd be respected, wouldn't you? Doesn't work that way. Young witches have taken over the trade. They get on television. Get all the publicity, all the customers."

"You don't suppose..." Whistler said, leaving the sentence hanging there.

"Don't suppose what?"

Whistler shot his thumb over his shoulder at the door. "...I could have a look inside?"

"What the hell for?"

"I don't know. I don't know what there is to look for until I have a look."

He took out his money clip and peeled off twenty dollars.

"You know about money?" the man said. "It's not the awful stuff people say it is. It's just a store of time. It's the only way people can save up time today and use it tomorrow. I put enough of these little pieces of time away ten, twenty years ago and I wouldn't have to be managing a run-down apartment house in my old age."

"It's never too late to open a savings account. That's what the banks say."

The man took the twenty.

"Whenever Eve knows she's going to be out past a certain hour, she asks me to let her cat out for a pee. That's what I'm here for at the moment."

He took out a key and opened the door. A Siamese cat came silently to his feet and looked up at them with its mysterious crossed eyes.

"Come on up here, Lucifage," he said, and clapped his hands. The cat leapt into his arms and sat there staring at Whistler.

"He's quick about it when it's raining," the manager went on. "Maybe two minutes, maybe three. You won't steal anything. Forget that. I can see you won't. Besides, I don't know what the poor old girl would have around worth stealing."

He walked down the long balcony toward the stairs, taking the cat down to have its pee beneath a plastic palm.

Whistler went to the middle of the room and, slowly turning around, took it all in. The kitchenette no bigger than a closet. The tatty couch with its upholstered arms all shredded away from the clawing of the cat. The armchair, placed for viewing the television that sat on a movable stand, and the lap rug folded across its back, waiting to warm legs gone chilly in the long lonely hours of the night. The framed poster on the wall.

A faint smell of stale incense but no evidence of rites or ceremonies. No devilish paraphernalia. No horrors.

He walked into the bedroom, glancing into the tiny bathroom on the way. All as might be expected for a woman living alone—the rinsed-out panty hose hanging over the shower rod, the extra roll of toilet tissue on the lid of the tank, the chenille bath mat.

There was nothing in the bedroom either that smacked of Satanism. Commonplace. Everything sad, old, used, worn, and commonplace.

When Whistler returned to the living room, the manager was already back, opening his arms so that the cat fell to the floor, landing on all fours, arching its back, looking up at the man, and yelling as though that was part of the relationship between them.

"Nothing much, is it?" the manager said. "You'd expect something better for a person who's supposed to be on speaking terms with Satan, wouldn't you?"

There were footsteps outside. The manager turned around to see if it was one of the neighbors. Mike Rialto stopped in the doorway.

"Hello, Whistler. I figured you might be here."

Rialto glanced at the manager.

"It doesn't matter. Go ahead and talk," Whistler said.

"Assignment or no assignment, I went looking for Younger. I went to his hotel."

"How'd you know which hotel?"

"I got friends in the cops just like you got friends in the cops."

"Okay."

"Younger came down and stood at the curb. After a while Eve Choyren pulled up and gave him the keys to her car. They went inside. She came out in about two minutes. She was alone. Five minutes after that a cab pulled up and she got in. I didn't know should I wait for Younger or should I follow the taxi. I waited. After about an hour he came down, all showered and shaved, clean denim shirt, quilted vest, shine on his boots, and got in the car. I got on his tail just for the practice. Followed him down to the beach. Down to Malibu. To Hobby's house."

"That where he is?"

"I saw him go inside. He was in there when I left and came looking for you."

"Just him and Hobby?"

"That I wouldn't know. You want me to drive you?"

Whistler looked around the sorry little apartment one more time, said good-bye to the manager, and went downstairs to get into Rialto's Caddy.

48

In his dream Canaan heard the peeping of a bird. He tilted his head and sharpened his ears and recognized the sound of his niece calling to him for help. He struggled up out of the swamp of glue he was trapped in. The cop they said never slept had fallen asleep on a stakeout. A stakeout he'd assigned to himself by himself.

Then he realized that the screaming he was hearing wasn't coming to him out of a dream. It was coming from Magdalene House.

His legs felt sluggish. He managed to struggle out of the car. He saw a shadow come out of the alley. He started to run across the street, but he couldn't get up any speed. Whoever it was was getting away.

"Hey! Stand still, you!" he shouted.

The shadow turned around and Canaan got a look at his face. The light of a streetlamp fell on pale skin and wild hair blowing around like the fur on a scared cat's back.

Canaan could see it was just a kid maybe thirteen, fourteen years old. He knew the face.

"Don't move! Don't run!" he ordered.

The kid took off like à sprinter. The last Canaan saw of him was a squint-eyed face no bigger than a thumbnail. Canaan had seen enough. It was the kid they called Bitsy. What he couldn't figure out was how come he hadn't recognized him right off when Whistler had shown him the photograph. Squinting just that way. Squinting against the sun the way he'd just squinted against the light of the lamp.

• • •

Rialto and Whistler drove through the rain, winding their way down the famous long boulevard, past the Beverly Hills mansions, past the university campus and over the San Diego Freeway, through Brentwood Heights, pretending to be a small town, and down the sweeping curves to the sea above Santa Monica.

They drove north, past Buddy's Place, where fifteen years before three women had been found buried in the Hog Wallow.

They came to the long stretch of houses known as Malibu, a place without a center, without a heart, seven miles long and six hundred yards wide.

Rialto pulled up across the road from Paul Hobby's house and turned off the ignition and the headlights. There was a man in white sailor pants and a white sweatshirt, holding an umbrella, standing in front of the house next door.

Whistler reached for the handle, about to open the door.

"Don't wait for me," he said.

"What do you mean? There's no public transportation out here except the Greyhound what don't hardly run even in daylight, let alone after dark."

"Go on back to the four corners. Go finish picking your horses."

"How'll you get home?"

"I'll find a way."

"It's fucking raining pups and pussies."

"It won't keep up forever. Besides, I've been wet before."

"You might need me," Rialto said.

"I don't want you around. I don't want you having a part of it."

"Part of what?"

Whistler didn't answer. He opened the door and got out of the car.

Rialto hit the button and lowered the window as Whistler walked around the Caddy and out onto the highway. He stuck his head out the window and screwed it around.

"Don't do it. He's not worth killing."

"Maybe that's all he's worth," Whistler said.

"Don't do it. It's not your style."

"What's my style? Standing around letting this asshole walk the streets, maybe come stalking Faye?"

"You don't know that."

"So maybe I'll just have a talk and find out. Maybe I'll just warn him."

The man across the street walked out to the curb, raising his hand to catch their attention, as though he'd been waiting for them.

Whistler walked across the highway.

Rialto didn't start the car. He sat there waiting, wondering what he should do. Wondering what good he could do if Whistler went in and killed Younger.

Whistler reached the other side. His feet were already soaked.

"You the police? I'm Manny Shiner. I'm the one who called."

"What's the trouble?" Whistler asked.

"I don't know. I mean it wasn't just the noise they were making, playing that goddam music so loud and everything. I'm not the sort of person who complains to the police when a neighbor's having a party."

"Your neighbor having a party?"

"That's what I'm saying. I don't know what they're having. There was chanting and screaming and shouting and the sound of things falling over."

Whistler turned his head toward Hobby's house as though listening for what Shiner was complaining about.

"Then it stopped. Just like that it stopped," Shiner said. "Maybe ten minutes ago. Right after I called you. Now you can hear, it's as quiet as..."

"What?"

"I was going to say as quiet as the grave. You going in?"

"What's the back of the house like?"

"All glass, looking out toward the ocean."

Whistler walked over to the fence and tried the gate that opened into the alley alongside the house. It was locked.

He went back and asked Shiner if he could go through his house to reach the sand.

"That's good," Shiner said. "That way, if they're asleep or something like that, Paul won't have to know I called the police."

"You think they're asleep?" Whistler asked as he walked through Shiner's front door.

Shiner stared at him, and when his face clenched up for a second he looked like a baby about to cry. "No, I don't," he practically whispered. "What do you think?"

"Well, I don't really know," Whistler said, the way a cop would say it, making no assumptions, waiting for the evidence.

He walked the length of Shiner's house, leaving wet footprints across the slate floors and white carpet, and went out the sliding doors at the back. The waves were foaming up on the beach now, their tops shaved off by the wind that drove the rain.

He stepped over the low wall that surrounded Shiner's patio and kicked through the wet sand to a wrought-iron gate. He pushed it open and skirted the black swimming pool, which stirred with greater agitation than the sea.

Even before he put his face to the window he could see the carmine splashed everywhere and the crumpled shapes scattered on the couch and rug like actors on a stage set.

The sliding doors were locked. He grabbed the handle and rattled them back and forth, kicking at the bottom aluminum rim until the catch tripped and he could slide one open. He took one step inside the room and stood there looking at Younger, who was sitting silent and still on the couch staring right at Whistler.

The front doorbell rang.

Nobody moved.

Younger never blinked.

Whistler heard footsteps behind him. A flashlight swept across his back and stopped on Younger's face.

Younger still didn't blink.

"Just raise your hands straight out from your sides," the sheriff's deputy said.

The minute Canaan walked through the door Bosco knew it was bad. The worst.

"Whistler here?" Canaan asked. He didn't even look at the booth where Whistler always sat.

"What's the matter with you, Isaac? Can't you see for yourself he ain't here?"

"Where is he?"

"How should I know? He don't tell me everything he does and everyplace he goes."

"He should be coming in any minute, right? I mean he always comes in about this time, doesn't he?"

"What is it, Isaac?"

"What've you got under the counter?"

"What're you talking about?"

"Whistler's going to need something when I tell him what I got to tell him."

"Whistler don't drink." They stood there staring at one another, playing the game of denial. What Canaan's mouth didn't speak and Bosco's ear didn't hear never happened. It wouldn't happen till one spoke and the other listened. If they stayed dumb and deaf long enough, they could make time stand still.

"What could be so bad he'd take a drink?" Bosco finally asked.

"I'll need one. I need one right now," Canaan said.

"I got brandy."

"Put two fingers in a mug and fill it up with coffee. Bring it to the table, will you?"

He turned his head in slow motion, as though fearing that while they'd been talking Whistler had slipped by them and would be sitting in his regular booth, waiting for the news.

Canaan walked over to the booth and sat down. He took off his hat. It was the first time in memory anybody'd seen him take off his hat.

He was almost bald on top. His hair fell away from a circle of pale skin like the tonsure of a monk. A purple yarmulke, embroidered in red, sat on the back of his head, making a half-moon of his naked scalp, a circle on a circle.

"I never knew you were such a religious man, Isaac," Bosco said, bringing over the spiked coffee.

"It's a prod to memory."

"You worn it long?"

"Since my niece was murdered."

"You don't need anything to keep you from forgetting something like that," Bosco said.

"No, you don't. You never forget. Never. Never. Never."

"Faye's dead, ain't she?"

Canaan drank from the mug.

"Murdered, ain't she?"

Canaan looked at him and scarcely nodded.

"That Younger do it?"

"I don't know. I don't know who did it. The techs are going over the crime scene. Maybe they'll find something to point the finger, maybe they won't."

"Where'd it happen?"

"Right there in Magdalene House."

"How?"

"With a knife. She was stabbed over and over again with a knife. It looks like she walked in on the killer right after he finished stabbing that baby hooker we were keeping as a witness for that other killing on the rooftop."

"That Younger did it," Bosco said with certainty.

"It looks that way. But I don't know. Nobody knows yet. I wish to hell Whistler would get here. I got to go back to the scene."

"Jesus Christ, what can you say?" Bosco said.

"You can say, 'Jesus Christ, embrace her,'" Canaan said. "She was a believer, wasn't she?"

The phone rang at the register.

"Get that, Shirley, will you?" Bosco yelled.

The phone rang twice more before Shirley Hightower lifted the receiver. "For you, Sergeant."

Canaan slid out of the booth and went over to answer the phone. Bosco took a swallow from the sergeant's mug.

When Canaan came back he said, "You can have the rest of that. I got to go."

"They find something?"

"Well, they found Younger down at Malibu. The way it's going to time out, we can be pretty sure he didn't do the work at Magdalene House."

"How's that?"

"Because Younger was getting himself shot just about the same time. That's the way it looks. That ain't all."

"What?"

"A Hollywood producer by the name of Paul Hobby and that witch, Eve Choyren, were found dead, too. All cut up. That ain't all."

"What?" Bosco asked again, not really wanting to hear.

"The sheriff's deputies found Whistler standing in the middle of the mess. I got to go out front and wait. Hooligan's coming to pick me up. He wants to look it over down in Malibu."

He started to walk toward the door.

Bosco picked up Canaan's hat. "Hey!"

A black sedan pulled up into the red zone in front of the shop and somebody sounded its horn.

"There he is," Canaan said.

"Don't forget your hat," Bosco said. "You don't want to get all wet. You don't want the street to see you naked."

49

"*The* walls and furniture inside that house look like they was painted red," Hooligan said. "What do you think? You saying the man butchered three people and didn't get a drop of blood on himself? Not a stain on his shoes?"

"There's blood on his shoes," the sheriff replied.

"On the bottoms where he stepped in it."

"So he went home and cleaned himself up before he came back to have another look."

"You're telling me fairy tales and I ain't a child."

"So what do you expect me to do? We get a call about a domestic disturbance. When my deputies arrive they find two people cut up like a couple sides of beef, one corpse sitting there with three eyes in his face, and a private license, who passed himself off as a law officer, standing there with his hands in his pockets. When we ask him what he was doing here in the first place he says he was checking into the whereabouts of one Inch Younger—that's the one got shot in the face—a paroled murderer who might be a danger to his ex-wife, the private dick's present girlfriend. So look at the motive we've got right there."

"He give it to you. He give you the information without you even had to ask. What kind of murderer is that? What kind of smart private license is that?"

Hooligan glanced out the door to the poolside terrace, where Canaan and Whistler were sitting on some plastic-webbed lounges as if they didn't even feel the rain soaking them, running down their collars and into their shoes.

Under the mercury lamps they looked like a couple of corpses having a conversation in a place in hell where it rained lead.

"Just give me one good reason I should turn a prime suspect over to you," the sheriff said.

"He won't be going anywhere. You want him, all you got to do is reach out and there he is in my paw. You want him, all you got to do is ask and I turn him over," Hooligan said.

"You're jailing him?"

"I can't jail him because I got nothing to book him. You ready to book him?"

"I got suspicion. I got reason to hold. I find a person in the middle of a butcher shop, I got reason to hold."

"You got nothing to charge him with. You'll look silly when forensics finishes up and tells you the one called Younger and them other two was having a drug party and it got out of hand. They was having a fucking orgy—the one guy's wearing nothing but trunks and a bathrobe, the woman's naked underneath that cape or whatever—and it got out of hand. Younger started cutting one of them up—you know that's what he was convicted of before, cutting people up?—and the other one jumped in. Next thing you know, the two of them are dead or almost dead and the man takes out a gun and shoots Younger between the eyes."

"I don't even know what's your interest. What the hell are a couple of detectives out of Hollywood Division doing coming down here to the beach sticking your noses in?"

"I told you, fachrissake." Hooligan glanced over his shoulder again and lowered his voice as though Whistler could hear him, sitting that far away, above the sounds of the storm. "We got an interest in this Younger because he's not out a week and he's got hisself jammed up. The least he probably did was try to rape a topless barmaid in a beer joint. The worst he could of done was murder and mutilate a baby hooker up on a roof. Also, we got reason to believe he could've murdered his ex-wife and the other baby hooker what was going to be a witness against him on the rooftop killing of her girlfriend."

"What the hell are you telling me? They let this asshole out on the streets and he goes and murders five people, zap, zap, zap, zap, zap, and then gets himself shot between the eyes?"

"You're talking serial killers, you're talking mass murders, you're not talking normal," Hooligan said. "But I don't think we got five killings by this Younger. I think we got maybe zap, zap, zap. We got the girl on the roof and we got these two in the body bags, because from the rough-estimate time of death the M.E. gives you, Younger'd never've had the time to do all four in one night."

The sheriff opened his mouth to speak but Hooligan went right on without pause.

"What we ain't got is we ain't got that poor sonofabitch sitting out there in the rain doing these murders. He came down to see what was what with this Younger. Maybe he was going to confront him. Maybe he was going to talk to him. Maybe, if he didn't get the right assurances, he would even've kicked his balls in or drowned him in the pool. But it never came to that. So you want to take him in and book him, go ahead and do it. You don't want the effort, let us take him back to Hollywood. He ain't going anywhere. I guarantee you."

"How do I explain it?" the sheriff asked. "How do I make out the paper?"

"You report him as a person coming to visit who found the bodies. You explain that two L.A.P.D. detectives asked to take him into custody on another, possibly related matter."

"But suppose—"

"If it turns out he had anything to do with what happened here, we give him back to you. It'll be your arrest. Your trophy."

The sheriff finally said okay but to be damn sure he was kept informed.

"About what?" Hooligan asked.

"About any damned little thing."

Hooligan went out and gathered up Canaan and Whistler. The two cops walked Whistler back through the alley to the highway, one on each side. It was like escorting a dead man. There was no feeling of life in him. He just shuffled along, staring at the rain falling in front of him as though that were all there would ever be in the world again. The strange persistence of the rain.

Hooligan drove and Canaan sat next to him. Whistler sat in the back, his face turned to the window, still looking out into the rain. Not saying a word.

All of a sudden he said, "You didn't put a watch on her. You didn't put a watch on her, goddammit."

Hooligan and Canaan didn't say anything to that.

They rode in silence all the way back to Hollywood.

Then Whistler said, "I want to see where Faye was killed."

"Ah, no, Whistler," Canaan said. "You don't want to do that. She's probably not even there anymore."

"Please, Isaac, do me the favor."

There'd been no cops on the watch, but now that somebody was dead there were uniforms and detectives all over the street and sidewalk. On the stairs and porch. Inside the house. In the living room and kitchen. Crowded on the little landing in front of the attic room.

Men from the Mobile Forensics Laboratory were inside the bedroom marking, measuring, taking samples and pictures.

Hooligan stopped in the doorway to the tiny attic bedroom, practically filling it. He turned around when Canaan touched his arm.

"They haven't got around to taking them away," he said.

Whistler stared over Hooligan's shoulder. His eyes were dead holes in his skull, filled with charcoal. Stains had appeared around his eyes. They looked like bruises, as though he'd been beaten with fists.

"Let him through," Canaan said. "Let him have a look, for God's sake."

Hooligan stepped aside.

Canaan reached out a hand. "Don't go inside. Don't try to touch her."

Whistler nodded. He stopped in the doorway. Moo was lying half naked on the bed, stab wounds all over her chest and belly.

Faye was sprawled on the floor. She was on her back and a scarlet flower had blossomed in the middle of her blouse. Her eyes were half closed. She seemed to look at Whistler in the half-sleepy way she'd looked at him when they'd first wakened on those mornings when all things were possible.

"There aren't any defensive wounds on her hands and arms," Whistler said, his voice sounding like a shout from far away, half captured by fog.

"No," Canaan agreed.

"It's like she walked right into it. Didn't even try to fight or run away."

"Yes," Canaan said.

"Let me through. Excuse me," the crime-scene technician said, anxious to be on his way. He was carrying something in a Ziploc freezer bag.

"What's that?" Whistler asked.

"Paperback book," the technician said, after he'd first looked at Hooligan and got the nod. "It's a book about those old Hog Wallow murders back in seventy-four, seventy-five. Remember that one?"

Whistler stared at Canaan.

"They let the sonofabitch out. They had him in their hands and they let him out. How many corpses do we give away for free before we burn the bastards nowadays?"

"But not Faye. He didn't kill Faye," Canaan said softly.

"No," Whistler said. He kept staring at the book in the plastic bag. "But there's a connection."

"I think we found Faye's kid," Canaan said. "I think he's right here in town. I think he was here tonight."

"What do you mean?"

A cop appeared at the top of the stairs.

While Canaan told Whistler how he'd staked out Magdalene House himself because the men hadn't been scheduled for that night, and how he'd seen the kid he thought was the one Whistler had asked him to identify in the picture come out of the house when the screams started, the uniform was mumbling something into Hooligan's ear.

"Fachrissake," Hooligan said. "It never quits."

50

"*You* want to hang around cops, join the force," Hooligan complained.

"Let him alone," Canaan said.

"What the fuck's going on here? I got dead bodies showing up all over the goddam place. I got a kiddie-vice cop acting like he's my partner. I got a private license—which I got to save his ass from the sheriffs—hanging around, sticking his nose in where it don't belong. What am I, a fucking charity agency?"

"Nobody'd accuse you of that, Houlihan," Whistler said.

"What'd you call me?"

"Houlihan. That's your name, isn't it?"

"Nobody's called me by my real name in thirty years. Everybody calls me Hooligan. That don't show any respect. Calling me by my real name shows respect."

Canaan turned his head and glanced at Whistler. He raised his eyebrow as if to say, "How'd you do that? How'd you make Hooligan sweet?"

There were squad cars at the curb in front of the condemned building Bitsy and his family called home. A cop took the men through the basement and out the door that gave onto the garbage-filled air shaft.

"There rats in there?" Hooligan asked.

"Plenty of them," the cop said. "They've been chewing on the subject."

"Ahh, Jesus."

"But you don't got to worry. They've been laying low ever since we arrived."

They kicked through the garbage to the middle of the area where Hogan's corpse was rotting away. The rats had been dining on him, just as the cop said.

"Who is it?"

"No identification. Just another kid, run away or thrown away."

"Who found him?"

The cop gestured with his head to a spot in the corner, where a bag lady was being comforted by a policewoman.

"She come in here looking for pickings." The cop grinned. "Got more than she expected."

Hooligan bent over and peered into Hogan's ravaged face.

"You know this one, Canaan? I mean if you can see enough to tell?"

Canaan gave a careful look. "No. He looks like a hundred others on the street. I don't know them all. He could be pretty new. Nobody could know them all."

Whistler bent over and reached out a hand.

"What the fuck you doing?" Hooligan asked, the good-natured glow brought on by Whistler's show of respect leaving in a hurry. "You trying to mess up the crime scene?"

Whistler straightened up. He had palmed what he wanted, a little matchbox covered in colored foil that said "Motel Royal."

"I wasn't touching, I was looking. And what do you think you're going to find in all this garbage, a goddam calling card?"

"All right, why don't you two guys take a walk? Go grab a cab. Ask a squad car to drop you on the corner. Whatever. Leave me do my job, will you?"

Canaan plucked at Whistler's sleeve. They started making their way back through the garbage.

"Hey, Whistler!" Hooligan said. "Don't leave town. Be where I can get you in case the sheriff comes to me asking about you."

"I'm not going anywhere," Whistler said. "Don't you worry."

51

Whistler stood at the curb with his eyes burning holes through the twangy boys, baby hookers, transvestites, undercover narcs, pimps, dealers, cutters, and nickel thieves spilling along the stroll. Reading their faces. Trying to decide which one of them might know a kid who once owned a foil-covered matchbox. Expecting it to appear in blazing letters in their eyes, on their foreheads. Expecting miracles.

The light changed but he just stood there.

He was a rock. The people eddied and split and flowed around him like a river of floating garbage, glancing at him out of the corners of their eyes, not a one of them daring—yet—to lay a hand on him and say how sorry they were—if they were—that he'd lost the love who had gone away and then come back to him and then got herself killed, never to come back again.

They already knew everything there was to know, because they were a river, and every drop knew in an instant what every other drop knew as they tumbled over one another on the way to the ocean.

Whether they'd tell him what they all knew was another thing. How much of their trust and good will did he have in the bank? He didn't have money enough to ask the questions of everybody.

Two kids he'd seen around the street—didn't know their names but had said Hi, how are you? How you keeping?—were buzzing around a streetlamp like a couple of fighter pilots. Being kids while waiting to sell their asses.

Whistler walked away from a green traffic signal that would've taken him across the street, out of the warm drizzle, into Gentry's, where he'd receive care, coffee, and comfort from the people he considered his family. From Bosco, Canaan, Rialto, and Shirley Hightower, and whatever gypsy cook was working the griddle for a week or two.

"How's it bouncin'?" he asked the two kids bopping around.

"About as high as my knee," Roach said.

"High as my nose," Duckie said.

"You want to get high with us?" Roach asked, doing his sailor-man's strut.

"What the fuck's wrong with you?" Duckie said. "This here's no customer. This here's the private dick."

"Well, that's what it's all about, ain't it? Ain't we waiting for somebody for some private dickin'?"

"You know me?" Whistler asked Duckie.

"Sure I know you. You're a friend of the one-armed guy works the counter across the street. You're also a friend of Sergeant Canaan."

"What do you think?"

"What do I think about what?"

"Doing me a favor?"

"What kind of favor?"

Whistler took out the matchbox. It lay like a jewel in the outstretched palm of his hand.

"That's Bitsy's," Duckie said.

"Hey," Roach said, protesting how quickly his friend had spilled it without even working up a price.

"Who's Bitsy? I see him around?"

"I don't know. Sure. You been around. Bitsy's been around. I suppose you seen him."

"Describe him to me."

"Skinny runt with loose hair and funny eyes."

"How do you know him?"

"From around."

"Hey, what for are you telling this man everything and anything he wants to know?" Roach protested again. "He wants the news, he pays the dues."

"I'm tapped out," Whistler said. "I busted myself handing out fives and tens trying to get some answers. You know what I want to know and there's forty in it for you. A double sawbuck for you and one for you."

"You just said you was tapped out."

"That's today. There's always tomorrow."

"So come ask us again tomorrow."

"There's another way we can do this. I can have Sergeant Canaan take you in. I can keep you in a holding cell with some drunks and perverts for forty-eight. I can do it that way if you make me."

"Jeeeesus, what a hard-ass you are."

"I'll owe you. I always pay my debts."

"So all right. I just wanted to see what the deal was," Roach said.

"Where's this around you know Bitsy from?"

"We used the same building to sleep in."

"How many used the building?"

"Maybe eight, nine regulars and people who came and went."

"The building where Mimi was murdered on the roof?"

"Yeah, that one."

"The one where Hogan fell off and speared himself on some rusty iron."

They both nodded, disturbed by this talk of the violence that had come so close to them, upset because he was reminding them of memories they'd put away like birds frozen in winter and buried in spring.

"You still sleep in that building?"

"Hell, nooooo!" Roach said, spinning around in circles, as though driven crazy by the foolishness of a man like Whistler who should know better.

"You out of your fuckin' mind?" Duckie yelled, his voice chattering with a kind of laughter. "That's a bad-luck place. It ain't a home for us no more."

"How about any of the others?"

They both shrugged and laughed out loud, like a couple of dancers working a routine in sync.

"Who's left? Sissy's gone away. Mimi and Moo's dead. So is Hogan. I don't see Bitsy and Dipper around anymore," Duckie said.

"I seen Dipper," Roach said.

"Where you seen Dipper?" Duckie asked, mightily interested.

"I seen Dipper over by the bookstore. He was looking for Bitsy or Hogan."

"Who's Dipper?" Whistler asked.

"He's this retard used to hang around Bitsy," Duckie said.

"Tried to hang around us but it was no good. Old Dipper hanging around is bad for business," Roach added.

"Dipper maybe goes back there," Duckie finished. "If he didn't have nobody to tell him where to go, that's where he'd go."

Whistler glanced over his shoulder just as the light changed to green. He raised a hand and hurried to cross the street.

"Hey!" Roach yelled. "That's twenty bucks apiece! Don't forget!"

52

They were huddled together on the broken catwalk on the pitted roof, under an evening sky going sulphur yellow from the pollution that hardly ever left the air, like the last two survivors of a city destroyed by nuclear holocaust.

The rain had stopped. Everything smelled like wet bread.

"I thought you run away and left me," Dipper said.

"Why would I want to do that?" Bitsy asked. "Besides, the other day when I seen you with Roach and Duckie it was you who acted like you wanted to run away from me."

"Did I?" Dipper asked, genuinely surprised, his face screwing up with the effort of trying to remember.

"Now, why would you want to do that?"

"I don't know."

"Well, you must've had a reason."

"Oh, I suppose I had a reason," Dipper said forcefully, as though wanting to prove he wasn't so foolish as to do something without having a reason.

"Was it because you think I was mad at you?"

"I don't think so."

"I mean why would I want to be mad at you?"

"That's right, you wouldn't."

"So maybe it was because you saw something."

"What?"

"I don't know. Maybe you *thought* you saw something."

"Like *what*?"

"Maybe you thought you saw me doing something."

"When? When? When?" Dipper was rocking back and forth in his agitation, thinking that Bitsy was asking him these questions because he wanted him to remember something he couldn't remember.

"I got to pee," he said.

"You know the cops are still looking for you, Dipper? You know that?"

"So maybe I should run away."

"You got any ideas?"

Dipper thought about it and shook his head. "I got to pee."

"I mean it wouldn't necessarily be so bad for you if they picked you up. They'd just question you is all they'd do. Probably. They'd ask you what you saw when you was hiding up here on the roof."

"I saw that man doing it to Moo."

"Then he did it to Mimi and then he hit her and cut her up?"

Dipper squeezed his eyes shut and grabbed himself between his legs. "I don't think so."

"What do you mean, you don't think so? How could you remember one thing and not remember another thing?"

"Sometimes I remember something and sometimes I remember something else."

"Like you got to take a pee?"

"That's right."

"So go take a pee."

"Where? You always told me not to do my business in the corners."

"You remember something like that?"

"Sure I do."

"Well, we're not inside now. We're on the roof. You can pee on the roof. In fact, you want to, you can go pee over the edge. That way you can say you peed a hundred feet."

Dipper grinned his foolish, innocent grin and got to his feet. "That's one thing I won't forget. I'll always remember that." He walked over to the edge of the roof behind what was left of the railing, unzipped, and took himself out of his pants.

"I worry a little bit about what you remember and what you forget," Bitsy said, and stood up, too.

"What did you say?" Dipper asked.

"I asked you how you was doing."

"Listen," Dipper said. "It's a long way down."

Bitsy was only three steps away from Dipper's back when the door to the roof opened up.

Whistler was standing there. Bitsy looked at him, and even in the dim light of the failing day they could read each other's eyes.

"Enough, Bitsy," Whistler said. "You can't kill everybody in the world."

Epilogue

Sissy came walking by over to Roach and Duckie capering on the four corners. For a minute they didn't recognize her. She'd punked her hair into a Mohawk roach, with shaved sides and long thick strands hanging down her back. Rows of safety pins pierced through the outer shell of her ears, and her metal skirt rattled around her thighs, barely covering her treasure.

"That you, Sissy, for God's sake?" Duckie howled.

"Where you been?" Roach asked, as they shared hugs and kisses all around, Sissy beside herself with the joy of being home and being welcomed.

"Been back in Pennsylvania. Back in Pittsburgh."

"What for?"

"Wanted to see if my mother was alive."

"Was she?"

"Oh, sure. She was alive like always. Had a fat lip and a new space in her smile."

"Your old man beat her up?"

"Not my old man. Some new old man. She's always got some new old man. Asshole tried to finger my treasure practically the minute I walked through the kitchen door. I knew I wasn't going to be staying long."

"We wondered where you was. We were even starting to wonder if somebody had stole you."

"Violated you."

"Cut your throat."

"Jesus Christ, is that any way to say hello?" Sissy asked. "Why the hell you talking like that?"

"Because that's what happened to Mimi and Moo."

"Whaaat?"

"Don't you watch television? Don't you read the papers?"

"What for? They're full of nothing but rapes, murders, and bad news."

"Well, that's true," Duckie said.

"So are you kidding me?"

"Hell, no. Mimi got raped with a broken bottle up on the roof. Moo got her throat cut and whatever over to that shelter..."

"Magdalene House," Roach said when Duckie hesitated, the place where Moo and Faye had expired already lost to his memory.

"That lady what came around with the hot chocolate and the big nigger?"

"Yeah."

"She was stabbed to death, too."

"My God. My God," Sissy said. She looked around as though wondering why everybody she knew wasn't there for her homecoming. "Where's Hogan and Dipper? Where's Bitsy?"

"Hogan's dead, too."

"Whaaat?"

"Fell off the roof. Some rusted iron bars went right through him like spears."

"My God." Her mouth was hanging open. She couldn't believe what she was hearing.

"Dipper's in a nuthouse," Duckie said.

"In a facility for the socially impaired," Roach said, acting superior about his knowledge of the jargon.

"How about Bitsy? Where's Bitsy?"

"He's in jail."

"Whaaat?"

"He done it."

"Done what?"

"Done it to Mimi on the roof. Later on they proved he killed Moo and that woman from Magdalene House, too," Roach said.

"I can't believe it," Sissy said.

"You know how they proved it?" Duckie asked.

"No, how?"

"They found his teeth marks in a apple."

"In a apple?"

"His teeth marks was in a apple in the ashtray at Magdalene

House and they matched the teeth marks on Mimi's body."

"Whaaat?"

"He bit her on her thighs when he was shoving the busted bottle up her you-know-what," Roach said.

"I can hardly believe it," Sissy said, as though they'd just told her the plot of a fabulous moving picture. "I go away to see my mother for a couple of weeks, and look what happens."

Whistler watched them from the window of Gentry's, the herd of users, losers, and the lost, wondering how come sickness, violence, rape, muggery and buggery, herpes, AIDS, and old age weren't thinning out the action along the stroll.

Bosco brought over the coffeepot, poured Whistler a fresh cup, and sat down.

"Follow not truth too near the heels, lest it dash out your teeth," Bosco said.

"What the hell's that supposed to mean?" Whistler asked.

"How could it happen a kid gets sold out of the hills of Kentucky to some people on their way to Louisiana, runs away, and lands in L.A., where his old man once snuffed three women?" Bosco said.

"How could it be his old man's out on parole, roaming the same neighborhood where the kid's living in a derelict building with a bunch of other kids, one of which gets murdered and the other assaulted, for which the old man is picked up because he tried it on with a topless waitress and got himself cut?

"How could it be this kid's mother's back in town, running a shelter for baby hookers she picks off the streets and out of family court, so the whore that was assaulted gets tucked under her wing, fachrissake?"

"We'll fix it in the cutting room," Whistler said.

"How could they all come together in the same place at the same time, so that all the terrible things that could happen happen?" Bosco asked, his hand lying on a copy of *Oedipus After Sophocles*. "Sometimes you hear about them finding a body somewhere and you think that's the picture, but it ain't the picture, it's just the trailer."

Canaan came in. His eyes looked as though they were ready to weep. "What kind of soup?"

"Vegetable beef," Bosco said.

"Out of a can?"

"Homemade."

"How could it be homemade, I'm eating it in a coffee shop?"

"We get it shipped in from a little old lady out in Ocean Park."

"Give me a bowl. Bread instead of crackers."

Bosco called the order back to Shirley Hightower, even though she was on her break, because he knew she'd developed this little thing for Canaan lately and liked to serve him.

"What the hell are all these poor silly kids doing piling into a place that chews out their hearts?" Whistler asked.

"When you're their age, it's only today," Canaan said. "If it's good today, it's good. You know what I mean. Every little sucker out there thinks the world revolves around his belly button."

"So how come we can't make cities a little easier to live in?"

"Hey," said Bosco, "the worst corner of hell is home sweet home to some poor soul."